SCANDALOUS LORD, REBELLIOUS MISS

Deb Marlowe

MILLS BOON®

First published in Great Britain 2007
by Mills & Boon, an imprint of Harlequin (UK) Limited,
Large Print edition 2012
Harlequin (UK) Limited,
Eton House, 18-24 Paradise Road, Richmond, Surrey TW9 1SR

© Deb Marlowe 2007

ISBN: 978 0 263 23063 5

Harlequin (UK) policy is to use papers that are natural, renewable and recyclable products and made from wood grown in sustainable forests. The logging and manufacturing process conform to the legal environmental regulations of the country of origin.

Printed and bound in Great Britain
by CPI Antony Rowe, Chippenham, Wiltshire

Chapter One

Charles Alden, Viscount Dayle, sank into his favourite overstuffed chair in the morning room at White's. It was early; the porters had not yet let down the awnings and bright light flooded through the floor-to-ceiling window. At his elbow sat a pot of coffee, a plate of muffins, and a pile of papers. He snapped open *The Times,* sank his teeth into his first, hot, buttery bite and let out a heartfelt sigh.

He revelled in the peace of the morning all the way through the first paper. Unfortunately, peace was a commodity hard to come by anywhere in England in the spring of 1817, even for a viscount. Charles first noticed something amiss as he set aside *The Times* and reached for the *Edinburgh Review.*

A space had cleared all about him. The morning room, usually full of gentlemen either beginning one day or ending another, was empty but for a few souls gathered in whispering knots along the walls. One man caught his gaze, blasted him with a look of utter scorn, and stalked out, calling for his hat. A wrench of foreboding seizing his gut, Charles looked up into the sympathetic eye of one of the porters, come to refresh his coffee.

'Well, Bartlett,' he said quietly, 'I can see you are not half so ignorant as I. Tell me.'

Bartlett cleared his throat. 'I have taken the liberty of adding a copy of today's *Oracle* to the stack of your usual papers, my lord. Perhaps you would care to peruse the editorial section?'

'The *Oracle?*' It was little more than a scandal sheet. 'Thank you, Bartlett.'

Charles picked up the paper with trepidation and turned a few pages until he found the item he sought, directly under a scathing response to Lord Sidmouth's call against 'seditious publications'.

Tory Darling or Wolf In Sheep's Clothing?

They do say that a Reformed Rake makes the Best Husband—but what kind of Politician does he make?

Just such a man is Lord D—, a Rakehell of the First Order, now converted into a Responsible English Peer. Or is he? Based on certain, recent Rumours, We wonder if he has changed pastures only in search of fresh prey.

Lord D— has been seen often lately with the notorious Lady A— on his arm. Perhaps this is not so surprising when one considers his past taste for women of immodest character and her known taste for the rising young members of her husband's political party. What is surprising is that a man previously known for living on wit and instinct could have fumbled this situation so badly. No other explanation presents itself for yesterday's dramatic events, when Lord A— returned home unexpectedly only to find a dark-haired gentleman departing the house by route of Lady A—'s bedchamber window.

The lady has reportedly been duly chastised and banished to the country. But as for the gentleman?

It cannot be denied that Lord D— is a man of many talents. Indeed, it is rumoured he is to be groomed for High Office. We at the Oracle cannot help but wonder if the Tories should reconsider the notion. Surely a candidate exists who can demonstrate a higher standard of character. For if the Tories cannot trust Lord D— with their women, then why should they trust him with the Nation?

For a long minute Charles sat rigid with anger. Bloody, damnable hell. Months of hard work. Weeks of toadying. Countless gruelling hours spent constructing a careful façade. All destroyed in a moment with the vicious swipe of an acid pen.

Normal, everyday sounds drifted in from the adjoining rooms: the rustle of freshly ironed papers, the soft clink of china, the low murmur of men whose lives had not just been turned inside out. Charles sat frozen, trying to wrap his mind about the disaster that had befallen him with the turn of a page.

He nearly jumped out of his skin when grizzled Lord Rackham paused behind his chair and thumped him soundly on the shoulder.

'Just so, my boy!' the old relic bellowed. 'Brazen it out. Don't let them see you with your head down, that's the wisest course! Tomorrow some bloke will get caught hammering his rocks in someone else's quarry and they'll all be talking about that. It will blow over soon enough.' After another encouraging cuff he stalked off to rejoin his friends, the whole pack of them muttering darkly as they crossed into the coffee room.

With quiet, deliberate movements Charles finished his coffee. Old Lord Rackham had the right of it; he would not let anyone think he was ashamed. Once he had finished he stood, tucked the copy of the *Oracle* under his arm, and with a flash of a gold coin in Bartlett's direction, Charles walked out of White's.

He stood a moment on St James's Street, dazzled by the bright sun and annoyed at the bustle of traffic. Then he let loose a great laugh. Who in the world did he think he was—the heroine in a gothic novel? Should lightning crack the sky and mere mortals scurry for cover because Viscount Dayle's political career lay in ruins?

As if in answer, a brisk breeze riffled his hair, and Charles set off towards Mayfair. *Who did he think he was?* That was the question of the hour—no, of the entire past year—was it not?

There was only one answer. He was Viscount Dayle, a carefully constructed facsimile of the man who should hold the title. And Viscount Dayle was nothing without his political career.

His mind darted from one scenario to the next as he approached Piccadilly, scrambling to come up with some way to salvage the situation. Lost in his own whirlwind of thoughts, he failed to notice both the rising wind and the increasingly strident sound of his own name. It wasn't until someone grasped his arm that he came awake to his surroundings.

'Dayle, did you not hear us calling you, man?' It was Henley and Matthews, two of the more degenerate hangers-on of his old crowd. They were still in their evening clothes and looking the worse for wear. Charles winced. These two would tear him apart after reading that piece.

'Sorry, chaps. Lost in the fog of my own thoughts this morning,' he said, striving for a light-hearted tone.

'A bit dense in there, eh?' laughed Matthews. 'I trust it's not as thick as the fog at Hyde Park this morning.' He leaned in and spoke confidingly. 'Blackmoor met Ventry at dawn. Ventry was shaking so hard his gun went off before he'd got his hand half-raised. Hit the ground not ten feet in front of him, the poor sod.'

Charles felt like shaking himself, in relief. Obviously they didn't yet know. 'Blackmoor didn't kill him, did he?' he asked with nonchalance.

'I should say not,' Henley drawled. 'Pinked him in the arm, which is far less than the upstart deserved, should you ask me.' He shot Charles a conspirator's grin. 'It's good to see you, Dayle. It's been an age since you've been out and about with us. Leave the debates to them what can't get a rise out of St Peter, if you catch my meaning, and come on with us. You're too young to bury yourself in the House.'

Matthews chimed in. 'We're off to breakfast, old man, before heading home,' he said. 'Been to the new bawdy house on Bentinck Street? Opens in the morning and lays out a breakfast buffet. Mrs Pritchett guarantees a bellyful and an armful to send you sweetly to your dreams. Care to join us?'

The desire to yield and go along with them was almost visceral. How easy it would be to forget, to lose the pain of the last year and the humiliation of the morning in the burn of good liquor and the hot sweet flesh of a woman. He could just let it all go. End the charade.

He shook his head to rid himself of the notion. No. Charles Alden was dead. Slain by the same wild round that had stolen his brother, buried by the despair that had seduced his father. There was no going back.

He went forward instead, resolutely and one footfall at a time. Good-naturedly refusing the offer, he saw Matthews and Henley into a passing hack before crossing over Piccadilly. By the time he passed Devonshire House and headed into Berkeley Square, temptation had been safely locked away. Viscount Dayle was once again in full possession of all his faculties and putting together a plan of action.

The wind had become quite forceful by the time Charles reached his Bruton Street townhouse, and the sunlight dimmed by fast-moving clouds. Perhaps fate had indeed meant to give him the backdrop for his drama, and had only missed her cue.

'My lord,' his butler gasped as the door swung in. 'Forgive me, we were not expecting you back…'

'No need for apologies, Fisher.' Charles headed for the library. 'But could you please send round a man to fetch my brother? Drag him from his books, if need be, but tell him I need him now. And send some coffee in, too.'

'Wait, my lord!' the butler called as Charles stalked away. 'You have a visitor awaiting you.'

'At this hour?'

The butler had no chance to reply before the library door slammed open. 'Dayle!' The shout rang in the cold marbled entry. 'This time you will pay for your perfidy. Name your seconds!'

'Lord Avery, how kind of you to call,' Charles said, running a hand across his brow. 'Better make that something stronger, Fisher. Brandy will do.

'Now, my lord,' Charles spoke soothingly as he ushered the man back in the room and away from the staring eyes of the servants, 'we are a bit precipitous with this talk of seconds. But I would be happy to discuss the upcoming Poor Relief Bill, even at this early hour.'

'There's no distracting me, you philandering dog! I know what you've done with my wife, all of London knows!' The older man was nearly grey with fatigue and emotion. Charles guided him to a chair. The last thing he needed was for the fool to collapse in his study.

'You know no such thing. It's nonsense. I dined at the Clarendon, and stayed there talking most of the night. You will easily find a roomful of gentlemen to corroborate the fact. We can send for one or more of them right now.'

'I know what I saw, you young rakehell.'

'I don't know what you saw, my lord, but I know it was not me.' Charles's tone grew more firm.

'Do you think me a fool? I've seen you together with my own eyes! And all of London knows of your rackety ways.'

'I've never had more than a casual public conversation with your wife, sir. I own that she is charming, and exceedingly handsome, but whatever trouble lies between you has nothing to do with me.'

Charles saw the first sign of uncertainty in the man's face. He felt for him, but he could not let this go any further. He hardened his expression and said with finality, 'If you choose not to believe me, then I will indeed give thought to finding a second.'

Jack arrived just then, excited and fully ready to defend his brother's honour, but the fight had gone out of Lord Avery. He hung his head in his hands while Charles greeted his brother and while the brandy was brought in. He accepted a drink, threw it back, and held out his glass for another. Then he stood.

'I will accept your explanation for now, Dayle, but I shall check out your claim, and if I find it's a lie, I'll be back. Why would your name be mixed up in this if you weren't involved? Makes no sense.'

'You echo my own thought exactly,' said Charles.
Lord Avery bristled. 'This is no laughing matter!
My honour, and my wife's, has been destroyed.' He
looked thoughtfully at Charles. 'I know that there
are those in the Party who believe in your transformation. The rake reformed.' He snorted. 'I know
your history, and today's work smacks of it. Blatant.
Insulting. Just like your soft-hearted politics. It's
bad enough to side with the unwashed masses
against your own kind in the Lords, but this!
Unforgivable is what I call it, and so will many a
Tory, after I am through with you.' He marched to
the door and paused on the threshold. 'If your
whereabouts last night are uncertain, then tomorrow
morning's will be assured.'

The echo of the slamming door was much quieter
on this side. Charles looked away and began to pace,
from the sidebar to the crackling fire, then away to
the full wall of books. He couldn't bear to look
upon his father's portrait above the mantel.

'I'm sorry, Charles.' Jack's tone was quiet,
careful. 'God knows I don't understand it, but I do
know how important your political interests have
become to you.'

Charles nodded again and drank. He crossed to
the window and watched as the rain began to come
down in sheets.

'Throw me a bone, would you? I'm trying to play the supportive brother here.' Jack rose and came to stand behind him. 'He'll check your story and find that it's true. After that it's only a piece in a scandal rag. Is it really so bad?'

Charles stared at his brother's reflection in the window. 'It's bad, and it couldn't have come at a worse time. The Board of Trade is looking for someone to head an investigative committee on distressed farming areas. My name has been mentioned. It could set me on a path to much higher places.' He scrubbed a hand through his hair. 'I've worked hard, and come so far. Take a good look around, little brother, this country is in an horrendous mess. I have finally got myself into a position where I can do something about it…I could *help*.'

He slammed his fist into his hand. 'And now someone wants to use my past against me? No one will consider me seriously. I'll be just another *ton* wastrel who cannot keep his bodkin buttoned up. This could ruin me. My political career could be over before it has truly begun.'

'Would that be such a terrible thing?' His brother's hand was suddenly heavy on Charles's shoulder. 'Phillip is dead. You are not. Perhaps it is time to let all of this go. You could get back to your own pursuits, spend some time at Fordham with Mother.'

'No,' Charles barked. 'I could not.' He stared down into his drink, but there were no answers there. And no solace either, as he had good reason to know. How could he explain his desperation to his little brother? There were some things that Jack could never understand. 'I need this, Jack. I can't explain it, but I need to do this, and I need you to help me out of this mess.'

There was a moment's silence, and then Jack took his hand away and went to pour himself a drink. 'Is the situation salvageable? What do you mean to do?'

'I suppose I must demonstrate a higher standard of character,' Charles said with a wry twist of a grin.

'Higher than what?' Jack laughed suddenly and the tension in the room became a little more bearable. 'That wasn't really you climbing out of the old jade's window?'

'Good Lord, no! I'm willing to sacrifice a good deal in the name of politics, but that's taking the matter too far. In any case, I believe she only flirts with us young bucks to stir her husband up, to get his attention off the quarter of a million military men set adrift with no pensions and back on her. But she's evidently gone too far this time.'

Charles scrubbed a hand across his brow while he thought. 'Still, I have to admit this was a master stroke. Whoever is behind this is clever. They've negated months of work, and done it by painting me with my own brush. All with no hint of his own identity or agenda.'

'Someone doesn't like the influence you've begun to gain. How do we track the whoreson down?'

'First I'm going to find the baseborn idiot who wrote that piece for the *Oracle*. Whether he wants to or not, he's going to tell me who his sources are. But it's not going to be enough to find out which coward is behind this. The damage is done.' He moved back to the window and gazed out at the gathering intensity of the storm. 'I'm going to have to give them all something better to talk about.'

Jack nearly choked on his drink. 'Better than sex and scandal? There isn't anything the *ton* loves better.'

'Oh, yes, there is, little brother.'

'What?' Jack demanded as an enormous branch of lightning split the sky.

Into the brief moment of calm, Charles spoke. 'Marriage.'

His brother's jaw dropped. Thunder broke open in the heavens. The house shuddered.

'Marriage? To whom?' Jack managed to ask.

'To the most priggish lady you can drag up from the muck of the *ton,* I should imagine.' Charles shrugged. 'It seems clear that the only way I will ever live down the excesses of my past is to secure the dullness of my future. I don't know, draw up a list. Only the primmest and most proper to be considered. I'll marry the one at the top.'

Thunder throbbed through the house once more. The windows shook in their frames. Behind them their father's portrait rattled off its moorings, crashed into the mantel, and flipped face down in front of the fire.

Chapter Two

Her step light, her portfolio swinging and her maid scurrying to keep up, Sophie Westby strode through Cheapside. A gusting wind swept past in brisk imitation of the traffic in the streets, whipping her skirts and challenging the knot holding her bonnet. Sophie raised her chin, breathed deep of the pungent air and grinned in delight. London might be dirty, occasionally rank, and surprisingly lacking in colour, but it was also a huge, bubbling cauldron of *life*.

After years of quiet country living and near isolation, Sophie's own life was suddenly beginning to simmer. Furniture design had long been her passion, and in an effort to ease her dearest friend Emily Lowder's unusually long and difficult confinement, she had indulged them both with an extensive nursery project. It had been a smashing success. They'd had such fun and Emily had been so enchanted with the result, she had quickly swept Sophie up into a redesign of her dark and cluttered drawing rooms. The new suite had been unveiled at little Edward Lowder's birthday celebration and, to Sophie's chagrin, the room had nearly eclipsed the cherubic infant.

The grandest lady of the neighborhood, Viscountess Dayle, had been most impressed. Lady Dayle had run an assessing eye over both the new room and its designer, and in a bewilderingly sudden turn of events, she had them all established in town for the Season and for a large, mysterious design project.

Almost before Sophie could catch her breath, she found herself out of Blackford Chase, ensconced in the Lowders' London home, and finally encouraged to pursue her design work. The result was one ecstatic young lady.

A young lady who perhaps should not have left her coach behind, stuck in the snarl of vehicles blocked by an overturned coal cart. Against her maid's protests Sophie had climbed down, left instructions with the driver and set off on foot. And she could not bring herself to regret the decision. Walking was so much more intimate. She felt a part of the city rather than a bystander.

'Paper! The *Augur!*' The newsboy hefting his

heavy sack of papers looked perhaps ten years old. He had inked-smeared hands, a scrupulously clean face, and eyes that made Sophie's fingers positively itch for a pencil. An old soul smiled hopefully out of that young face.

'Paper, miss? Only sixpence and full of society's latest doin's.' He spotted a pair of well-dressed young ladies emerging from a shop across the street and waved his paper high to get their attention. 'Paper! The *Augur!* More exciting tales of the Wicked Lord Dayle!'

He could not have used a more enticing lure. Sophie promptly bought a copy, then turned to Nell, the maid assigned to her from the Lowders' town staff. 'Will you tuck this away in your bag, Nell, just until we get home?'

The maid looked startled. Sophie smiled at her. 'I promise to share as soon as I've finished.'

Gossip was like gold below stairs, and Sophie knew she had an ally when Nell, her face alight with mischief, took the paper and shoved it under the mending in her bag. The newsboy flashed them both a gap-toothed smile, then a cheeky wink. Nell giggled, but Sophie caught herself unthinkingly reaching for her sketchbook.

No. Not this time. She took a tighter grip on her portfolio and firmly set herself back to the task at hand: reaching the shop of a particularly well-recommended linen draper.

It was a scene that she had replayed with herself countless times in the past week. With so much history, so much energy and so many human dramas unfolding about her, the temptation to put it all down on paper was nearly overwhelming. From the towering glory of the churches, to the saucy curve of the newsboy's cheek, to the flutter of the fine ladies' dresses, London was full of sights, textures, and subtle images that she longed to capture in her sketchbook.

But she did not intend to succumb to the temptation. Sketching meant taking a step back, imposing a distance, becoming an observer, and Sophie Westby was done with being an observer.

Fate had finally smiled upon her and she meant to make the most of it. That was one reason why today's errand was so important. Though she as yet had no idea what project Lady Dayle had in mind, Sophie intended to dazzle her. Themes, colour schemes, and any number of preparatory steps could be readied ahead of time and individualised later. When the time came Sophie would be ready with an array of ideas and choices that would quickly highlight the viscountess's tastes. And when the project was complete, she vowed, Lady Dayle would have reason to be proud.

Sophie could do no less for the woman who had been so kind and generous. And indeed, Lady Dayle had no true idea just how much her kindness had meant, for she could not know that in the very act of bringing her to London, she had brought Sophie that much closer to two of her most heartfelt desires.

First, of course, were the incredible opportunities that could arise from a London project. She smiled when she remembered thinking that Emily's drawing room had been such a coup. As wonderful as that had turned out, it was as nothing compared to what exposure to the *ton*'s finest might do. So much might be accomplished if her designs were well received.

Second, and somehow more importantly, Lady Dayle had placed Sophie squarely in a position where she might see Charles again. Her pulse leaped at the thought.

She wondered what Lady Dayle knew of their relationship—but perhaps relationship was the wrong word. Friendship, then, because he had indeed been her friend. Her friend, her companion, her confidante, the knight of her youth.

Anticipation brought a secret smile to her face when she thought of the paper hidden in Nell's bag. How she loved to read of his exploits. Through the years she had followed his nefarious career with the same glee that she had felt hearing of his schoolboy stunts. She could scarcely wait to tease every scandalous detail from him. It was her favourite fantasy; the pair of them, reunited, sharing laughter and dreams just as they had used to do.

Sophie had always known that some day they would meet again. But now that the distant promise had become a near certainty, she found that it had gained new significance.

How had he changed? What would he have to say to her? Sophie knew she stood at a crossroads in her life, a rare point filled with promise and possibilities ahead. Yet she also knew that she would not be able to settle to any one of them until she had the answers to those questions.

'Miss!' came a gasp from behind her. 'Is it very much farther, miss?' Nell sounded breathless. Apparently Sophie's pace had quickened along with her thoughts.

'Not much farther, I don't believe.'

For Nell's sake she slowed her steps and resolved to keep her mind off of the distant past and the uncertain future, and firmly on the task in the present.

It proved easier than she might have imagined, for Cheapside was a treat for the senses, populated as it was with all manner of shops and craftsmen. Sophie wrinkled her nose at the hot smell at the sil-

versmiths, and again at the raw scent of fresh dye
at the cloth weavers. She marvelled at the crowded
windows of the engravers, but it wasn't until she
reached the tea merchant's shop that she came to a
delighted stop.

The merchant had at one time been blessed with
a bowed shop window, but the area had been converted, or inverted, and now held a charming little
protected alcove. Like a miniature Parisian café, it
held a small table, meant, she supposed, for custom-
ers to sit and experience some exotic new flavour
before they parted with their coin. It was the seating,
in fact, which had so caught Sophie's attention.

'Nell, just look at those chairs. If I'm not
mistaken, those are true Restoration pieces, sitting
right out in the street! Yes,' she said, rushing forward
to stroke one lovingly. 'The Portuguese arch. Oh,
and look, Nell, you must hold my portfolio while I
examine the *pé de pincel.*'

She could never truly say, afterward, just what
went wrong. Perhaps the clasp had already been
loose, or perhaps she herself accidentally triggered
it. In any case, one second she was absentmindedly
passing her portfolio back to Nell, and the next it
was dropping wide open. Another gust of wind hit
just then and all of her sketches and designs were
sent skyward in a veritable cyclone of papers.

For a moment Sophie stood frozen in panic and watched as her life's work scattered about the busy street. Then she sprang into action. First she sent Nell after those that had skipped back down the way they had just come. Then an enterprising street sweeper approached and offered to help retrieve the papers that had fluttered into the street. Sophie gave him a coin, entreated him not to place himself in any danger and sent him off.

She herself set after the bulk of the lot, which had gone swirling ahead of them. She was not heedless of the sight she must present, chasing, stooping, even jumping up to snatch at one desk design that had impaled itself on the pike of an iron railing, but she was beyond caring. These designs were her hopes for the future; she could no more abandon them than she could go quietly back to Blackford Chase.

At last, after much effort, there was only one paper left in sight. It led her a merry chase as it danced mere inches from her fingertips more than once. But each time she drew near another mischievous breeze would send it bounding ahead. Sophie's back ached and her gown grew more filthy by the minute, but she refused to give up.

And she finally had a stroke of fortune. Just ahead a gentleman stalked out of a printer's shop, right into the path of the wicked thing. It fetched up against a pair of well-formed legs, then flattened itself around one shining Hessian.

With a triumphant whoop Sophie swept down and snatched the paper up. *Oh my,* she thought as she caught sight of her own distorted grin, *you truly can see your reflection in a gentleman's boots.*

'Of course. It only wanted this.' The voice above her was heavy with sarcasm. 'I can now officially brand this day one of the worst I have ever endured. Now my valet shall berate me as soundly as the rest of London.'

Sophie fought the urge to grin as she slowly straightened up, her gaze travelling the unusual— and unusually pleasurable—path up the form of a well-formed gentleman. A well-heeled gentleman too, judging by the quality of the small clothes, which were buff, and the morning coat, which was, of course, blue, and the scowling face, which was…

Charles's.

The shock was so great that her stomach fell all the way to the pavement and the rest of her nearly followed.

He saw the danger and grasped her arm to steady her. She looked again into his face and saw that it was true. His face was not quite the same, the handsome promise of youth having hardened into a more angular and masculine beauty. His eyes were different as well, so cold and hard as he scowled down at her, but it was undeniably, without a doubt, her Charles Alden.

Sophie was so happy to see him, despite the awkwardness of the moment, that she just beamed up at him. All the joyful anticipation she'd felt for this moment simply flooded out of her and she knew that her delight shone all over her face.

It was not a shared emotion. In fact, he dropped her arm as if he'd suddenly found her diseased.

Sophie's smile only deepened. He didn't know her! Oh, heavens, she was going to have some fun with him now.

'I don't know what you are smiling at. That was the worst example of unfeminine effrontery I have ever witnessed, and in the street, no less.' He raked the length of her with a hard gaze. 'You look the part of a lady, but it appears to end there. Where is your escort?'

'My maid will be along in a minute,' she replied almost absentmindedly. She couldn't take her eyes off of him. It was no wonder he'd had such a reputation as a rake; he had grown almost sinfully handsome. She would bet that women threw themselves in his path on a regular basis.

'Please, stop that infernal smiling,' he ordered. 'If you need a good reason, impudent miss, just look at my boots!'

She obediently arranged her face into a more sombre mien. 'Please, do forgive me, sir.' She smoothed the chalked design that had indeed smudged the high polish off one of his Hessians. 'Let me assure you that I do not usually behave in so reckless a fashion. But I had to have my papers back, you see.'

'No, I do not see.' He stopped suddenly, an arrested look upon his face. He glanced back at the building he had just exited; with a closer look it appeared to be a publisher's office. 'Are you a writer, a reporter, by chance?' he asked.

'No, sir. I—' She was not allowed to finish.

'Damn. I could do with someone from the press in my court.' With a sudden motion, before she could protest, he had reached out and smoothly snatched the paper from her grasp. 'But please, enlighten me as to just what is worth making a spectacle of yourself.'

Sophie looked as well and saw that it was a design of a *chaise-lounge* she had specifically drawn for his mother, complete with a complementary colour palette and notes on specific fabrics and trims.

'Furniture,' Charles said with a deprecating snort.

'Décor,' she corrected as she just as smoothly retrieved the design and tucked it with her others.

'Pray, do excuse me,' he drawled in exaggerated

tones. For a moment he reminded her forcefully of his younger self, and her reaction was instantaneous and purely physical. And yet, something distracted her and slowed the melting of her insides. She'd heard that mocking tone before, but never with so hard an edge. He wasn't taking her seriously, true, but he wasn't being nice about it either.

She narrowed her eyes. 'No, I don't believe I will,' she replied.

His eyes widened in mock dismay. 'Was that meant as a mortal blow to my pride? Unforgiven and despondent, the gentleman prostrates himself and begs for mercy. You have read one too many novels, my dear,' he said.

'Just look about you,' he continued with an encompassing wave of his hand. 'There are a good many things in this world in need of attention, even some worth making oneself a fool over. But let me assure you—' his voice was getting louder now '—that furniture is not one of them.'

Sophie raised her brow in the very arrogant manner that he himself had taught her. 'Perhaps not to you, sir, but our circumstances are quite different. You haven't a notion of my concerns. To me, this is very important.'

'Important, of course,' he said, the sarcasm growing heavy again. 'You will forgive me if I don't raise décor to the same level as perhaps, the plight of the English farmer, or the suspension of Habeas Corpus.'

'And you will forgive me if I place it a little higher than the shine on your boots.'

Charles stopped in the act of replacing his hat, clearly taken aback. He opened his mouth, then closed it. He jammed the beaver on to his head. 'I concede you the point.'

Suddenly his shoulders slumped. He tore the hat off again and bowed his head. 'What on earth am I doing?' He heaved a sigh and the tense lines of his neck and shoulders relaxed.

When he looked up at Sophie again, it was as if a layer of cold stone had fallen from him. 'Listen, I do apologise.' He scrubbed a rough hand through his hair and flashed her a half-grin that was awkward and thoroughly familiar.

'It's not my usual habit to go about berating young women in the street, but then nothing has been usual in my life for—well, it feels like for ever. It has been so long since I had a normal conversation,' he continued, 'I scarcely recall how to go about it.'

The indefinable pull that emanated from him had doubled in its intensity. Sophie could not make herself respond, could not tear her gaze from his. There they were at last, warm in their regard, Charles's eyes. Her Charles.

He didn't seem to notice her lapse. 'Allow me to help you.'

With brisk efficiency he soon had her designs in order and her portfolio securely fastened. Another awkward silence followed her thanks. Sophie desperately tried to gather her wits. She knew she should either take her leave of him or reveal her identity.

He spoke before she could choose either option. 'You seem to have a great many ideas. It must be a very large project you have undertaken.'

Sophie flushed. How to answer that without making a fool of herself? She should have told him who she was at the start. 'Yes, at least I believe so. The truth is, I do not really know yet.'

He shifted and she could almost feel his restlessness, his need to escape. But she was not ready to see him go yet, nor was she quite sure she had forgiven him his harsh manner. She curved her lips into a smile and cocked a brow at him. 'If not normal, then what sort do you usually have?'

He was puzzled. 'Pardon?'

'Conversations. You say you are unused to the normal variety. I am perishing to know what kind of conversations you usually have.'

'Oh.' He paused and she thought that he might not answer, that he would put an end to this improper tête à tête and go about his business, but instead he glanced carefully about, then flashed her a wicked smile. 'Do you wish for the truth or for a properly polite answer?'

Sophie tossed her head, her chin up. 'Always the truth, please, sir.'

'Very well, then. The truth is that for most of my days my conversations tended on the coarse and bawdy side. More like the seasonal bawling of young bucks and the bleating of…available females than true human exchange—'

Sophie interrupted him with a sigh. 'You did warn me. I am sure I should be slapping your face, or stalking off in high dudgeon. Fortunately I am not so faint-hearted.' She smiled. 'Do go on.'

He shrugged. 'Now I have political conversations. Long, relentless, occasionally monotonous, but in the end productive and worthwhile. Both sorts, I find, have their own drawbacks and pleasures.'

The playful gleam returned to his eye and he leaned in a little closer and lowered his voice. 'But I will let you in on a little secret. Sometimes, especially when the stakes are high, political debates are remarkably similar to primitive mating rituals. There is a little polite cooing, leading to an extravagant display of superiority, then a mad scramble as everyone pairs off.

Occasionally there is a show of temper and brute strength. In the end someone wins, the victor takes the spoils and the next day we all ever so politely begin all over again.'

Sophie laughed. 'Fascinating. It gives one a whole new perspective on Parliament, does it not?

'It helps me get through some very long days in the Lords.'

'It makes me wish I was indeed a reporter. Imagine the story I could write: "Wild Westminster, The Secret Life of Parliament." Every paper in London would be at my feet. Alas, my talents lie in another direction altogether.'

Charles eyed her portfolio, then slid his gaze down her form. A swift, fierce heat swept through her, following its path. 'I beg you won't be insulted if I say that you decorate the city with your mere presence.'

Before she could gather herself enough to respond, his face suddenly contorted into a grimace of dismay that had her following his gaze. An elegant carriage pulled by an exquisite team passed them by. Very obviously staring was a pair of wide-eyed feminine faces. One even craned her neck to look back as the equipage moved on.

'Oh, hell,' he breathed before turning back to her. 'As stimulating as this has been, I cannot afford any more gossip just now. Neither would I wish to harm your reputation with my tarnished presence.' He sketched her the curtest of bows. 'I wish you the best of luck with your endeavours.'

She returned with a curtsy just as brief. 'Indeed, I understand, sir.' She watched as he turned to go and called after him, 'Off you go to save the world. I will content myself with dressing it up.'

He tossed a scornful glance over his shoulder at her. 'Unworthy, my dear, and just when I had begun to judge you a promising opponent.'

Sophie watched, amused, as he stalked away. Let him have the last word for now, she thought. Oh, she was going to enjoy their next meeting even more than this one.

She became aware, suddenly, of a faint panting just behind her. She turned and found Nell, who handed over a sheaf of papers and wiped her brow. 'Who was the gentleman you was talking with, miss? He looked a mite put out.'

'That, dear Nell, was none other than the Wicked Lord Dayle.'

'No!' The maid's gasp was more titillation than shock.

'Indeed, although I recall him more fondly as my very own knight in shining armour.'

Nell had been pushed too far this morning to be discreet. 'Happen that armour's tarnished some.'

'It does appear so,' Sophie mused. 'Though the polishing of it could be quite a bit of fun, indeed.'

Nell only shook her head. 'If you say so, miss.'

Chapter Three

Miss Corinne Ashford's hand was limp and cool as Charles bent over it. As was the expression on her face while he took his leave of her. Even so, Charles's step was light when he stepped into Portman Street and set out for home.

He felt as if he could breathe again, as he hadn't been free to since that cursed piece in the *Oracle*. He had been exonerated, of course, once it had leaked out that the dark-haired man sneaking out of Lady Avery's window had been none other than Lord Avery's valet. And society had quickly sunk their teeth into new and even more delicious gossip when the old girl had run off with the young fellow, the petty cash, and the family jewels.

Yet the damage had been done. The thinly veiled references were in every scandal sheet. Suddenly his old peccadilloes were fodder for gossip again.

Wild, reckless, restless—these were the epithets he had become accustomed to in his seven and twenty years, the labels a scandalised society had readily laid at his door. They were well and truly earned, too. He had misspent his youth in a frenzy of hard living, soft women, and outrageous pranks. He had, in short, enjoyed the hell out of himself.

But such carelessness belonged to another lifetime. Charles Alden might have spent his time in carefree pursuit of pleasure, but Viscount Dayle was not so lighthearted. Two years ago his brother had died, his father had shortly followed, and Charles's life had been transformed.

It had begun as a penance he had embraced in a fury of remorse and determination, and, though it was true that grief and guilt still lay heavy on his shoulders, Charles could not deny that it was the work that had saved his sanity.

With fierce devotion he had immersed himself in the estates, the accounts and the politics. Somehow he had survived, had even reached a point where he could draw breath, enjoy the success he had wrought and begin to envision a future.

Until that ridiculous article. Now his name had once again been associated with scandal and vice, and his reception had significantly cooled, both in the corridors of Westminster and the parlors of

Mayfair. He found the setback infuriating, and despite his best efforts, he still hadn't a clue as to who was behind it.

So, he had temporarily abandoned his search for the villain, dragged out his original plan, and after careful deliberation decided that Miss Ashford might be just the thing to cure his ailing reputation. She was the daughter of a baron and a member of a notoriously staunch conservative family. Elegant and tall and proud to a fault, she wore respectability like an enveloping mantel. Charles just hoped that it was large enough to cover his own sins.

In truth, he had half-expected to be left standing in the street when he began to pay his addresses to the lady, but the past year's good works—or his title and fortune—had proved credit enough to get him in the door. Whether he progressed any further remained to be seen.

He crossed his own portal now, satisfied for the moment, and more in charity with the world than he'd felt in weeks. He found his mother descending the stairs, straightening her gloves. 'Going out, Mother?' he asked.

'Indeed, as are you. Please have the carriage sent around, dear. We won't wish to be late.'

Charles nodded to a footman to deliver the message. 'Late for what?'

Only a mother could fit so much meaning into a sigh of exasperation. 'I knew you would forget. We are promised to call at Mrs Lowder's, *both* of us. And do not even think of trying to wiggle out of it. You know that Edward Lowder is influential in some very important political circles. And in any case, Emily Lowder has something in particular at her house that I wish to show you.'

She had reached the bottom of the stairs. Charles smiled and offered her his arm. 'Wiggle out? I wouldn't dare. Not since the Aunt Eugenie incident.'

She laughed. 'I would never have banished you to your room if I thought Phillip would do such a thing. I thought we were going to have to break the door down. Do you know, to this day we have never found that key?'

He couldn't hide the twinge he felt at Phillip's name. She saw and stopped to put her hand on his cheek. 'They were good times, Charles. It is fine to remember them.' She smiled and straightened his cravat. 'And we will have good times again, I feel it.'

Charles could almost believe her. His mother was smiling again. She had come up from Fordham Park with a spring in her step, a list of some kind in hand, and he had barely seen her in the weeks since. He had warned her of the Avery scandal, but she had only laughed and dared anyone in society to vilify her son to her face.

'How went the hunt?' she asked now. 'You have certainly given the rumour mill enough grist. Word is out that the Wicked Lord Dayle is looking for a wife to tame his ways. Surely the worst must indeed be past if such a high stickler as Lavinia Ashford gave you entrance to her drawing room.'

The arrival of the carriage saved him from a response, but his mother would not let the subject drop. She teased a list of names from him and then cheerfully dissected each one, as callous in her regard for the young ladies as if they were no more than choice offerings at the butcher's stall. 'If what you truly wish is to wed a pattern card of propriety, Charles, then there are in truth only three or four girls who will do. Nearly everyone of consequence is in town now. There should be plenty of time for you to meet them all and select the best.'

Charles suffered a little qualm hearing his mother discuss his marriage in such cold-blooded terms. He suffered a bigger qualm picturing the many long years ahead leg-shackled to a cold-blooded shrew. Then, like a sudden summer breeze, the image arose in his mind—dark, windswept tresses, laughing eyes, a radiant smile. The chit from Cheapside.

The exotic little beauty had invaded his thoughts

more than once since their encounter. That smile—it kept coming to mind. Perhaps she reminded him of someone? And perhaps it was only a knee-jerk reaction to the course he had chosen. Intelligent and witty as well as pretty, she would be a far more pleasing prospect to face every morning over breakfast.

Except that such a prospect did not exist. Nor should it. He could not forget the near panic he'd felt during the lowest moments of the last weeks. The thought of failure was insupportable. He had hit upon the best path out of this mess and he was going to follow it right into a cold and sterile marriage.

He gave a cynical shrug; it would be a fair trade, surely. A cold marriage bed for a lifetime of credibility. And he should be down on his knees thanking the powers that be for even such dim prospects, for he was lucky to have a future at all.

These reflections left him in a mood of grim determination. He would prevail, would sacrifice anything to ensure his success. His resolution lasted across Mayfair, through all of his mother's chatter, and right up until he entered the Lowders' family drawing room. It might have lasted through the entire Season and seen him through the tedious weeks ahead, had it not encountered the pair of ankles.

A very fetching pair of ankles, framed by a scalloped

flounce and situated right at eye level. Grim determination stood not a chance; it melted under a combined onslaught of shock and pure male appreciation.

'Have the guests arrived, Thomas?' asked a voice situated somewhat above the ankles and the stepladder they were perched upon. Charles couldn't see how far above because his gaze remained locked where it did not belong. 'Hold a moment and let me hand down my things. I wouldn't wish to be caught at work.'

'Too late, my dear,' his mother chirped. 'Come down, please, you frighten me out of my wits on that thing.'

But the unexpected reply had disturbed the girl's balance, both mental and physical. A surprised 'Oh!' came from above and then the ankles and the stepladder began to sway.

The footman who had admitted them—the recalcitrant Thomas, no doubt—lunged for the ladder, but it was Charles who, without conscious thought, reached out and plucked the girl from the air.

'Charles, dear, I did particularly wish for you to meet Miss Westby today,' his mother said, her voice wry.

But Charles was staring at the woman he held in his arms. She was a beauty indeed, and she'd had quite a fright. Large dark eyes stared apprehensively into his, her arms were locked tight about his neck and her soft, full bosom was pressed quite delightfully into his chest. But pleasure faded as realisation dawned, and then it turned to growing outrage. 'You!' he gasped.

Sophie's heart was beating so fast—partly from fear, partly from exasperation at the absurdity of the situation, and partly from sheer feminine appreciation—that she was sure Charles could feel it. To view Charles from a few feet's perspective was a delight; the prospect from a few inches was awe-inspiring.

It was as if he had been designed to be pleasing to every eye. His hair was the colour of chestnuts, thick and luxuriant, his eyes a deep brown that clearly signalled his shock—and his interest. Strong cheekbones, stubborn chin, every inch of him solid, authoritative, and somehow *English*. It was enough to tempt one to sing in praise of a nation that could produce such a specimen.

She'd forgotten that smug English superiority. Ever so slowly the astonishment faded from his face, only to be replaced once more by haughty disdain. *What was it?* she wondered. What had happened in the intervening years to turn her laughing boy into this proud, imposing man?

This proud man who still held her tight in the incongruous safety of his arms. Sophie took encouragement where she could find it, and forged ahead.

'Well, my lord, you have caught me—literally—
at a disadvantage once again.' She peeked over his
shoulder, 'Really, Thomas, it was too bad of you to
neglect to warn me. I'm sure we have embarrassed
Lord Dayle past all bearing.' She handed the
footman her wet paintbrush and cut off his apologies. 'No, it's fine, really, just remove my equip-
ment, please, and we shall muddle through, shan't
we, my lord?'

Charles did not reply, although the stark lines of
his face tightened, and so did his grip.

'Do put her down, Charles, for heaven's sake,'
Lady Dayle commanded.

He flushed and immediately set her down, with a
bit more force than was necessary, Sophie thought.
She flashed him an unrepentant smile, and wiped
her paint-stained fingers. She would break through
his stone-sober demeanour, she thought, if she had
to take up a chisel and hammer to do it.

'I'm fine, truly,' she said as Lady Dayle fussed
over her. 'I should have known not to ask Thomas
to warn me, he's started up a flirtation with the
parlor maid and was bound to forget.'

'Mother,' Charles said tightly, 'you seem to have
some idea just what the dev—deuce is going on
here. Perhaps you will enlighten me?'

'It is what I have been trying to do, my dear,

indeed, it is why you were invited today.' Beaming, she took Sophie's hand. 'Allow me to reacquaint the two of you. I do not say introduce, for, if I recall, the two of you did bump into each other in Dorsetshire in years past.'

'We have indeed bumped into one another,' Charles began in an acid tone, 'and only too recently—' He stopped. 'In Dorsetshire?'

'Yes, dear. May I present Miss Westby? Sophie, surely you remember my son?'

Sophie could only nod. Her heart was, unexpectedly, in her throat and she could not tear her eyes from him as she waited for the truth to strike. She could almost see his mind spinning behind the dark and masculine beauty of his eyes. 'Westby,' he repeated. And there it was, at last, shining in his gaze, knowledge, and a flash of pure, unfettered joy. 'Sophie?'

A weight of uncertainty dropped from Sophie's soul. He knew her. He was glad. She felt as if she could have floated off with the slightest breeze.

He stepped forward and took her hands. His grip was warm and calloused, and so longed for, it almost felt familiar. 'Sophie! I can scarce believe it! It's been so long.'

'Indeed.' She smiled. 'So long that you did not know me—twice over! If I weren't so pleased to see you again, I should feel slighted.'

'It was you in the street that day, and you did not reveal yourself—minx. I do not know how I failed to realise. I should have known that only you would back-talk me so outrageously!'

'Back-talk? I only gave back what you deserved. You were so high in the instep I barely knew it was you at all.'

The door swung open and in swept Emily. 'Oh, do forgive me,' she said, her voice shaky. 'I should have been home an age ago, but you'll never believe it.'

'Emily, are you well?' Sophie turned as Charles dropped her hands. 'What is it?'

'We have been caught up in a riot!' Her hand shook a little as she returned Sophie's embrace.

'A riot?' gasped Lady Dayle. 'My goodness, are you unharmed?'

'Perfectly well, do not fear.' Emily removed her bonnet and moved to a chair. 'Perhaps riot is too strong a word, though it was unsettling!' She tried to rally a reassuring smile. 'It was only a group of mourners who had come from that poor Mr Cashman's funeral. They were quite well behaved, but there were ever so many of them! It was a little frightening to find ourselves in their midst.'

'No weapons, no looting?' asked Charles. His voice had gone cold and harsh, so different from just a moment ago that Sophie could scarcely credit it.

His smile was gone. All traces of warmth had vanished and he stood, shoulders squared, solid and unmoving. Sophie instinctively took a step towards him. He looked as if the weight of the world had descended upon him.

'No, thank the heavens.' Emily sighed. 'I own that the man was used rather badly, but I have no wish to be drawn into the situation.'

'Used indeed!' said Sophie, still eyeing Charles uneasily. 'And then cheated, robbed, and made a terrible example of by the very government he risked his life to protect.' She allowed Lady Dayle to pull her to a chair. 'I wish I might have paid my respects.'

The man's story was tragic, and all too common. A navy man, the 'gallant tar' had faithfully served his country for years. The war at last over, he'd been discharged, but unable to collect his arrears in pay and prize money. He'd pursued his claim, but had been insulted and ignored. The same day as his last curt dismissal by the Admiralty Board, spurred by drink and anger, he'd become caught up in an angry crowd bent on riot, and he'd been caught and arrested for stealing arms from a gunsmith's shop. Tried, convicted, and publicly hanged, he'd become a symbol for thousands of the discontented across the nation.

'In any case, it is too upsetting to contemplate,' shuddered Emily. 'Let us order tea and talk of pleasanter things.' She rang for a servant, and then settled on the sofa next to Lady Dayle. 'Well, Lord Dayle, tell us how you are getting on after that absurd Avery situation.'

Charles paled even further and shot a wary glance in Sophie's direction. Clearly he did not account this a more pleasant subject.

'I am faring little better,' Charles responded, 'though the truth is out.' He spoke tightly, his face a mask of control. 'I prefer not to discuss the subject, ma'am.'

'I don't know who could have believed such nonsense in any case,' the viscountess complained. 'As if you would have been interested in such a nasty old piece of baggage.'

'Mother,' chided Charles.

'I'm sorry, my dear, but it is the truth. Lord Avery and his wife have antagonised each other for years, each trying to outdo the other in their outrageous bids for attention. I wish they would finally admit their feelings for each other and leave the rest of us out of it.'

'Charles is not the first young Tory she has used to stir her husband's jealousy,' Emily agreed.

'Nor am I the first whose career has been jeopardised,' he added, 'but I am the first to be so publicly reviled for it.'

'It is your past exploits that make you so irresistible to the papers, my lord,' Sophie teased, hoping to restore his good humor. 'They think to line their pockets with so long a list.'

'I would that that were the only motivation behind this constant attention. But someone seems determined to unearth every scrape I've landed in since I was breeched.'

Sophie deflated a little with this answer. It would appear that Charles could not be coaxed back to his good humour. If anything, he looked more morose as the tea things were brought in and he took a seat. Emily poured, and, after she had offered around the biscuits, she exchanged a pointed look with Lady Dayle.

'I know it has been an age since you were last in this room, Charles,' his mother said, setting her tea down, 'but have you noticed the changes that have been wrought?'

The question appeared to startle him. As it would any man, Sophie supposed. Yet she could not suppress the nervous chill she felt when she recalled his scorn at their last meeting.

He glanced about, and Sophie followed suit. She could not help but be well pleased with what she saw. Emily had held a definite vision for this room, and between them they had created something special. Much of the woodwork had been painted a dark green, softer shades of the same hue graced the walls and were incorporated into the upholstery and curtains. Rich cherry furniture, including a stately grandfather clock, contrasted nicely. It looked well, and, most importantly, it satisfied a secret longing in her friend's soul.

'It is very peaceful,' Charles replied, sounding surprised.

'Exactly how I hoped it would feel,' Emily agreed. 'I wanted to step in here and feel as if I were hidden away in a forest glen. It is only just finished, and I could not be happier with the effect. I am extremely pleased with the artist who helped me with the design. In fact, although it is supposed to be a secret, I believe I will share one aspect that was done just for me. You will not spread the tale, and I am convinced no one else would have done the thing so well.'

Sophie held her breath. The viscountess looked intrigued. Charles appeared to be looking for a back way out. But Emily was not to be deterred.

'When I was a girl,' she began in a dreamy voice, 'I was fascinated with fairy rings. I searched our home woods diligently, and when I found one I would spend days there, making wishes and dreaming dreams of the fairy realm.'

'Your mother and I did the very same thing, dear, when we were young.' Lady Dayle's voice was gentle.

'I know,' Emily said fondly. 'She discovered me one day. She joined me, plopped herself right down amongst the toadstools in her best day dress. We spent many a happy day so occupied.' She sat quietly a moment and Sophie's heart ached for her friend.

'So when we began this room,' Emily continued, 'I tried to convince…ah…my designer, to use a fairy wallpaper pattern I had seen in a design guide. It really was quite loud and colourful, though, and not nearly so tasteful as what we have here now. It was my designer who convinced me and still found a way to incorporate the youthful fantasies of a silly, nostalgic woman.'

'Don't keep us in suspense, dear,' said Lady Dayle. 'Where is it?'

'All around us,' said Emily, 'and neither of you had any idea! But if you look closely, you'll see a pixie here and there peeking out at us.'

The viscountess immediately rose and began to search, but Charles looked straight at Sophie's green-stained fingers then right at the high spot where she had been when he entered the room. And there she was, a tiny green and gold-haired sprite, peering at them from the top of the curio cabinet.

He looked back at her and Sophie smiled and gave a little shrug.

'Well, Charles,' his mother said with a touch of sarcasm as she returned to her seat, 'that's a sour look you are wearing. Have you too much lemon in your tea, or are you in some kind of pain?'

'No, no.' He let loose a little bark of laughter. 'No more than any other gentleman forced to listen to a pack of ladies fussing over *décor.*'

It was Sophie who was in pain. He was being deliberately cruel. But why?

'Well, pull yourself together, dear,' his mother was saying, 'for you are in for more than a little fussing.'

'Yes, for we have saved the best surprises for last,' Emily said.

'I think he has already discerned one of them,' said the viscountess shrewdly. 'And you are correct, my son, it was indeed Sophie who envisioned the design of this room. She has done a magnificent job, both here and at Mrs Lowder's home in Dorsetshire.'

'I congratulate you on your fine work, Miss Westby,' he said, his voice coldly formal. 'I wish you equal success in your début.'

Sophie was growing tired of Charles's swaying moods. What on earth was wrong with the man?

None of this was going as she had planned. 'I am a designer, my lord, not a débutante,' she said firmly.

He cocked his head as if he had heard her incorrectly. 'Nonsense. You are an earl's niece. You are of good birth and good connections.' He nodded at the others in the room. 'Why else come to London at the start of the Season?'

'She has come at my invitation, Charles,' his mother intervened. 'Both to be introduced to society and to aid me with your birthday present.'

His look was so frigid that Sophie wouldn't have been surprised if the viscountess had sprouted icicles. 'I beg your pardon?'

Lady Dayle was a warm-hearted and giving woman. She was also still Charles's mother. 'Do not practise your high-handed ways with me, sir.' She softened her voice a bit and continued. 'The Sevenoaks house, dear. A politician needs a place to get away, to invite his cronies and plan strategies, to entertain. The place is run-down and shabby. For your birthday, I would like to ask Miss Westby to help me with the redecorating of it.'

Sophie could have cheerfully kissed Lady Dayle's hem. A house. A nobleman's house. It was exactly what she hoped for.

'I appreciate your thoughtfulness, Mother, but such a large undertaking is unnecessary. I would not wish you to tax yourself. Nor would I wish to be responsible for taking so much of Miss Westby's time away from her first Season.'

Sophie could have cheerfully punched Lord Dayle's nose. Was he insane or merely trying to make her so? Who was he? Haughty aristocrat or charming gentleman? She was beginning not to care.

'Nonsense,' returned his mother. 'I shall see to it that we both divide our time favourably. And with Emily's help as well, we shall have a grand time with it all. You will,' she added her *pièce de résistance,* 'be in no way discommoded.'

'But, Mother,' he returned gently, 'perhaps this sort of project should be undertaken by my bride?'

'I should place a great deal more weight with that argument if such a person existed.' The viscountess sniffed. 'You haven't won the hand of a dyed-in-the-wool puritan yet, my boy.'

Emily spoke up. 'I dare say that your mama should derive more enjoyment from such a project, in any case, my lord,' she said with a significant look.

This argument did indeed appear to sway him. 'Oh, very well,' he capitulated with bad grace. He turned, his eyes narrowed, to Sophie, 'But I beg you both, here and now, to leave me out of it. It is entirely in your hands. I do not wish to be conferred with, consulted with, or called on. In fact, I would be mightily pleased if I hear not another word on the matter until it is finished.'

Even before he had finished his sentence Sophie was swallowing her disappointment, pushing away a deep sense of betrayal. She had been so humiliatingly wrong. The Charles Alden she had longed for was nothing more than a foolish girl's fantasy. A ghost of a man who might have grown from a good-hearted boy.

The real Charles Alden, she was forced to conclude, was this hard-eyed monument, more marble than flesh. He had no inclination to renew their friendship, and she—well, she was long past the time she should be indulging in daydreams.

She met his stony gaze and nodded her agreement as Lady Dayle and Emily chattered, full of excitement and plans. Sophie would easily—gladly—meet his terms. She would do her very best for the viscountess and she would make the viscount's home a place of beauty and harmony. But another ten years would be too soon for her to ever see Lord Dayle again.

He stood. 'I shall leave you ladies to your fairies, furniture, and furbelows.' He bowed and took his leave, never quite looking Sophie's way. She watched him go, felt her dreams dragging out behind him, and took some small satisfaction in the cheerful green handprint showing clearly on his left shoulder.

Charles clutched his hat with shaking fingers as the door closed firmly behind him. For several long moments he stood, shoulders hunched to ward off the pain. Sophie.

When he had first realised who she was—for the briefest moment—he had forgotten. Elation and an odd possessiveness had surged through his veins. At last fate had smiled upon him and sent the one person who in some elemental, deeply satisfying way, understood him completely.

The flash of joy and relief had been overwhelming. His ally, his friend, his very own Sophie.

Then Mrs Lowder had come in talking of riots, and he had remembered. Realised. She didn't know, could never understand. They couldn't ever go back. The thought hurt on a nearly physical level.

She had grown up, his childhood friend. She was all vibrant energy and exotic beauty, as passionate and unconventional as ever. Still, he had longed for her company. He wanted to tell her everything and hear everything she had done over the years.

He could not. Judging from their two unconventional encounters, she had not changed. She was impetuous, opinionated, and always in trouble. A friendship with her would be dangerous. Poison to Viscount Dayle, the only part of him still living. He had realised it at once; he could not have her. Ever.

So he had acted like the juvenile she had known and he had flailed at her in anger. Now she would despise him, and it was better that way. Easier.

Charles straightened and dragged himself off. He would go home and examine this situation in the way that it deserved—through the bottom of a bottle of blue ruin. Then he would live the rest of his life the way he deserved. Alone.

Chapter Four

'Sophie, you are not attending me.' Lady Dayle's words barely penetrated the mist in Sophie's head.

'What?' She blinked her eyes and focused on the jumble of fabric swatches and wallpaper patterns spread before her. 'Oh, yes, that combination is lovely, but I don't know how much more we can accomplish until I have seen the house.'

It was a true statement, but what she left unsaid was that though this was the chance of a lifetime, she could scarcely concentrate on plans for the house without succumbing to a barrage of conflicting thoughts about its owner. One minute she was wishing him to perdition where she would never have to lay eyes on him again. The next she wanted to knock him to the floor, sit on him, and flick his ear until he confessed just what it was that forced him to act like an ass, just as she had done when she was twelve and he had hidden her favourite box of coloured chalks.

'I know, dear, but it will not be long before we see it. I've already sent word to the staff to remove all the covers and shine the place up, so you'll see exactly what you have to work with. In a day or two we can visit and— Oh, I've had the most fabulous idea! Let us make a party of it!'

'Party? But we will have much work to be done if we are to be there for only a day.'

'True, but we can at least make a picnic of it. Emily, and her dear little one, will enjoy it. Jack can come, he needs to get away from his books occasionally. And Charles can escort us. How refreshing it will be to get away together!'

A little *frisson* of panic travelled up Sophie's spine at the mention of his name. 'I do not think we should bother Lord Dayle. I promised he should not be troubled by this project, if you will remember.'

'Don't be such a widget! We are his family. It is his house, for heaven's sake. In any case, we'll invite that dreadfully prosy Miss Ashford along and he can feel as if he is putting his time to good use.'

A different kind of twinge struck Sophie. 'Miss Ashford?'

'The leading candidate for dullest débutante in London, and therefore the main focus of Charles's attention. He has a notion that marriage to a strait-laced girl of impeccable family and no two thoughts to rub together will settle all his troubles in one fell swoop.' Lady Dayle paused. 'Although he could not have picked a more unlikely miracle worker, should you ask me.'

'Miracle worker?'

'Indeed. An alliance with such as her, he expects, will reassure the party, restore his standing in the *ton,* and stop the papers' infernal fascination with his old exploits.'

Surely it was a sudden onset of the putrid fever that had Sophie's throat closing and her eyes watering, not the tight fist of jealousy or the realisation that if *that* was the sort of girl Charles was looking for, it was no wonder he wanted nothing to do with *her.*

'In any case, we'll ask him tonight at Lady Edgeware's ball,' continued the viscountess, unaware of her protégée's distress.

'I know you went to a deal of trouble to have me invited, my lady, but I am of a mind to stay quietly at home tonight. You know that going about in society is not my true reason for being here, and, indeed, I am not feeling all that well.'

'Nonsense. All work and no play, and all those other adages, my dear. In any case, I think we are avoiding the real issue.' She stroked the back of Sophie's hand. 'You must face him some time, you know. Emily and I will be with you, there will be nothing to fear.'

Indignant, Sophie sat up straighter. 'I am not afraid of Lord Dayle.' She might not have the pedigree or propriety of a Miss Ashford, but she was no coward.

'Good Lord, why should you be? I was not speaking of my addlepated son. I meant Lord Cranbourne, your uncle.'

Her uncle. A man for whom she had given up all feeling, confused or otherwise. Would that she could do the same for Lord Dayle. 'I'm not afraid of him, either, but neither do I wish to rush a confrontation.'

'There will be no confrontation, of that I can assure you. Just a polite, long-overdue meeting.' Dismissing the subject, she forged ahead. 'We've been so busy lately with plans for the house that we have quite neglected our social obligations, and this will be just the thing to liven you up a bit. And in any case you must come tonight and see Lady E's Egyptian room. It is quite famous, and you will not want to miss it.'

'Oh, very well…' Sophie paused. 'Did you wish me to bring my notebook? Are you thinking of something similar for the Sevenoaks house?'

'Heavens, no! She has taken Mr Hope's ideas and run wild. It is a dreadfully vulgar display.'

Sophie thought longingly of her own bed and her previous plans for the night: a quiet meal in her room, a nice long soak, the pages of portraits she would like to draw of Lord Dayle before she shredded each one and consigned it to the fire. Then she thought of him dancing with the faultlessly lineaged Miss Ashford, or perhaps taking her for a stroll in the garden, where he would kiss her eminently respectable lips.

'In that case, how can I resist?'

Miss Ashford, Charles thought as he led the lady out for their set, was everything he was looking for in a bride. She did everything proper and said everything prudent. She even danced in an upright manner, perfectly erect and composed, with no expression, of enjoyment or otherwise, on her face.

Why, then, was he trying so hard to discover some chink in her flawless façade? He had spent the evening trying to uncover something—addiction to fashion, a sweet tooth, a secret obsession for nude statuary, anything.

He had failed. The lady seemed to be everything reputable and nothing else. No flaw, no interests or passions or pursuits. And no warmth for him, either.

She accepted his attentions with calm dignity and with no sign of reciprocal regard or even disfavour. He felt as if he was courting a pillar. Lord, it was a depressing thought.

Their set finished, he led her back across the ballroom, exchanged all the correct pleasantries with her equally bland mama, and took his leave, trying not to yawn.

A slap on the back from his brother brought him awake.

'Evening, Charles,' Jack said, 'you look like a man who could do with a drink.' He signalled the footman and when they both had a glass of champagne, said, 'Just thought you might want to celebrate a bit—your name hasn't been in the papers for a week, but it has shown up in the betting book at White's.' He swept his glass across, indicating the crowded ballroom. 'They're betting which of these dull-as-ditchwater debs will have the chance to tame you.' He drank deep again.

Charles grinned, feeling more than a little satisfaction. Things were finally progressing according to his own plans. He still had much political ground to make up, and, ridiculous though it might be, his social success would help him cover it quickly.

'I am happy to report that Miss Ashford is the filly out in front,' said Jack. 'Wouldn't be surprised if your attention to her tonight makes it into the *respectable* social columns tomorrow.'

Charles's good humor deflated a little. He glanced over at Miss Ashford, who stood in unsmiling, serious conversation with some matron or other. This marriage-of-convenience business was a bitter brew to swallow. But swallow it he would, and be thankful for it, he thought. The bitterness he undoubtedly deserved, and some stubborn, wilful part of him welcomed the challenge.

'Good.' That same stubborn part of him yearned to find the person responsible for stirring up this hornet's nest of scandalbroth. 'Unfortunately I haven't had the same luck finding the editor of the *Augur.*'

'Someone's tipped him off,' said Jack.

'It is a convenient time for the man to have developed a far-flung sick relative. I doubt I'll get anywhere with him if he's anything like the one at the *Oracle*. He makes Lord Avery's talk of a peasant revolution look quite sane. Hates the nobility, took a satanic glee in rubbing my nose in my own misdeeds.'

'He certainly did his research.' Jack grinned. 'Honestly, Charles, even I did not know that you were the one who painted old King Alfred's statue such a heavenly shade of blue. There's a certain justice in it that you must pass the old boy every day on the way in to the Lords.'

Charles firmly suppressed his answering smile. 'Somebody's feeding them information, and being bloody clever about it. My man hasn't found a scrap of a clue.'

'So what shall we do now?'

'I meant to ask you to take over the search for the missing editor.' He clapped his brother on the shoulder. 'Sorry, old man, I know it means time away from your research.'

'It's no matter, I find I quite enjoy this sleuthing. It's not so different from scholarly research, except for the venue. And I never had to buy so many rounds in the university library.'

'I appreciate it, Jack. In the meantime I have taken a lesson from this tricky cove and decided to fight him with his own weapons.'

'Do tell!'

'One of my footmen has been "bribed" by the press.'

Jack laughed. 'Damn me if you aren't brighter than you look, big brother. Brilliant idea. Now you can leak the information you wish to hit the streets.'

Charles smiled. 'Before long there will be an entirely different view of the "Wicked Lord Dayle" circulating.'

'I'd drink to it, but my glass is empty. Ah, well. Perhaps I will dance, since I am all rigged out and actually made it to one of these intellect-forsaken functions.' He surveyed the room, then nodded his head and raised a brow. 'And there is just the creature to make me willing to dredge up the memories of those nightmarish dancing lessons— Mother's protégée. Take a look, Charles, she cleans up excellently well.'

Charles did not turn. He had spent the evening purposefully trying not to notice Sophie. And yet he knew how incredible she looked in her exquisitely embroidered ivory gown. He knew how the scarlet of her overdress contrasted so richly and set off the lustrous sheen of her ebony tresses, and he could probably calculate to the smallest measurement just how much of her smoothly glowing skin was displayed.

He did not look, for every time he did he found himself mocked by his own thoughts. *He would prevail, would sacrifice anything to ensure his success.*

He'd had no idea just how much he would be asked to sacrifice.

Jack was leaning in closer. 'Tell me, what do you think of that whole situation? There's been a bit of gossip there as well. None of it malicious, so far, just curious, what with the estranged uncle and the unflagging interest in design.' He nodded again towards the corner where their mother stood with Sophie and a group of friends. 'Although I did hear a few catty whispers from the younger set, something about the girl having trouble with society at home.'

Charles unclenched his teeth. 'I think that her presence makes Mother happy, and for that we owe her much.'

'Without a doubt. I haven't seen Mother so animated since… well, in a long time. But I confess, at first I thought that Mother was matchmaking.'

This time Charles could not stop the grin that came at his brother's words. 'It occurred to me as well. In fact, I scrubbed up the courage to confront her, thinking to forestall any hopes in that direction, only to be unequivocally warned off.'

'I was read the same lecture.' Jack rolled his eyes and imitated his mother's stern tone. '"The dear girl has suffered enough at society's hands. I mean to ease her way, not subject her to the wayward attentions of a man too busy with his nose in a book to treat her properly."'

Charles laughed. 'It was my boorish moods and general crankiness.'

'Well, she's right, old boy. You are a cranky boor and I am in no way ready to acquire a leg shackle, but that doesn't mean I can't dance with the little beauty.'

Charles watched him go. Watched him receive a smile from Sophie and a warning look from their mother. Watched the other men watching her as she gracefully took the dance floor, smiling her evident enjoyment. Then he turned, heading for the card room, where one of the members of the Board of Trade was reportedly diminishing his own cash flow.

Sophie watched him leave the ballroom as the dance began. She had been surreptitiously watching him all evening, all the while painfully aware that he was nearly the only person present not watching her.

The *beau monde* did not know what to make of her. Her birth was good, her fortune respectable, though it had a slightly mercantile taint. But she was undeniably not one of them. At three and twenty she was a bit long in the tooth to be entering society. Worse, her manner was too direct, her looks too exotic, her passions too strongly expressed. She was *too much* of everything, she felt, for them to be comfortable with her.

They studied her like a rare insect, some with fascination, some with revulsion, and Sophie wouldn't have cared a whit, yet she knew Lady Dayle would be distressed should she be found wanting.

Not to mention that she was absolutely determined, even more so as she pretended to ignore Charles ignoring her, that he would not find her alone and friendless today as he had so many years ago. Especially not when his own social standing appeared to be so fully restored. The 'Wicked Lord Dayle' might not play well in Whitehall, but since the rumours began of his search for a viscountess, he was a hit in Mayfair.

So she had smiled. She had sparkled. She had danced and talked with a great many boring gentlemen, and she had secretly studied Charles the way the rest of the room studied her, trying to fathom his mysteries.

He was incredibly handsome tonight, in deep blue and creamy white. Someone had tamed his wayward hair; like him, it was shining and gorgeous and contained.

When, she wondered, had he donned this mask of control? She knew he must be relieved at his restoration, but there was no sign of it. No sign of any emotion, except for a few moments of obvious camaraderie with his brother. He remained calm and cool, receiving attention from every woman in the room as if it were his due. He spent a good deal of time in corners with other gentlemen of a political bent, danced only a few dances, and twice only with Miss Ashford.

She could not like the man he had become. But though she wavered between hurt and disdain, she had to admit also her fascination. How and when had he changed so completely? She was not ready to give up on her questions, to give up on him.

Let him bask in the admiration of the silly women of this world. Sophie knew her man, and with the old Charles a little disdain went a long way. Perhaps, with this stranger, it would as well.

So she thanked his brother prettily for the dance and bided her time. When she grew tired of feeling like a new species of insect at a naturalists' gathering, she retreated to the ladies' retiring room. She dawdled for a bit in front of the mirror, gathering her determination. She was no stranger to disapproval. At the tender age of seven she had been orphaned, uprooted from her home in Philadelphia, and unceremoniously shipped to England. She'd dreamed of a warm welcome and a loving uncle. Instead she'd been shuffled off to a lesser estate, hidden away along with her eccentric aunt, who sometimes thought that she was seven years old as well.

The people of Blackford Chase had taken their cue from the earl and done their best to forget her existence. She'd been so lonely until she found Charles, and again after he left. Still, she had managed well enough for herself and eventually found a way to be useful. She could do the same here. And here she still had a chance at unravelling the mystery that was Charles Alden.

Still lost in thought, she headed back, but was surprised when she heard a step close behind her and felt a hand on her shoulder.

'Good evening,' a strangely familiar voice greeted her.

Sophie froze. It wasn't her chance. It was her uncle.

She forced herself to breathe deeply and turned. She'd known she must face him some time, but still she found herself unprepared for the pain. 'Hello, Uncle.'

He had grown older. The broad shoulders she remembered were a little stooped, the dark hair shot with grey.

'It has been a long time,' he said.

She inclined her head. There was no polite reply to that.

'You are doing well for yourself. You've shown initiative getting yourself to London.' He smiled for the first time and looked her over like a horse at Tattersalls. The smile did not reach his eyes; they glittered, reminding her of a hungry spider. 'Quite a change from the snivelling chit that landed on my doorstep.'

He would find her no easy prey. 'Indeed,' she politely agreed. 'Many changes take place over the course of so many years. The most important one is that I no longer need, or desire, your approval.'

Her rudeness didn't faze him. 'You've got your mother's spirit as well as her looks.'

'Enough of it to tell you that you may go to the devil, which is exactly what she said to you, is it not?'

'Clever, too. Young lady, you have far more potential than I have given you credit for.'

'Lord Cranbourne,' a clear voice rang out, and Lady Dayle materialised behind Sophie. 'We so hoped to see you tonight. How nice to see that Sophie has at last tracked you down.'

'She has indeed, and I see how wrong I have been not to search her out sooner. But I shall make amends and call on you soon, my dear.' He made his bow and departed.

Lady Dayle turned and stroked Sophie's face, her own dark with concern. 'Are you all right?'

'Perfectly.'

'I am sorry I was not here sooner.'

'Do not worry.' Sophie made herself smile for her friend. 'The worst is over. It will only get easier from here.'

'I hope you are right.' She sighed. 'But he did not seem upset in the least, did he? I had worried that he would resent my interference. Well! Everyone is still at supper. If you have finished, then perhaps we should take a look at the Egyptian Room?'

'Lead on, my lady.' But Sophie drew her shawl

closer to her for warmth, and tried to ignore the fact that her hands were shaking.

She forgot her discomfort once they entered the Egyptian Room. Sophie's shawl fell along with her jaw as the door closed quietly behind them. It was unlike anything she had ever seen. She had expected something cold and sterile. Instead her senses were under attack. The vibrant warmth of the vivid blues and oranges contrasted strongly with the antique red and black. It was astonishingly busy, yet the lines were straight and clean. It was alien, spectacular, and oddly compelling.

'Dreadful, isn't it?' asked Lady Dayle. 'I don't think this was what Mr Hope meant at all.'

'In fact, I believe this is quite close to the spirit of some his work,' came a voice from deep within a lionskin chair. 'Except for all the odd animal parts. I believe that little touch is all Lady Edgeware's.'

Charles stood and Sophie's heart dropped. She was shaken still, and edgy from her encounter with her uncle. Not at all up to dealing with him, or the way he made her feel.

'Charles! What are you doing in here?' Lady Dayle's tone was sharp.

'I've come to see Lady E.'s latest acquisition.' He gestured and Sophie swept around a sofa with legs fashioned after an elephant's.

'Oh!' she gasped. It was a monstrosity of a stuffed crocodile, frozen for ever in a snarling pose of attack.

'Good heavens,' complained Lady Dayle, 'the woman has gone too far. Charles, you shouldn't be hiding away in here. Some baron from the north has stolen a march on you and taken Miss Ashford in to supper.'

'I make it a point to come in here every year. It helps to distract myself from my own folly when I contemplate someone else's.'

'Yes, well, perhaps you should not encourage Lady Edgeware. I don't find this place at all comfortable, but there is an appealing piece here and there. This, for instance,' and she swept toward the heavily adorned marble mantel.

'Hold, Mother,' Charles warned, but it was too late. The short, pearl-encrusted train of her gown had caught in the jaws of the stuffed crocodile. The tear of fabric sounded loud in the room, along with the pinging dance of scattered pearls.

'Oh, the horrid thing,' huffed the viscountess. 'Do untangle me, Sophie, and tell me how bad it is.'

Sophie knelt to examine the hem. 'I'm afraid it is quite a long tear, my lady. Let me help you to the retiring room and we'll find a maid to stitch you back up.'

'No, no, dear. You stay and finish your look

around. If you find any of my seed pearls, do be so good as to tuck them into your reticule. No, Charles, you go on to the dining room. I shall be back in a trice to fetch Sophie.'

She was gone from the room before either of them could protest. Neither of the pair left behind would have been comfortable had they seen the crafty smile she wore as she went.

Sophie, who felt that her current mood could rival any of Charles's most cranky moments, bent again and began to gather the pearls. 'You should go, my lord. I doubt Miss Ashford would be happy to know you were alone in here with another woman.'

He stood, silent and cold, for a moment. 'Perhaps you are right.' He turned to go.

Perverse disappointment bit into Sophie. 'Incomprehensible.' She said it just loud enough for him to hear.

'I beg your pardon?'

Defiant, Sophie lifted her chin. 'I was remarking to myself that I find you incomprehensible.' She pursed her lips and shook her head. 'But upon reflection I find that I don't even want to try to understand it.'

'Understand what?' he demanded.

'How the boy who faced down Otto, the village bully twice his size, the same boy who climbed the maypole just to win a bet, the man who swam naked in the Serpentine with two of the city's most famous high flyers—how that person somehow metamorphosed into the pluck-less specimen before me.'

Charles just blinked for several seconds. 'Did you say pluck-less?'

'Yes, but I could have substituted faint-hearted, mean-spirited, dandified, or, let us not forget, hen-pecked.'

For a moment he looked as if he might explode. Then he laughed. And laughed. Then he sat down in the lion chair and laughed some more.

'Damn you, Sophie,' he said when he had recovered, 'you always did bully me out of a bad mood. I should have remembered.'

He met her gaze as he smiled in remembrance and Sophie's breath caught. Here it was, the look, the feeling of friendship and something indefinable, but *more*. This was what she had been looking for when she found him again. It was sweet to discover it at last, but also painful, because she knew it was fleeting.

'I? Bully?' she asked. 'You are the one who has yelled at, insulted, and ignored me. A little name calling is the least you deserve.'

He grinned. 'How did you hear about the Serpentine?'

'The same way the rest of England did—in the

papers. I dare say I've heard of every scrape you've been in since you were fifteen.'

'Good Lord, I hope not. Some of them were never meant for ladies' ears.'

'No one has ever had cause to call me faint-hearted,' she said with pride. 'You know I've never cared for what people say of me. You never did either.'

The challenge hung in the air between them, and Sophie held her breath. For a moment she thought she had done it, that he would tell her what haunted him, but then he grimaced and the light in his eyes died. The mask was back.

'Now I do,' he said, his voice harsh, 'and it is past time you did too.'

'I never thought to see the day I could say this with honesty. I don't like you, Charles. I can't abide the person you have become. You are closed, cold, and cruel.'

'Good. It's better that way.' His voice was as remote as his expression.

'Why are you trying to drive me away?' she whispered.

His eyes closed. He was fighting some inner battle while she waited alone. He knelt and took her hands. His were warm. He smelled of masculine things, smoke and expensive cologne and raw male sensuality. 'Things have changed,' he said gently. 'You are right, I've changed. We cannot be to each other what we once were.'

'Why not?' She had to fight to keep the anguish from her voice.

'Don't, Sophie,' he said, dropping her hands and rising. 'If you only knew how hard it has been.' He was pacing now and she was shaking. 'And you come along and make it so much more difficult.' He turned to her. 'You're not…I cannot…' It was panic in his voice and on his face. Something out of proportion for the situation as she knew it. He began to pace again.

He stopped. 'Listen, Sophie, let's agree to be friends, then. I cannot offer any more. Please.'

He was hurting and, in some way she didn't understand, it was her fault. She wanted to ease his pain, wanted to know what it was that frightened him. 'We have always been friends, Charles. We always will be.'

'Thank you.' His relief was palpable.

Confused, she bent back to her forgotten task. The tiny pearls blurred as she fought the tears that threatened.

'Here, let me help you, then I shall escort you to Mother.'

She blinked furiously. He didn't truly wish for her friendship either, he just wanted to be rid of her.

They worked quietly for a moment before he said, 'I believe there are some still trapped in the creature's jaws.'

Sophie struggled to regain some semblance of herself. Never would she allow him to see the depth of her humiliation. She summoned a smile from some buried vein of strength she didn't know she possessed. 'Shall I leave them to you, then?'

He made a face and knelt down, picking a jewel from the crocodile's teeth. 'You always did leave the nasty work to me.'

'How can you say so?' she protested, leaning back on her heels. 'I believe it was I who pulled the leeches off you when you would go into the South Bog after those berries.'

'Very true,' he returned, 'but who had to muck out the gardener's shed when you decided to raise a goat in there?'

Her smile was a true one this time. At least they had not lost this, the ease they felt together. It had been present since their first meeting and was the part of their relationship that she would have mourned most. Perhaps she could be content with this. 'Poor William,' she sighed. 'He's still a terror, you know.'

He made a strange, strangled noise. 'William!' He began to chuckle. 'I'd forgotten the goat's name.' He began to laugh in earnest again. 'Because Billy was undignified!' he whooped, and set himself off again into gales of laughter.

This time she joined in, because it was easier to laugh than to cry.

'Ah, Sophie,' he said a minute later as he wiped his eye, 'we always laughed, didn't we?' He leaned in close to pass her his handful of pearls, his gaze suddenly serious and locked with hers. 'I'd forgotten how much I missed it.'

Now it was her turn to experience a twinge of panic. He was close, so close. He looked relaxed, almost happy now that he had settled her firmly in a distant sphere.

Biting her lip, she asked herself just what it was she wanted. She scarcely knew. She'd come to London telling herself she only wanted to renew their friendship. Now he offered just that and she felt—what? Disappointment. Dissatisfaction. She yearned for that connection that lit her insides, ignited her passion, made her feel whole.

Very well, she breathed deep. She would take what was offered. For now.

She schooled her expression and lifted her gaze to meet his.

But didn't.

Because his was locked on her mouth, and the atmosphere had suddenly, subtly changed. She could almost feel the hot touch of his gaze as it travelled down the column of her neck and across the expanse of her shoulder. The air between them danced with the hard beat of her pulse.

Slowly, his hand rose. Sophie's eyes closed as, whisper-soft, his fingers brushed along her collarbone. Her head tilted as he caressed the one heavy lock that lay against her nape.

It was the tinkling of the scattering seed pearls slipping through her fingers that allowed sanity to intrude. Just in time, too, for once she was released from the sensual spell of Charles's touch, her brain began to process what her ears had been trying to relay.

'I'm sure he must be in here, dear, I left him here gathering up the jewels from my dress.'

Lady Dayle. Right outside the door. Sophie only hoped it was the proximity of the viscountess that caused the horrified expression on her son's face as they both clambered to their feet.

'There you are, my darlings.' Lady Dayle had a distinctly sour-looking Miss Ashford in tow. 'Haven't you found all those pearls yet? I was just telling Miss Ashford about our plans for a picnic, Charles, and felt sure you wouldn't mind if I invited her along.'

'What plans are those, Mother?'

Charles walked away without a second glance, and Sophie had the distinct impression that that look of horror would have been there even had his mother not appeared.

Chapter Five

Perfect morning light, a soft haze of chalk dust, the quiet scratch of a pen—it was a recipe for contentment. Alone in her room, enveloped in her beloved things, Sophie should have been content. Ecstatic, even.

She wasn't, because the air also hung with the heady fragrance of lilacs. He had remembered her favourite flower. A glorious full vase of lilacs rested on her dressing table, their scent teasing her, their beauty distracting her, the card that had accompanied them tempting her to read it just one more time.

Friends, then.

That was all it said, all he offered.

Sophie flung down her pen and gave up her work as a lost cause. It was time she was honest with herself, she thought as she began to pace the room. Her real problem, the true source of her agitation, was the certain realisation that what he offered was not enough.

She wanted the old Charles back, him and their rich, easy friendship. She wanted the laughing, carefree Charles, the one who, when left alone with a pretty girl, would have gone far beyond one burning caress.

She pressed one hand to the spot he had touched and dug her other palm into her brow. She was mourning the passing of a rake! She must be the only person in all England who wasn't completely enamoured of the new Lord Dayle. It was the new Charles they admired, the one who was productive, and prudent, and moody, and so incredibly handsome.

The horrid truth was that she wanted that Charles too.

She groaned and started to pace again. She was as inconsistent as he! He who asked for friendship with words and pen, and something else entirely with stormy eyes and fervent touch.

Sophie sighed and came to a stop. There was only one thing she could be certain of: her need for some answers. She had to know where that mask had come from, what had caused that haunted look in his eyes, where the old Charles had gone. Perhaps a better understanding of Charles's feelings would clarify her own.

Very well, they would be friends. She would chip

away at the stone, remove what obstacles she could from between them, and then? Then she would see what happened next.

She dipped her nose in the bouquet one last time, then turned and rang for Nell. If she was going to begin to look for answers, there was no time like the present.

'Nell,' she began when the maid appeared, 'will you let me know right away when Emily returns from the park with the baby?'

'Yes, miss.' Nell stopped and looked surprised at the stacks of papers and designs covering the bed, the table, and nearly every flat surface in the room. 'Lordy, miss, I hope you don't mind my saying it, but you have been busy. I thought you'd done all you could until you saw the big house?'

'I have. All this—' she gestured '—is for another project. Something very special indeed.' In fact, this work represented a dream very close to Sophie's heart. It was nearly complete, but she was not quite ready to confide in anyone just yet.

'Mrs Lowder did send word that you should be ready for callers this afternoon. Shall I just run a brush through your hair?'

Sophie laughed. 'Nell, you are wonderfully circumspect. Yes, thank you, I always do muss it dreadfully when I am working.'

She sat quietly while Nell plucked the pins from her hair. Once the maid had begun brushing with long, rhythmic strokes, she asked, 'How long have you been with the Lowders, Nell?'

'Oh, going on seven years now, miss. Usually I'm just the upstairs maid, so I was ever so glad when you came.' For the first time Nell sounded shy. Sophie guessed she was not used to talking of herself.

'You've done a wonderful job,' Sophie said warmly, 'and I shall be sure to tell Mrs Lowder so.'

'Oh, thank you, miss. I did get to help with Mr Lowder's sister when she made her come out, and I watched her dresser do her hair ever so many a time, so I had an idea what was needed.'

'Seven years. And you've been in the London house all this time?'

'Yes, miss.' The maid sounded a little wistful. 'Though I've thought a time or two that I might like the country.'

Sophie chuckled. 'I always felt the same about the city. I suppose it's natural to wonder about what you've never really experienced.' She was quiet a moment and then she cast a glance at Nell in the mirror. 'I suppose you've heard a good deal about Lord Dayle's adventures, then? He did keep the London papers busy for a good number of years, did he not?'

Nell ducked her head and kept her brush busy. 'They say he's reformed now, Miss. Though I admit I was surprised when such a good girl as you are had an acquaintance with him.'

'Oh, yes…' Sophie did her best to sound nonchalant '…I've known Lord Dayle since we were both practically in leading strings.' She cocked her head. 'I never truly knew his older brother, though. But you would have been working here when the previous Lord Dayle died?'

'Oh, yes. Such a shame. I even saw him a time or two, he was as wrapped up in politics as Mr Lowder is. That sorry I felt for his poor mother. Bad enough the son, but then her husband gone so soon after.' Nell shivered as she twisted Sophie's hair up and reached for the pins.

'Phillip died at Waterloo, but I was home in Dorset when Lord Dayle took sick. We all thought it just a minor illness. No one expected he would die as well.'

Nell pursed her lips and concentrated intently on her work.

Sophie watched her in the mirror. 'There were vague rumours of trouble in the family at home. Did they reach town?'

'Almost done, now. Such hair you have, miss! You must remember to wear your new bonnet for the picnic tomorrow, it brings out the light in your hair so well.'

'Nell?'

The girl sighed. 'It's just servants' gossip, miss.'

Sophie sat silent, questioning.

'They whispered below stairs that Lord Dayle died because he wanted to.'

Shocked, Sophie said, 'Surely no one believes…?'

Nell shook her head. 'No, they just said he gave up. Got ill and didn't fight it, then he just slipped away.'

Sophie turned around in her chair and gave Nell a measuring look. 'The next time we are at Lady Dayle's house, do you think you could…?'

Nell's bright eyes shone. 'Ask some questions?'

'Discreetly.' Sophie paused. 'You've already shown yourself to be loyal and trustworthy, Nell. I know I can depend upon you in this matter.'

The maid straightened, her face proud. 'Of course, miss.'

A knock at the door startled them both. Sophie called entrance, and a footman opened the door deferentially to announce a visitor waiting below.

With a flustered glance towards the lilacs, Sophie rose. Was it Charles? She gathered her shawl and steadied herself. Good, she could begin finding some answers straight away.

She entered the drawing room a moment later at a sedate pace, chin up, only to draw up short.

'Lord Cranbourne, miss,' the butler intoned.

Once again she found her uncle where she had been expecting someone else entirely.

'Uncle,' she said in the frostiest tone she could summon.

'Niece.' He was equally formal as they seated themselves and the butler offered to go for the tea. He watched her the entire time, his gaze sharply calculating.

As the servant's footsteps faded in the marbled hall, her uncle spoke. 'I was annoyed when I first heard you had come to town, I admit.'

'I am amazed you thought to care one way or another.'

He crossed his legs negligently. 'It doesn't look well, you coming here without my sponsorship, but, after meeting you, I'm willing to overlook the matter.'

Sophie inclined her head regally. 'That does seem to be what you do best.'

He leaned forward, suddenly intent. 'Look here, niece. We can sit here all afternoon while you flail me with the sharp edge of your tongue, or we can get straight to the point. Which would you prefer?'

'Whichever gets us finished quickest.'

He chuckled. 'I'm impressed, my dear, and that is not something I say with any frequency.' He shook his head. 'I just never guessed you had any fire in you.'

The tight control she held on her rage snapped. 'It

is impossible that you would know anything about my character!' She struggled to regain herself as the servants returned with tea.

Heavy silence hung in the room as she poured for them both and wished mightily for Emily's return.

Her uncle was still entirely at ease. 'I know more about you than you would think, young miss, never doubt it. I know you resent me, but what's done is done. We find ourselves now in a situation where we can help each other.'

Determined not to let him see her out of countenance again, Sophie sipped her tea. 'Your offer comes fifteen years too late, sir. I'm not interested.'

'Don't go missish on me now, girl. It took brains and courage to get here without my help. Now I can make sure you go much, much further.' He leaned back. 'I have connections. What is it that you want? To be a leading lady of the *ton?* A political hostess holding her own salons?' He gestured to her colour-stained fingers. 'A patroness of the arts?'

She merely shook her head in reply.

'There is power to be had behind the scenes. True power. Empires are won and lost by chance meetings at a ball, by a loose word let slip over drinks. You could be a great help to me, and I can make sure you meet all the right people.'

Sophie closed her eyes in pain. She'd spent too

much of her life hoping for some kind of attention from her uncle. Now here he sat and she only felt ill. He wasn't interested in her, only in what she could do for him. Perhaps, she thought for the first time, she had been better off without his attention.

'You are more like your mother than I thought possible,' her uncle continued. 'She had beauty and intelligence and spirit as well. But she chose poorly, and look what it got her. A few years of love in a colonial backwater and a watery grave.' He sat straighter and stared intently at Sophie. 'Don't repeat her mistakes.'

'I thank you for the confidence you have finally shown in me, sir, but I am not feeling at all well just now.' She could stay no longer. What he did not know was that Sophie had her mother's temper as well, rarely raised, but devastating in scale. One minute more of this and she would be throwing his offer, along with her cup of tea, in his face. Only the thought of Lady Dayle's and Emily's disappointment stayed her hand. She took comfort instead in imagining his reaction when all of her plans were revealed. 'Pray, do excuse me.'

He rose and gave a short bow before declaring in a hard voice, 'I'll give you some time to consider. Don't dawdle, Sophie. Together we can accomplish much.'

Shaking, Sophie rose. It was the first time he had

ever called her by her name. Her anger fled, leaving her aching and empty inside. With a barely audible farewell she hurried out and up the stairs. The lilacs mocked her as she entered her room and flung herself upon the bed. First Charles and now her uncle—who would ever have guessed that getting all the things she thought she wanted would be so horribly disappointing?

She cried then, hard, racking sobs for the little girl who had only wanted someone to love her, and for the grown woman still searching.

Lord Cranbourne watched her leave. He turned and stalked out to his waiting carriage, fiercely ignoring the pain once again radiating down his left arm.

The chit was going to be a problem. He had enough trouble this spring chasing after a political appointment that should have come easily, and, far more worrying, dealing with his own body's betrayal. Throw a headstrong brat into the brew and he might not be able to vouch for the outcome.

Inconstancy. Unpredictability. He was unused to such, yet they seemed suddenly pervasive, hanging thick in the air, obscuring his vision, fouling his plans. He was a man used to being in a position of strength, of knowing all the variables in myriad situations and understanding ahead of time where the players were connected and how the final act would play out.

In a world where knowledge was power, he was a very powerful man indeed, albeit, as he had hinted to his niece, behind the scenes. For most of his life it had been enough, but lately, when faced with these reminders of his mortality, he found he wanted more. He wanted just a bit of the glory and recognition due him, and he wanted it with a fierceness that surprised even himself.

Now he stood on the verge of gaining his objective and his carefully laid plans were fragmenting. He clenched his fist to his chest against another pain and cursed out loud. He was not going to go down without a fight.

When the carriage rocked to a stop, Cranbourne stepped down on to Green Street and walked gingerly up the stairs. He'd feel better after a good stiff drink. He left his coat with a footman, and calling for his secretary, headed for his study.

'You're sure that message went off to Philadelphia as planned?' he asked the compact, extremely efficient man.

'Indeed, yes, sir.'

'And we can expect a reply, when?'

'Two weeks…maybe three at this time of year.'

Cranbourne grunted. Three weeks. He was glad

he'd had the foresight to send his inquiries earlier. Judging by the obstinate look on his niece's face, he might need some help from that direction.

'If I may, sir? You have a visitor in your study.'

'Wren, is it?

'No, sir. It is Mr Huxley.'

'What? Old Huxley, here?' he paused outside the study door.

'No, sir, the young gentleman with the maps, if you will remember?'

Cranbourne wrinkled his brow and longed for that drink and a few minutes of peace. Serious matters were afoot. He needed to think. 'Maps? Oh, yes.' He sighed. He'd done a favour for a very useful friend, and hired one of his sons to do some detailed survey work. Heaving a sigh, he went in.

'Lord Cranbourne, sir.' The young man rose, blinking like an owl from behind a thick set of spectacles. 'I have good news. The project is completed.'

But inspiration had hit Lord Cranbourne just as the mid-afternoon sun glinted off Mr Huxley's dishevelled blond hair. The boy was the right age, tall, shaped well, and easy enough to look at if he would lose the barnacles. 'Good, good,' the old man said as he took the papers the puppy handed him. He barely glanced at them. 'Yes, you'll do.

Sit down, my boy.' Cranbourne sank gratefully into his own chair.

'You will find the map completely updated, sir. I walked practically every inch of Lancashire myself. Every lane, farmer's track and footpath is noted.' He handed over another folder. 'The only thing missing, I dare say—' he smiled '—is who is on the roads at present.'

'Yes, very thorough,' agreed Cranbourne, but his mind was racing. Perfect. At the least, young Huxley would serve as a very creditable distraction, but if matters came to a head between his niece and himself, then the man might be more useful yet.

'Here's the additional information you requested as well: innkeepers and way-station holders in the district, and what I could find on meeting places, debating societies and reformist connections.'

'Excellent. Tell me, do you go out into society much, Mr Huxley?'

The boy blinked again, startled. 'No, sir.'

'It's time you started, then. How many years have you, three score?'

'Just eight and twenty, sir, but I fail to see how this relates to the project you hired me for.'

'I've got a new project in mind. Got a niece coming out this Season. I could use a good man like you to squire her about a bit, ask her to dance, take her for a drive now and then.'

'I hadn't really thought to…'

'Nonsense. The girl's a beauty, educated; she's just new to town and doesn't know many people in society. You can't stay a bachelor for ever, sir. I thought to give you first crack at her.'

'You do me an honour, sir, but I have given no thought to taking a wife at present.'

'Oh, well.' Cranbourne shrugged. 'The chit's got no money, unfortunately, but I'd be disposed to look kindly upon her husband. To be his patron, perhaps.' He gazed shrewdly at the young man. 'I belong to a committee of importance or two, you see, and I had thought to propose a few more mapping expeditions. Who knows what might come of it? A project encompassing the entire island, perhaps.'

Mr Huxley blinked once more. 'Perhaps if I just met her, sir.'

Chapter Six

The day of the proposed expedition to Sevenoaks dawned bright, with a slight crispness in the air that boded well for comfortable temperatures later. The company gathered early in Bruton Street and quickly separated into travelling groups. Lady Dayle elected to ride with Emily, her husband and their little boy in the closed carriage. Jack enticed Sophie into his showy cabriolet. Two more carriages, carrying servants, the baby's nurse, and the picnic, stood waiting. And Charles? He stood on the steps, suppressing a sigh as his own smart curricle rounded the corner, heading back to the mews.

'I don't mean to be a bother, Lord Dayle,' Miss Ashford assured him again, 'but a journey of several hours in that contraption? And all the way back, too? I'm not sure Mama would approve.' She gave him an arch look. Charles had the impression that it was meant to be flirtatious.

Charles smiled at her. 'I would gladly give up the chance to drive my bays in exchange for the pleasure of your company, Miss Ashford. We are very glad you could join us today.'

She thanked him with pretty words, but her eyes did not meet his. In fact, Miss Ashford was directing a look of displeasure somewhere else entirely.

It was a man who drew her attention, a battered-looking man in a ragged regimental coat. He walked slowly towards the group, until he was a few feet from Jack's rig. There he stopped, snatched his hat from his head and spoke in urgent tones too low for Charles to hear.

'I'm sure I feel all the pity that is due someone like that, and the compassion for which my own gender is known,' Miss Ashford said in an equally low voice, 'but I cannot think Mayfair a suitable place for him to wander. Should you do something, my lord?'

'I am confident that Jack will handle the matter appropriately,' Charles answered. And, indeed, he saw his brother reach for his purse. He was stalled by Sophie, who leaned down to speak with the grizzled veteran. Clearly startled to be so addressed, the soldier answered her. Sophie continued to speak—indeed, it looked as if she were questioning the man closely. Soon she reached into her reticule, pulled out a scrap of paper and scribbled something on it.

The open barouche arrived just then, and Charles, busy handing Miss Ashford in, missed the end of the strange encounter. He gave the order for the party to set off, and noticed as they drove past the unfortunate man that he clutched the paper tight in his hand and stared after the departing Sophie with a look of dazed surprise.

Charles could not know what she had said to the man, but he recognised that vacant look. It was an expression commonly seen in Sophie's vicinity. He'd worn it himself more times than he could count.

She was a force of nature, his Sophie, and he suspected that her power, like her beauty, had only grown with her. Just look what had happened at Lady Edgeware's ball. A few minutes alone with her and he had forgotten his role. Forgotten his debt. Let down his guard and laughed like he hadn't since Phillip had died.

She fascinated him, yet he was terrified of her. She knew him too well. So easily she had discovered the chinks in his armour. He could never let her look inside. She might discover that there was nothing left underneath.

They would be friends, he had told her, though they both felt that spark, that potential for more. It was that instantaneous jolt he felt in her presence, perhaps, that sizzling reminder that a man did indeed exist under the viscount's shell, that frightened him most of all.

Because she was still Sophie. Still outrageous, outspoken and slightly out of step with the rest of the world. They were qualities he had always enjoyed in her—now they were the very reason he must avoid her.

He had already lived life his own way, for his own pleasure, ignoring the strictures of society, and what had it got him? Only a hellish reputation at first, but too quickly followed by a dead brother, a dead father, a lifetime of remorse and a title that he hadn't ever wanted.

He'd never coveted the viscountcy, but he was saddled with it now, and it came with an enormous debt to repay. It was clear that, if he ever meant to pay that debt, sacrifices were required, the first and greatest of which was his freedom.

He knew now that his theory was sound. Society was quick to judge, but easier to manipulate. They had fussed and worried over his past like a dog with a bone, but all he had needed to distract them was a bigger prize: his bachelorhood.

A few dances with the right debs, a compliment here, a witty rejoinder there; all he'd had to do was show a proper interest in making one of their darlings his viscountess, and suddenly his wickedness became youthful high spirits, his transgressions were forgiven, and invitations began piling up again.

His political prospects had improved as well. He'd been approached at Lady Edgeware's ball by Sir Harold Luskison, an influential member of the Board of Trade. The gentleman had stuck to polite conversation at first, but eventually he had given Charles a friendly slap on the back and approved his attention to Miss Ashford.

'I know you've been down a rough road recently,' Sir Harold had said. 'Avery's nonsense is easy to ignore, but together with the character assassination in the papers? It becomes more difficult.'

Charles had started to speak, but the man had stopped him. 'I know I'm not the only one who has noticed that all of those published escapades are shades of a murky past.' He had flashed Charles a conspiratorial grin, 'Do you know I myself was caught up in one of your pranks, once?'

Charles groaned, but Sir Harold appeared lost in fond remembrance. 'It was that contretemps you got up to at the Lady's Slipper. Do you recall it?'

Recall it? How could he forget? The tavern in the Strand was the scene of the most notorious brawl he and his cronies had ever got mixed up

in. The owner had been in a fury and had had
Charles and his friends thrown into the street.
He'd even threatened to send the bill for repairs
to Charles's father.

Sir Harold was still grinning. 'You make a fine
rum punch, lad. Not too proud to say I sampled a
cup myself.'

Charles rubbed his brow and hid his eyes. The very
next night, he had set up camp outside the pub, with
a small cauldron fitted out like a woman's shoe, in
the likeness of the tavern's famous sign. He had
mixed up his best rum punch and ladled it out for free
to every comer, ruining the pub's business and infuriating the owner all the more. The man had called
the watch and Charles had been lucky to escape.

'It took me all day to put together that cursed
shoe.' He dropped his hand and returned Sir
Harold's smile. 'Do you know I still have it?

The man laughed. 'I dare say there's not one
among us who couldn't rake up a hairy tale or two
from our youth. I just wanted you to know you have
your defenders. The energy and dedication you've
shown since you inherited has done you good.'

Sir Harold had gestured toward the dance floor
then. 'Good gracious, not since that dreadful
Fitzherbert woman has anyone's courtship been so
closely examined. But you are doing well. A steady

girl of good family and reputation will prove your sound judgment and lay your past to rest.'

Charles had been thrilled at the reassurance. His instincts had been correct, his gambit had worked. He had, in fact, felt completely vindicated in his course of action.

Until he had almost kissed Sophie.

'What do you think, my lord?'

Even her interruptions were timed perfectly, Charles thought, mentally noting the addition of another 'Reason to Marry Miss Ashford'. More than happy to be distracted, he fixed his attention on the young lady. 'I beg your pardon, my attention was drawn elsewhere for a moment.'

'I asked,' she said again, allowing the smallest hint of exasperation to colour her question, 'how you think I might best approach Miss Westby. You seem to know her well, so I thought you could advise me.'

'Approach Miss Westby?'

'I think she might benefit from my influence. I shall take her under my wing, as they say. With my help I dare say she shall go on very well here in town.'

Charles shrugged. 'It's very kind of you, but I think she's doing well enough on her own. I can see no need for you to so trouble yourself.'

Miss Ashford threw Charles a significant glance

and favoured him with a very small, tight smile. 'Naturally a busy gentleman such as yourself would not encounter the same sort of small talk that a lady would. Normally I would not deign to pass on such, well—let us call it what it is—petty gossip. But a few things have been brought to my attention, since I am known to also be an acquaintance of your family's.' She paused and this time her speaking look was even more pointed. Charles would have been amused if he hadn't had a sudden chilling vision of the thousands of such arch glances the lady's husband would be subjected to, day in and day out. Chalk one up for the 'Reasons to Consider Someone Else'.

'Fortunately there is nothing that cannot be overcome with my help. The incidents are mostly small and insignificant, in the manner of what we saw this morning, when Miss Westby engaged that beggar man in conversation.'

Charles knew, without a doubt, that he should be grateful to Miss Ashford. She only sought to please him. She only echoed his own doubts about Sophie's behaviour. She only offered to help Sophie in exactly the manner that he wished for himself, if on a larger scale. There was no earthly reason for him to feel such indignation on Sophie's behalf. Yet feel it he did. Indignation and irritation flashed through him at the thought of Miss Ashford's forcing Sophie into a mould fashioned after herself.

'That military man, and all his like, deserves our condescension and compassion, Miss Ashford. God knows they have obtained precious little from the government they risked all to defend.'

'I agree. Yet for a lady to be seen in conversation with them in the street is not at all the thing. If Miss Westby has a charitable bent, I have a far better notion of how she may proceed.'

Charles's interest was piqued. Perhaps Miss Ashford had more bottom than he had suspected. He hadn't had an inkling that she participated in charity work. He couldn't help but approve. 'How so?' he asked.

'I, and a few of my peers, have organised our own charitable society. I mean to ask Miss Westby if she would like to join us.'

'I dare say she would,' Charles said warmly. 'I'm very interested myself. Tell me about your works, perhaps I could help in some way.'

'Oh, it is nothing you would be interested in. We are a small group, and new.'

'Nonsense. I would be glad to help in any way I can. What have you accomplished so far? Have you a board? A charter? Perhaps I could serve as financial advisor and take that burden from you?'

Miss Ashford was looking more and more discomfited. 'I am afraid you have surpassed me already, my lord. As I said, it is a group of *ladies*. We meet every week or so over tea to discuss society's ills. We have not progressed so far as you imagine.'

Charles did his best to hide his disappointment. For a moment he had thought…but no, it was clear that Miss Ashford's society would never progress as far as he imagined. Oh, she might throw a charity ball, but she would never truly interest herself in the plight of the less fortunate. The 'Not Miss Ashford' column was coming on rather stronger than he was comfortable with.

'I fear I must warn you,' he said, 'Miss Westby was never a fan of discussion. If she sees a wrong being committed, she is far more likely to intervene herself than to sit and talk about it.'

'Yes,' agreed Miss Ashford, 'and that is precisely the character flaw I hope to eradicate. Do you know what she said to the Duchess of Charmouth?'

Charles did not know, but he could well imagine. 'No, but I would wager that she criticised that cold and draughty ballroom that her Grace is for ever entertaining in.' The *ton* had suffered, silently shivering, through year after year of the popular event. He almost laughed at the picture of Sophie haranguing the old termagant.

'Worse,' Miss Ashford declared, 'she pointed out everything architecturally wrong with the room, then she came right out and told her Grace that she knew of a builder who could repair it…' and she lowered her voice to a dreadful whisper *'at a good price!'*

Unexpected laughter burst out at the mental image, but Charles tried hard to contain himself when he noticed Miss Ashford's shocked countenance.

'It is no laughing matter, my lord. Such pretension on Miss Westby's part must not be encouraged.'

'And was the duchess insulted?' he asked.

'No, she was not.' Clearly Miss Ashford was puzzled by this. 'But she very easily could have been.'

'What, exactly, was her reply to Miss Westby's advice?'

'She said she was glad indeed to meet someone who would talk sense to her despite her title, and would be gladder still to hear of a man who would not cheat her because of it.'

Charles chuckled, but he could see Miss Ashford's point. Yet even though his head conjured images of Sophie suffering a scathing set-down and social disgrace, urging him again to distance himself from the girl, he knew in his gut that he would not.

She very likely would get herself in some sort of trouble this Season. With Sophie, it just seemed inevitable. But she was the closest friend of his child-hood. He would stand by her, come what may.

It is a shameful thing, some deeply buried part of himself whispered, *that you won't trust her enough to allow her to return the favour.*

The party made good time on the roads and arrived in Sevenoaks just past mid-morning. Everyone welcomed a stop in the village centre to stretch weary limbs and to admire the stand of trees that bestowed on the little town its name.

After a brief respite they climbed back aboard and travelled the short distance to Lord Dayle's di-lapidated house. For a few moments chaos reigned as the house servants came out to greet them, the stable hands swarmed to take charge of horses and vehicles, and those servants who had accompanied them from town set about unloading and locating the best spot to set up the picnic.

For Sophie, their arrival came not a moment too soon. She had fidgeted her way through the entire journey, apologising to Mr Alden and explaining it away as anxiousness to begin her project. What she could not admit to him was how unnerving she found the sight of Charles and Miss Ashford together.

The ride had been bad—the thought of watching them strolling together in the gardens, rowing on the lake, or doing any of a thousand things that courting couples do, was insupportable. She made haste to befriend the housekeeper, therefore, and swept away with her and Lady Dayle, happy to bury her anxiety in her work.

Confused feelings were easy to ignore when one had an entire house to bury them under. Sophie had poured over plans of the estate; she had imagined the rooms as she concocted colour schemes and design themes, but nothing compared to this: walking into the house and knowing that the transformation of it belonged to her. Touching the walls, studying the light, draping fabrics across furniture, and mentally turning a musty, neglected old house into a place of warmth and life.

Sophie had measured, climbed, scraped, pulled, and scribbled page after page of notes and sketches for several blissful, uninterrupted hours. This, this was heaven, and she resisted when Lady Dayle and Emily finally came to insist that she come join the party and eat.

'Do come now, dear,' wheedled Lady Dayle, who had kept up with her for most of the morning. 'You must feed your body as well as your soul. And as much as I enjoy seeing you so happily engaged, it's past time we go and save Charles from Miss Ashford.'

'Save him?' Sophie asked. 'I rather thought he was happy for the chance to continue his courtship.'

'Yes, well, a few hours of the lady's unrelenting company should have cured him of that notion,' Lady Dayle answered with a wry twist of a grin. 'Let's go down.'

The viscountess marched out. Sophie shot a questioning glance at Emily, who only shrugged. Feeling intrigued and more than a little hopeful, Sophie took her friend's arm and followed.

She was quickly happy that she had given in. Charles, she found, had directed the picnic to be spread out in a sun-dappled grove overlooking the lake. The air was soft and full of birdsong, the company was in high good humour and a bountiful feast of cold meats, cheeses and fruit lay spread before them.

'Which is the tree in which you hid Cabot's teeth, Charles?' Jack Alden called.

Charles's only response was to roll his eyes at his brother.

'We had a litter of new puppies in the stables,' Jack confided to the company. 'The butler refused to allow them in the house. Charles had to exact his revenge somehow.'

'It isn't nice to tell tales on your brother, Mr Alden,' Emily said with a meaningful glance in Miss Ashford's direction.

Jack only laughed and they all went forth to the

feast. True to her word, Lady Dayle enticed Miss Ashford into conversation and into a seat next to her. Sophie noted that Charles did look grateful as he took his plate and joined his brother. She carried her own and settled beside Emily and her family.

Emily was slicing fruit for her young son. 'You must see my little Edward, Sophie,' her friend said joyfully. 'He's walking so well!'

'The springy turf and even ground have inspired him,' chimed in Mr Lowder. 'He'll be running soon, though I think now he likes the falling down as much as the walking.'

'Sophie, there is dust on your skirt, a cobweb in your hair, and a smudge on your cheek,' Lady Dayle spoke up. 'All sure signs that you are enjoying yourself rather well.'

'I am enjoying myself immensely,' Sophie said complacently. 'Later today the builder arrives, and I predict that my appearance will suffer further, but my enjoyment will increase in proportion.'

'Speaking of which, Lord Dayle,' Sophie called. 'Forgive me for interrupting, but I must ask if you've any objection to my tearing down the wall between the two parlours at the back of the first floor?'

She hesitated to ask, after his harshly declared intention to have nothing to do with the project, but did not feel comfortable undertaking such a large change without his approval. Fortunately he appeared amused instead of annoyed. 'I give you full *carte blanche,* Miss Westby. The house is entirely in your hands.' He looked directly at her, and she caught her breath. Breathtaking was how he looked, sitting relaxed, with the wind ruffling his hair and a smile tugging at the corner of his mouth. 'I only ask that you don't attempt to bring the wall down yourself.'

Sophie gathered her composure and wrinkled her nose at him. 'I appreciate your confidence, and promise to leave the demolition to the men.'

She smiled as little Edward, appetite assuaged, toddled over to her and patted her face with sticky hands. 'I don't know why you berate me for my untidiness, Lady Dayle. Just look at this little gentleman—covered in peaches and grass stains! You'll never win the ladies' hearts that way, my boy,' she admonished him.

The boy laughed and plopped himself into her lap. 'Well, perhaps you shall,' Sophie said, gathering him close for a squeeze.

Emily smiled at her son's antics. 'Better grass stains than bruises, Sophie.' She raised her face to the sun filtering through the new leaves and leaned back against her husband. 'Oh, this was a marvellous idea.'

'Yes, a lovely day,' Miss Ashford agreed. 'It is a shame that you may not relax and appreciate it as the rest of us have, Miss Westby.'

Sophie did not wish to think about how Miss Ashford had been spending her day. 'I thank you, but beg you not to worry for me. I am more than content.'

'It seems an odd sort of thing to gain such pleasure from,' Miss Ashford remarked.

'It is unusual, but there can be no doubt of your talent,' Mr Alden intervened. 'I wandered in earlier and caught a glimpse of some of your colour and fabric combinations. Won't you please tell us how this project came about?'

Lady Dayle answered him. 'Sophie is too modest to tell the story correctly, so we shall have to enlighten you. It started with the baby,' she said, gesturing to the boy growing heavy-eyed in Sophie's arms. 'Tell them, Emily, dear.'

Emily rose to fetch her son. 'It did indeed start with Edward,' she said as she settled back with him. 'Shortly before *his* arrival came the arrival of a very large packing crate at our home. I couldn't imagine what was in it.' She paused to adjust the baby's weight in her arms.

'Shall we guess, Mrs Lowder, or will you tell us?' Mr Alden laughed.

'I shall tell you, Mr Alden, if you will be patient.'

She smiled over at him. 'It was a cradle. A marvellous cradle, with a mighty castle, and knights and horses, and even a princess in her tower carved right into the wood, like they had grown there. I confess, it took my breath away.'

'Beautiful piece,' Mr Lowder agreed. 'Never seen anything like it.'

'It was from Sophie, of course, and we asked her right away where she had found such a treasure, for we hoped to get some matching pieces.'

'Was it Spanish?' asked Miss Ashford. 'I've seen some lovely pieces from Spain and they arc a fanciful people.'

'No indeed,' replied Emily. 'Sophie had designed it herself, and had a gifted friend of hers do the woodwork. We were amazed, of course.'

Everyone proclaimed their admiration. Sophie, blushing, tore her eyes from Charles, who had appeared very far away while Emily talked.

'Due to some previous difficulties, the doctors had insisted I stay off of my feet,' she continued. 'I thought I would go out of my mind! So I struck upon the idea of redoing the entire nursery, to keep my thoughts occupied.'

'She was the brains of the project,' Sophie laughed. 'I was only the hands and feet.'

'That is not at all the truth,' Emily protested. 'But

it turned out so well and we had such fun that, after little Edward was born, I decided to ask Sophie's help in redoing some other rooms.' She turned to Miss Ashford. 'I assure you, they turned out beautifully. You've never seen anything so comfortable and elegant at the same time.'

'How nice,' murmured Miss Ashford.

'And upon seeing their handiwork, I decided that a big redecorating project would be just the thing for me as well,' interjected Lady Dayle. 'I came up with the idea of doing this house for Charles's birthday and enjoying the Season at the same time. And here we all are.'

'Yes, here we are all, and here I am going to stay, at least for a bit,' said Sophie, more than ready to change the focus of the conversation. She looked to Charles. 'Your mother and I have packed a few things. We mean to stay for a day or two, to get the work started off in good fashion.'

'Won't you be missed in town, Mother?' he asked.

'No. We intend to stay only tonight and tomorrow night. We shall be back in time for Almack's on Wednesday.'

'Good. I would hate for Miss Westby to miss any of the excitement of her first Season.'

Irritation straightened Sophie's spine. 'I do not know why you must insist on thinking of me as an empty-headed débutante, intent on flirting my way through the Season and into some peer's pocket.'

Charles cast a lazy eye over her. 'That was not my meaning, but since you brought it up, I shall remind you that decorating as a hobby might make you an eccentric, but as a career it will place you out of consideration for nearly any gentleman of birth.'

'That is just as well, then,' she returned. 'I have as much talent, vision, and will as any man, not to mention enough money of my own to gain me something that few other women possess: choice, free will, and independence.' She raised her chin, more than ready to continue, but was forestalled by Miss Ashford.

'I'm sorry to hear that you will not be returning with us, Miss Westby,' the lady said smoothly. 'I am hosting a gathering of young ladies tomorrow to discuss some charitable works, and I had intended you to join us.'

Sophie blinked. The woman sounded as if she fully expected a reversal of their plans. 'I am most obliged, Miss Ashford, but I must stay. The plasterer cannot come until tomorrow. I must be sure everyone comprehends what I have in mind. The first stages of a project such as this are critical.'

'Of course, I understand.' Her tone said otherwise. She accepted a glass of lemonade from a servant and turned back to Sophie. 'What I would like to hear is how you developed such a passionate interest in design, Miss Westby. It is a most unusual accomplishment for a young lady.'

Sophie fought back a grin. Clearly in Miss Ashford's eyes, *unusual* was not a compliment. 'Oh, it was born of necessity, I'm sure. My singing voice is not fit for public hearing, my needlework skills are mostly of the practical variety, and my musical ability, though competent, is nothing special.'

'Her artistic talents, however, are unsurpassed,' Charles broke in unexpectedly. 'I don't believe I have a single memory of Miss Westby without a sketchbook close at hand.' He smiled at the company in general. 'Unless, of course, I had squirrelled it away and hidden it. It was the greatest torture I could devise.'

Despite the tension that still crackled between them, Sophie was warmed by Charles's defence of her. And by the brightness of that smile. It sparked a longing to see it more often.

She forced herself to laugh and keep her tone light. 'I, on the other hand, devised any number of ways to torture you.'

'Yes, and I still bear the scars of a few of them,' he said with mock-severity.

'I know Miss Ashford would love a hint on how

to beat Charles into submission, Sophie dear…'
Lady Dayle spoke with the indulgence of a fond
mother hen with a brood of wayward chicks '…but
it will have to wait for later, for isn't that the
builder's cart travelling up the drive?'

'Oh, it must be,' Sophie said, rising to her feet. 'He
is due to arrive some time this afternoon.' Pausing,
she flashed Charles her biggest smile, then stopped
and bent down to Miss Ashford. Still holding
Charles's gaze, she said in a deliberately loud stage
whisper, 'Ear flicking, he hates that', before striding
off to the house.

Chapter Seven

The afternoon sun was still high when Charles entered the house in search of Sophie. Though there was plenty of daylight left, most of the party wished to return to London before dark. He'd avoided the bedlam of repacking, calling to his mother that he would find Miss Westby so that she might bid everyone farewell. Now he wandered the empty rooms of a house that had never been meant for him, searching for a woman who was undoubtedly wrong for him.

There were signs of her everywhere. Long shrouded furniture lay newly uncovered, the discarded linen lying in heaps in the corners. Sunlight and fresh breezes poured through the place, as every window had been thrown open to let the day in. Splashes of colour, in swatches and sketches, sat prominently in each room.

She was up a ladder again when he found her, measuring a window for curtain lengths, he surmised. He stood, unnoticed in the doorway, watching the graceful bend of her body, the sunlight fighting against the glorious night of her hair, the gentle sway of her dress in the breeze.

He was a fool for being here. He was playing with fire and likely to get burned. But there was a part of him that could not resist her call, the young man in him who missed her chaotic friendship, and perhaps also the dark part of him that had always relished such danger.

'Don't fall,' he said softly, remembering the last time he'd discovered her on a ladder.

She turned her head and gifted him again with that dazzling smile—all white teeth against soft, exotically toned skin. 'Don't worry, Charles, I'm not going to fall.'

Her mocking tone made him wonder if she referred to something other than the ladder.

'The rest of the party is preparing to leave, I thought you might wish to come and see them off.'

'Yes, of course, just let me finish these measurements.' She bent again to her task. It grew quiet, with only bird sound from the open window to break the silence. Charles leaned on the doorframe and stayed where he was. He almost started when she spoke.

'Tell me, Charles, do you see much of Lord Avery lately?'

She surprised him with the question. 'Only in Westminster.'

'How does he go on?'

'I have not the faintest idea, except for the fact that he does go on about my reformist leanings every time we meet. He and his cronies keep up a continuous dark mutter when I am present.' He shivered. 'It is deuced unsettling. Why do you ask?'

'An odd notion. I know you feel you were sorely abused in that whole strange situation, but I can't help feeling sorry for him and his wife, as well. It seems to me that they were quite as ill used as you.'

'I agree, in large part, but I assure you my sympathy is the last thing Avery wishes. He persists in blaming me, at least in part, for the whole débâcle.'

'I suppose there is no one else for him to concentrate on, is there? It's human nature to look to others instead of yourself when something goes wrong. But I still feel for him. Has he heard from his wife?'

'After she ran off with the valet? I've no clue, but I don't wish to know anything else about the tawdry affair. What has brought all this on?'

'It's nothing. I just hate to see a relationship—and they do seem to have loved each other, in an odd way—come to such an end.'

Rolling up her tape, she climbed down and tried to put herself to rights. The familiar sight caused an unexpected ache, but still made him smile. It was so easy and comfortable, being with Sophie.

'What is it?' she asked, rubbing a grubby hand against her cheek and only making it worse.

'Nothing.' He chuckled. 'It's just with dirt smudges all over you and your hair coming down like that, you look about eleven years old again.' He let his gaze roam over curves and valleys that had never graced her younger figure. 'Well, perhaps not,' he said, unable to keep the husky appreciation from his voice.

She stilled and did not reply; a wild thing scenting something dangerous.

He advanced into the room, trying not to feel like a predator. 'I didn't wish to discuss it in front of everyone, earlier today, but I remember the first time we really discussed your designs. Do you remember?'

She still had not moved. 'Yes.'

Her caution, her attitude of expectancy, of uncertainty, was affecting him. His heart was pounding. God, she was beautiful.

It was warm in the room, and the space was somehow growing smaller as he drew closer. 'It was summer, and we were trying to keep cool in the gazebo by the lake. You were drawing another of your infernal rooms, another place that existed only in your mind. I remember the breeze teasing the edges of your paper.' His own voice filled the small distance between them, wrapping, winding about them both and carrying them somewhere else entirely.

'I had never asked you before why you created those imaginary parlours and kitchens, ballrooms and stillrooms, instead of sketching flowers or houses or landscapes like every other girl. But that day I watched you, the intensity in your eyes, the heat of the day in your cheeks, and the wind whispering in your hair. And I asked. Do you remember what you answered?'

Her eyes were closed, but he knew she wasn't here any more. She was lost in the sweet summer's warmth of long ago. 'Yes.'

'You spoke of your father's warehouse, how he would take you there with him. You described the dust in the air, the sunlight spilling into the shadowy places, illuminating boxes, and crates, and barrels, of furniture, and paintings, and pottery. You told me how, just a small girl, you would close your eyes and dream of the homes those beautiful things would go to, of the rooms they would adorn.'

Sophie's eyes snapped open, and the spell was broken by the spark of fear shining there. Charles knew she did not want him to go any further. She lifted her chin. 'Pray don't mention this to Miss Ashford,' she said. 'I've only just been warned not to discuss my mercantile background.'

He accepted her retreat, knowing they both recognised it for what it was. 'I'm sorry if she offended you.'

Sophie shrugged. 'I am sure she meant it well.'

He sighed. 'I am sure that is what she tells herself, at any rate.'

'What's this?' The old Sophie was back, grinning her mischievous insight. 'The courtship's path travels over rocky ground?'

'No, maybe I would prefer that it did. Anything would be better than the bland, unexceptional terrain we've already traversed.'

'I'm glad to hear you say that. I was afraid you hadn't seen it.'

The relief in her voice puzzled him. 'Seen what?'

'Seen how ill the two of you would suit.' She smiled again. 'I thought I was going to have to exert myself to disentangle you from her clutches.'

Charles flinched. 'You misunderstand. I shouldn't have spoken so, it was a mistake.'

She stared. 'The only mistake would be to continue to pursue her.'

'Don't be ridiculous. It's an advantageous match for both sides.' This was not a conversation Charles wanted to have with Sophie.

'Charles, I've seen you with her. Watched you.' She spoke carefully, patiently, like he was a child, too young to see things clearly. 'In her company you disappear. There is only some sober, solemn stranger standing there in your skin.'

'That is exactly the intended effect.' His voice sounded as tight as the constriction in his chest.

'I don't understand. You mean to say you wish to be rigid, humourless, and unapproachable?'

'No, I mean I wish to be seen for what I am—an adult, a responsible, respectable peer of the realm.'

'Oho! Convenient, but unoriginal, Charles. I never thought to hear you playing Lord of the Manor. Does it all come back to the title, then?'

The scorn in her tone infuriated him. 'Of course it comes back to the title!' he said harshly. 'The bloody thing hunted me, laying waste to my family. Now it's got me. The duties and responsibilities are mine now; some of them so heavy, you cannot comprehend.'

'Balderdash! Do your duty, accept the responsibility, but don't let it change who you are.' Her hands were moving, sharp and fast, emphasising the force of her words. If he hadn't been so angry, Charles would have laughed. You knew Sophie was in a passion if she started talking with her hands. Then he heard what she was saying and any urge to laugh died instantly.

'You may not believe it, Charles, but I remember many things as well. I remember a girl making herself miserable, turning herself inside out trying to please the adults who tried to forget her existence. I remember the boy who taught her to find her own happiness. I remember the small confessions, the shared stories. My uncle, your father. My sad aunt, your overburdened brother. I remember the words too. Do you want to hear them?'

'No,' he said harshly.

'"We'll think of the others, but live for ourselves." That's a wondrous piece of wisdom for a mere boy. Too bad the man's forgotten it.'

Her voice was heavy with disdain, and Charles shocked himself by welcoming it. Yes, he deserved nothing but her contempt, however misdirected its focus might be.

Sophie turned away from him and gripped the faded curtain. 'That's what you're doing now, isn't it? Living the life that others expect of you?'

She would never understand. He felt a sudden, insane urge to blurt out the truth, all of it. But he couldn't bear to see her reaction.

She'd grown tired of waiting for one. 'It's just a title, Charles. It may define your station in life, but naught else. You've hidden from yourself for so long, I think you've forgotten who you are. You're more like Phillip now than I ever thought you could be.' She paused a moment, as if digesting her own words, then realisation dawned on her face. 'It's Phillip,' she breathed.

This time, Charles knew, his flinch was noticeable. He'd known she was dangerous. Now he struggled to gain control, to throw the mask back up before it was too late.

It already was too late.

'My God, Charles! Is that what this is all about? Phillip was a serious man, a good and studious man. But it was his nature; the title didn't make him that way. Do you think to turn yourself into your brother?'

Charles's heart was pounding, his breath coming fast. 'We're not children anymore, Sophie. You don't know me as well as you think you do.'

'I know you well enough. Don't throw yourself away in such a marriage. Phillip would not approve. He would want you to be happy.'

Charles almost choked on the conflicting emotions within, all trying to fight their way out. She was beautiful in her passion, terrifying in her perception. He wanted to run, back to London, if necessary, where he could bury himself in work and never hear his brother's name again. He wanted to drop the mask and let the warmth of her affection and acceptance flow over him, absolving him of his sins. He wanted to shout the terrible truth at her: *I can't be happy. I don't deserve to ever be happy again.*

He couldn't do any of those things. So he buried his hands in her already dishevelled hair and kissed her instead.

For a moment, a shocked Sophie could only stand frozen, stunned. It was a short moment. Then she came alive under his hot and insistent mouth.

She couldn't push her mind past the miracle of it: Charles kissing her. She was overwhelmed by the taste and scent of him, the wonder of the dark need curling through her.

Through the long, lonely years, when Charles had been a companion only in her mind, he had represented safety, acceptance, and warmth. Then she had found him again, and he wasn't her best friend anymore, just a stranger who had shown her mostly arrogance and disapproval. Now, with his mouth slanting hotly over hers, he radiated something else entirely: risk, danger, molten excitement that welled deep in her belly.

She welcomed it, thrilled to it, reached for him so she could demand more. He groaned as her arms went around him, and the sound made the throbbing deep within her that much stronger.

He was barely in control of himself. She didn't

care. He drove her head back with his hard, brazen kiss. She yielded to the assault and met him kiss for kiss. He backed her against the wall as his hands crept up to crush the curves he'd admired so boldly. She clung to him as if her life depended on it.

She had cracked his armour, touched the man underneath. His passion served in part as a stalling technique, a way to avoid dealing with the emotions that frightened him. But it was true, and it was hers. She accepted it and while the wind gusted through the open window, draping the faded curtains over them and enclosing them in a cocoon of desire, she gave him back all the fervent warmth in her heart.

He wasn't ready to accept it.

With a despairing moan he tore his mouth from hers and slid his hands up to grasp her shoulders. His chest heaved as his eyes closed and he rested his forehead on hers.

'I remember it all, Sophie,' he gasped, 'even the part you didn't wish to hear. I asked you that day why the rooms you drew were always empty. You said they were waiting for the happy people who would come to live in them.'

Sophie closed her own eyes in pain. She'd pushed him too far. She deserved this, she knew.

'Don't do it here,' he whispered. 'Don't create

rooms for *my* happy family. They don't exist. They never will.'

He loosed her abruptly and strode out of the room. He didn't look back.

Chapter Eight

This was the last in a high stack of forms. Resolutely, Sophie dipped her pen again and signed. She paused, staring at the bold scrawl of her signature, contemplating everything that this step meant, then she pushed the papers over to her guest. 'Here you are, Mr Fowler.'

'Thank you, Miss Westby.' The man ran a practised eye over the contracts before putting them away in his case. Only then, Sophie noticed, did he visibly relax, take a sip of tea, and smile. 'I admit this is far more pleasant than my usual business meetings, but then, everything about this venture is unusual.'

Sophie sighed. There was that word again. *Unusual.* In the fortnight since that fateful day at Sevenoaks, it had echoed repeatedly in her head. Always in Miss Ashford's ever-so-slightly condescending tone. She took a deep breath. Perhaps it was time to make *unusual* work for her, rather than against her.

She raised her cup and an ironic brow. 'Then let us drink to the unusual success of our enterprise, sir,' she said.

'Hear, hear.' Mr Fowler drained his glass and began to gather his things. 'I have no doubts on that score, however. Your work is delightful. It is sure to make us both a success.'

'I sincerely hope so,' Sophie said, standing to bid him farewell.

He took her hand, but paused. 'I feel I have to ask again. Are you certain you wish your portion of the proceeds to be paid to this…gentleman?'

'Mr Darvey, yes.' Sophie fixed her guest with a penetrating look. 'He may not be a gentleman, as you have obviously discovered, but he is a good and worthy man, and he will see that the money goes where it is needed most.'

'He's a lucky man, to have attracted a patroness like you, miss.'

'As I am a lucky woman to have found a friend like him.' She smiled. 'Nor am I unaware of my good fortune in securing a publisher of your calibre, Mr Fowler.'

He grinned and picked up his case. 'I'll send you

round a copy of the book as soon as it is ready. It has indeed been a pleasure.'

Sophie watched from the window as Mr Fowler descended to the hired coach that had brought him. His cheerful whistle and jaunty step only served to frustrate her further. Her temple rested against the cool and soothing glass long after he had gone.

It was disheartening, really. She had accomplished so much. She'd found friends who felt more like family as each day passed. She was in London, with a major design project coming along relatively smoothly, and now this. A design guide of her own. It was a victory, a culmination of a dream that she had worked towards for years. More importantly, it was a means of helping those who might otherwise have no chance of a future.

Fate had surely had a hand in her meeting with Mr Darvey, all those months ago, for it had come at a time when they had both been in desperate need of some hope. The combination of her vision and his talent had resulted in some lovely pieces, such as little Edward Lowder's cradle. But that had only been the beginning. With a bit of Sophie's money, Mr Darvey's good sense, and a few members of his former regiment, they had created more than beautiful furniture, they had manufactured opportunity. They had given hope to others as well as themselves. This book could lead to more of the same.

She should be flush with success, awash in triumph, but she had found that she couldn't truly enjoy any of it. Instead she was only filled with a ceaseless, restless anxiety.

It was all Charles's fault, damn his eyes. She had neither seen, nor heard from, him in the fortnight since that unexpected, heart-pounding, earth-shattering kiss. And unsettling though his continued absence may be, worse was her inability to reconcile her unruly feelings.

Once she had recovered from the pure, physical shock of their embrace, she had been furious. How dare he resurrect a moment of their past, seduce her with the beauty and intimacy of it, then use it to push her away!

A little more thought, however, had reinforced the notion that his kiss had been an act of self-defence. She had touched him. Her patient chiselling had succeeded at last, and she had found a tiny breach in the stone rampart around him. She had reached the man inside and it had frightened him. Typically, like a scared little boy, he had pushed back, trying to scare her off in the same manner.

Perversely, his tactic had had the opposite effect on Sophie. And perhaps that was characteristic of their relationship as well, she thought with a smile. But she could not help the feeling of intense relief that had swept over her with the realisation that there was indeed a mystery to be solved here. It wasn't a natural tendency for prudery and sanctimony that had changed Charles. Something had happened to induce this drastic alteration in personality and demeanor, to cause him to retreat behind that bulwark of prickly pride. Something to do with his dead elder brother.

What could it have possibly been? As far as she knew, Charles and Phillip had had the normally contentious relationship of brothers a few years apart in age. They had been especially close as young boys, tumbling through the home woods, racing their ponies, and perpetrating endless pranks. Even later, when separated by school and their father's increasing demands on Phillip's time, they had maintained the rough-and-tumble, slightly competitive regard of adolescents.

Had something happened to change that? Sophie did not know, but she was going to find out. It was a relief to have the task before her. It gave her hope, at least, that if Charles faced whatever it was he was hiding from, he might have a chance to be happy.

That, at the last, must be her goal. With everything in her, she longed to see her tousle-haired, smiling

Charles again, even if it meant he found his happiness without her.

Such a thought, of course, led right back to that burning kiss. Good heavens, but every girl dreamed of such a kiss, when not only lips and bodies mingled, but souls brushed each other as well. Heat, desperation, spiralling desire—it all came rushing back. A small, triumphant smile escaped her as she touched her lips. Let him kiss Miss Ashford and see if he felt like that.

She drew away from the window. He could not escape her tonight. Lady Dayle was throwing a dinner party and expected him. It was time she prepared herself for the confrontation ahead. A silk gown would be her armour tonight, her weapons nothing more than determination and a smile. But perhaps she would carry along her chisel as well.

'That's all I know, I swear on my mother's grave!'

Charles tightened his grip, choking off the remainder of the man's lies, along with most of his breath. 'Your mother is alive and well and living in Kensington,' he said in disgust. 'How do you think I tracked you down?'

Like her son, the mother of the editor of the *Augur* liked money. Charles wasn't complaining, however.

Greed was far easier to get past than radical fervour—which still blocked any progress with the *Oracle*'s editor.

'That's all you can give me?' Charles released the man, allowing him to slump back against the wall. 'A small, dark, wiry man. No name? No idea for whom he worked?'

'No, no,' Mr Mills said, rubbing his throat. 'He came around at night, left me a fat file of papers— all dealing with you.'

'And a fat purse, I'll wager.' Charles snorted. 'Do you still have the file?'

'Aye.' The man turned sullen now. 'I left it at my mother's place.'

No wonder the old woman had looked at him so strangely. 'What, exactly, was in this file?' Charles asked.

Now the little editor was eyeing him up and down. 'A right long reckoning of your career as a hell-raiser, my lord.' He chuckled. 'And may I salute your creative thinking too! We never got to print half the juiciest stuff.'

'You're sure this small, dark man never mentioned where he got this file?'

'No, it was always "my employer" wants this, "my employer" wants that. But whoever it is—it seems they have been watching you a long time.'

Charles had come here expecting to solve this mystery; instead it was only growing deeper. Frustrated, he sat abruptly down upon a nearby chair. His opponent watched him warily as he drew a purse from his pocket. He tossed it on to the scarred desk the man was obviously using as a temporary office. 'That's a sign of good faith. I believe you have told me everything you can, and I believe that if you remember anything else, you will contact me right away.'

The scoundrel snatched it up. 'I swear, that's all of it.'

Charles drew out another, fatter purse. 'This I will give you if you agree to print another story about me. A remorseful story. A favourable story.'

The man weighed the first purse in one hand while eyeing the other. 'No insult intended, but your randy youth is the most interesting thing you've got. What else is there to draw the readers in?'

'The truth. An apology for the damage you've done me. I don't know, something about the good I've accomplished in Parliament, the charities I support, something. Do your own research this time, man. Write a real story.'

He nodded agreement and reached for the second purse.

Charles tucked it back into his coat. 'You will

receive it on the day the story is printed.' He stood. 'I want that file delivered to me tomorrow.'

Without waiting for a response he turned and strode out. Once outside the man's dingy little hideaway, Charles vaulted back into his curricle, took the reins from his groom and set his bays off sharply. He had several hours before he had to be back home in time for his mother's blasted dinner party. The idea had him groaning out loud. A house full of people. It was the last thing he wanted when this whole mess had him feeling so desperate.

Despite his best efforts with the *ton,* despite his obvious perusal of the available debs, despite his intensifying courtship of Miss Ashford, the tide of public opinion was turning against him again.

He wasn't a madman. Someone, for some unknown reason, was orchestrating this siege against him, but this time the tactics had changed. Nothing new was in the papers. Instead, the attacks came in the form of vague rumour and untraceable innuendo. He was living a masquerade, people whispered. He hadn't reformed, he'd just taken his illicit activities underground. He was lulling Parliament, pulling the wool over society's eyes. He was a secret radical, a closet Catholic, a Whig sympathiser, a bacchanal, or an opium addict, depending on whom you spoke with, and whose friend of a friend they knew.

Charles would have laughed if he hadn't known that the truth about himself was far worse than anything society could come up with. And he would have realised the serious nature of the situation, nipped it in the bud earlier, if he hadn't been obsessed with Sophie.

A discreet cough from his groom recalled his attention to the road. Just in time too. He pulled his pair up as traffic slowed at the crossing of the Westminster Bridge. He was doing it again. Obsessing. And on the road, no less.

He sighed. It was still early, but he could not go home, it would be under siege, buried in a flurry of activity as his mother prepared for her party. As his wheels met *terra firma* once more, he turned the curricle smartly and set off for his club.

It appeared that even this small pleasure was to be denied him. There was a crowd of gentlemen at White's. Charles pushed his way through the crowd, looking for an empty seat. He finally found one, at a corner table. The vacancy was probably owing to the cloud of gloom that hung over the pair of occupants, nearly as tangible as the heavy haze of smoke in the air.

Charles paused as he grew closer. It was that infamous pair of his erstwhile friends, Matthews and Henley. What the hell.

'Gentlemen,' he bit out. 'Do you mind if I join the ranks of your dismal consortium?'

Matthews did not even look up. Henley rolled one bleary eye at him and waved for him to take the remaining seat.

Charles dropped into the chair and waved at a passing porter. Glancing at the empty brandy bottles still on the table, he sent the man off for another.

A brooding silence reigned in the corner, which suited Charles perfectly. A swirl of troubles floated through his head. He had to focus, had to find a way to salvage what was left of his life. But only one thought consistently rose to the top of the maelstrom: Sophie.

Good Lord, he'd kissed Sophie. Devoured her, more like, as he thought back to that shockingly intense embrace.

He'd had no business kissing her. It had been an idiotic thing to do. Cruel, even, when he thought of the harsh words he'd uttered afterwards. But how could he not have kissed her? When she had stood there, so beautifully tousled, so dangerously perceptive, so close to the unspeakable truth? And why, then, had he spent the fortnight since reliving it?

Because it was nigh on impossible not to, that's why. Bad enough that he was obsessed with thoughts of the dratted female, but suddenly so was everyone else in London, and as much as he bemoaned his own notoriety, he almost cringed more at Sophie's.

The porter returned with the brandy and with a clatter began to clear away the empty bottles. Matthews looked up in surprise, and then started even further at the sight of Charles. 'Good Lord, when did you get here, Dayle?'

'A good ten minutes ago, you drunken lout,' snapped Henley. He gave Charles a good once over. 'Though I must say, Dayle, you look as bad as I feel.'

'Just looking at the pair of you makes me feel worse,' Charles retorted. He sighed, then. 'Sorry. What is the trouble with you two?'

'Female trouble, what other sort is there?' asked Henley.

Matthews was pouring them all a glass of the brandy. He flourished his own high. 'Women, bah!'

Charles lifted his own glass in a show of solidarity and they all drank deep.

'Got to get leg-shackled, Dayle,' Matthews said in a voice of deepest mourning. 'Don't want to. Family insists.' His head lolled a bit, but he got himself under control and fixed a reddened eye on Charles. 'M'father put his foot down. Cut my quarterly allowance. Refuses to cover my expenses. Not even my debts of honour, not until I fix my attention on some deb.' He shot a hateful look over at Henley. 'And my so-called friends have deserted me in my hour of need.'

'I'll tell you one final time—you keep away from my sister!' Henley shouted. 'When she marries it will be with far better than the likes of you.' He turned to Charles. 'Tell him, Charles—you wouldn't want a sot like him marrying your sister, would you?'

'Dayle ain't got a sister, toff head,' snorted Matthews. He stopped and Charles suffered an instant dislike for the light dawning in his unfocused eyes. 'But you do got that pretty little filly your mother has been squiring about town,' he said with sudden enthusiasm. 'She'll do. Will you do it, Dayle? Fix me up with an introduction to the girl? Slide in a good word for me?'

'No,' Charles spat.

Matthews gasped, then looked like he was going to cry into his brandy.

'See?' Henley crowed his triumph. 'Dayle don't want you pawing any of the females in his family, either.'

'She's not family,' Charles said, trying to keep his temper. He tried to look apologetic. 'Listen, Matthews, Miss Westby is not your conventional débutante. She's not the sort of girl your father would probably even wish for you be courting.'

'Don't try to turn me up sweet, now. It must be me you object to. Nothing wrong with the girl. She's got breeding, and money. Your own mother dotes on her, and so do the Lowders.'

'Seen the Duchess of Charmouth take her up in her carriage at the park, myself,' Henley put in. 'Heard her Grace asked for the girl's advice on her new ballroom. If the duchess embraces her, the rest of the *ton* will have no choice in the matter, even if the chit has spots and six fingers on each hand.'

That was the problem, Charles thought. Embrace her the *ton* already had, with a vengeance. Her name was on everyone's lips, as much as his own. Suddenly everyone had an amusing little tale to tell of Miss Westby. The events she attended were an instant success. The vivid colours of her gowns were touted as a natural expression of her artistic temperament and were aped by matrons, widows and any woman old enough to escape pastels. The Prince Regent himself demanded an introduction, examined her portfolio, and spent an hour discussing designs with her. Now her passion for décor was an asset, not an oddity, and the fickle *haut monde* clamoured for her advice.

It was galling. He behaved like a monk and was cursed for a fiend. She broke half of polite society's rules and they worshipped her for it.

Not that he could blame them. She'd hit their insular little world like a mortar shell, scattering insipid young misses like shrapnel, but she'd done worse to him. She'd bewitched him with her beauty, seduced him with her laughter. She'd made him forget.

He had forgotten his companions. They were both staring at him with knowing expressions on their faces.

'Perhaps you aren't the problem after all, Matthews,' Henley mused. 'Perhaps Dayle wants the chit for himself.'

'You got the Ashford girl all wrapped up,' complained Matthews. 'You don't need both of 'em.'

Charles had had enough. He stood. 'I must go. I wish you good hunting, Matthews.' He threw a handful of coins down on the table, enough to pay for the entire evening's tally of drink, and he strode out, calling for his vehicle.

He had wasted enough time, mooning like a schoolboy. He didn't have time for it. He had to concentrate. He must work out this mess that passed for his life—for the sakes of those who no longer had one.

He forced his thoughts back the encounter he had had with Mills this morning. A small, dark man. A file tracing his activities. It was devilish little to go on. Though he racked his brains, he could not think who might hate him so. The only people he'd ever truly wronged were dead. And now to find his enemy had been watching him so closely for years? It made no sense, but it sent a shiver of unease up his spine.

Perhaps Jack had made some progress. With luck, his brother would be in his rooms and they could have a private word before the party. He took the ribbons from his groom and set out.

He was passing Humphreys, the renowned print shop, where the usual crowd gathered to see the new prints in the windows, when the cry went up.

'It's him!'

'Hey, Dayle! Can I have an invitation to your next party?'

A chill descended over Charles and he pulled the horses up short. On the street, an older woman pulled a young lady away. 'Don't look at him, dear,' she said, with a sniff. 'Let us go.'

Tossing the reins to his groom, he approached the window, already certain what he was about to see.

It was worse than he imagined. Burning rage twisted in his gut, bubbled up and spewed out of him in a particularly inventive string of blasphemies. Stalking inside, he snatched one of the offending things off the glass. The catcalls and ribbing continued as he accosted the first apprentice he found. 'Where's your mistress?' he barked.

'U-upstairs,' the boy stammered.

'Lead on,' Charles said.

'Oho!' The involuntary chuckle escaped Jack when Charles handed the paper to his brother. 'Oh, my.'

'Is that all you can say?' growled Charles. They were in Jack's cluttered bachelor's quarters and Charles was trying to pace without toppling one of the many towers of books and papers.

'No, as a matter of fact. I have to say I'm insulted that you never invited me to any of your orgies.'

Despite himself, Charles laughed. 'Damned caricaturists. Yes, they're clever, but it doesn't sit so well when it's you they ridicule.'

'Yes, but Cruikshank, no less! No one is truly notorious today until Cruikshank mocks them!' Jack bent to examine the piece more closely. 'Well, old chap, sorry to say it, but he is very clever. Portraying you entertaining the *ton* in one room while the wild orgy is going on behind partially closed doors! And the detail is brilliant.'

'Brilliant and devastating.'

'Look—half the patronesses of Almack's are on one side, while on the other…' Jack looked up. 'Did you truly have an affair with *the* Annie Ewing?' he asked, his voice filled with awe.

'Of course not,' Charles snapped.

'Oh, well, I've always enjoyed her singing. It's clear from this how she came by her nickname.'

'You are missing the important part, Jack.'

'More important than Amply Endowed Annie's bared breast?' his brother asked, grinning.

'Take a look at what the half-clothed revellers are reading.'

'Hmm, yes, that lucky fellow is holding a paper, isn't he? *The Radical Review?* And look over here, on the floor next to these energetic ladies, a book, *The Real Rights of Man.* Bad form, my boy, to mix pleasure and politics.'

'But that's just it, it's the same thing as last time. An attack on my morals and my politics in one fell swoop.'

'So you think that the same person is behind both?'

'I feel that it must be. But who?'

'I feel sure that it is not Avery,' Jack said with a sudden serious turn. 'I've kept an eye on him, as you asked. He truly is miserable, Charles. I don't believe it is an act, and I don't believe it is only his honour that is damaged. I think he misses the old girl.'

'But why should he continue to stir up trouble for me? He certainly does it openly at Whitehall, if not clandestinely with these attacks.'

'You're an easy target, and a natural one for him. You're mixed up in the business that has humiliated him, and there is a true political divide between you. Frankly, I admire the old man for staying in town. Many a lesser man would have fled home in the face of such embarrassment, and never been heard from again.'

Charles stopped pacing and turned to face his brother. 'Perhaps that is the whole idea. Perhaps either one or both of us were supposed to withdraw, to tuck our heads and hide, but from what?' He sat in the chair across from Jack and scrubbed his hair to help him think. 'It must be me, since the latest round was aimed at me as well.'

'But perhaps the caricature is only the natural result of all the rest, and not a new attack.'

'Ah, but I haven't told you all of it.' Charles told his brother of what he had learned from the *Augur*'s editor. 'And, when I found that—' he gestured toward the cartoon '—I had a little talk with Hannah Humphreys.'

'She gave up Cruikshank?'

'Told me where I might find him, rather. He was not a bit apologetic, but he did tell me something interesting.'

Jack only raised a questioning brow.

'He said he would never have had the idea for that thing if he hadn't met someone new at his regular coffeehouse.'

'A small, dark, wiry man?'

'Who got into a political discussion with him one afternoon, and bought him dinner one night, so they could continue their interesting debate.'

'And you were served up along with the chops, I gather.'

'Not outright, but very subtly.' Charles stopped. Something was nagging at the back of his mind. 'There is something familiar about all of this, but I can't quite place it.'

'Familiar?' Jack laughed. 'Good Lord, if this sort of thing is familiar, then I don't envy you.' He rubbed his eyes and shook his head as if to clear it. 'It's still not a lot to go on. Even if we could find the right man, what would we do, charge him with scandalmongering?'

'I'd find out who he works for, by God, and I'd make his life as miserable as he has made mine.'

'It wouldn't fix the damage already done,' Jack said philosophically, 'and it might send you fleeing for the continent. No,' he mused, 'I know I scoffed at your idea at first, but I'm beginning to think you have had the right idea all along. Ignore the rumours. If you aren't visibly affected, maybe he'll grow tired and move on to play games with someone else.'

'It's too late for that,' said Charles.

'No, it isn't. Focus on your work, and your search for a wife. If everyone is discussing which lady you are courting now, they will not be talking about who you poked last year. Even if it was Amply Endowed Annie Ewing,' he finished with a grin.

'I'm not sure even that will save me now. The highest sticklers were already avoiding me. That—' he gestured to the caricature '—may well be a killing blow.'

Jack stood, an odd gleam in his eye. 'It has been a hard couple of years, Charles, for all of us. I would not wish to be saddled with some of the burdens you have carried. But you've done well.' He approached, and clasped Charles's shoulder. 'It's the perfect time for you to take a step back. Look around. Decide, once and for all, what it is that you want. What *you* want. And I'll do whatever I can to help you get it.'

Jack grinned, lightening the mood. 'But for now, you had better get home and get ready for Mother's dinner party. She'll shoot us both if we're late.'

'I forgot.' Charles dashed back his drink and rose to shake his brother's hand. He clasped it longer than necessary, trying to convey his gratitude and so much more. 'Thank you, Jack.'

It started to rain as he set his tired horses for home. Charles shrugged out of his greatcoat and gave it to his ever-patient groom. He hunched his shoulders as his brother's words echoed in his head. *Decide what it is that you want.*

Chapter Nine

Sophie entered Charles's house poised for battle. If nothing else, at least she would see him, and this interminable wait would be over. She was not good at waiting, and hadn't been since she was eight years old, and had decided that a year was long enough to wait for an uncle who was never coming. That fateful day she had shed her good-little-girl persona along with her pinafore, climbed the tallest oak in the forest, and found a tousled-haired, kindred soul at the top.

It was poetic justice, she thought as she smoothed her long gloves and twitched her gown into a more graceful fall, that Charles should reap some of the forceful nature he had helped to sow.

Sophie had brought Nell along, and, after a few whispered words of instruction, she sent her off on her covert mission. Before long she was entering the parlour on Lady Dayle's arm, confident that she looked well, and confident that, whatever the outcome, Charles would no longer be able to ignore her.

Her poise faltered a bit when the first person she saw was her uncle. She arched a brow at the viscountess, who only grinned and urged her forward to greet him. A hostess's duties soon called her away, and Sophie was left alone with her uncle once more. She had seen him only once since their first, distressing private interview, and that had been at Mrs Dawson's musical evening. She had been relieved that it had been a public scene with no chance for private conversation. He asked her now if she would join him on the corner settee.

'I've been hoping for a moment with you, niece.'

Sophie agreed. He looked tired, his once-handsome face pinched, as if he were in pain. Fleetingly, she wondered if her father would have resembled him as he grew older.

He didn't waste any time. 'I wondered if you had given thought to our last discussion?'

'I've thought much on it, Uncle.'

'And?'

Sophie breathed deep. Daringly she took his hand—it was cold and thin. 'There was a time, sir, when I would have given anything to have received such a show of interest from you. But I've had to make my own way, forge my own happiness, for too long now to submit myself to anyone else's ideas for my future.'

'Stubborn girl! You could choose—'

'No, sir,' she interrupted. 'I'm afraid we are both too wilful to get along together in the manner I think you are suggesting.'

He withdrew his hand from her grasp. 'I'd expected as much.' He gave her a look she thought might be regretful. 'But I'd hoped I was wrong.'

'I would like it if we could find our way toward some kind of relationship.'

He was silent a long time. So long she thought he might not answer at all. When he finally spoke, he avoided her eye. 'I wondered if perhaps you remember… Did your father ever speak to you, of me, when you were a child?'

'Yes, of course. He had your likeness in a miniature, which he often showed me. He told me tales of your childhood. He loved Cranbourne House.' It was the earl's principal estate, situated five and twenty miles from the small estate where Sophie had grown up. She had never seen it.

'And, your mother?'

Still, he looked away, where Sophie could not read his face. She understood what it was he was asking. 'She spoke fondly of you.' Now Sophie was the one looking down at her hands in her lap. 'It was one of the reasons I was so looking forward to living with you.'

A trill of nearby laughter distracted them both from their sombre thoughts. It was a party, after all, and life did go on, despite old hurts.

'Well, then…' Her uncle had recovered and was motioning someone toward them. 'You'll recall Mr Huxley, won't you?'

The gentleman reached them and made his bow. Sophie and her uncle stood to greet him. She did indeed remember him—her uncle had gone out of his way to present him at Mrs Dawson's. Sophie had wondered at it, as the two seemed as unlikely a pair as she had ever seen.

An odd, but likeable gentleman, Mr Huxley had talked at length of his map collection.

'A pleasure to meet you again, sir.'

'The pleasure is mine, Miss Westby. Will you take a stroll about the room with me?'

'Yes, you young people run along,' her uncle agreed. 'There's a discussion on the Corn Laws going on over there that needs my insightful input.'

The realisation struck Sophie suddenly that her uncle might be matchmaking. Nevertheless, she laid her hand on Mr Huxley's arm and allowed him to lead her off.

'Your uncle tells me, Miss Westby, that you have been travelling a great deal into Kent.'

'Why, yes, I am involved in a project that takes me there every few days of late.'

'Which roads do you travel? I'll wager a monkey that I know a route that will shorten your travel time by at least a quarter of an hour.'

Finally dry and presentable, Charles made his entrance after most of the guests had arrived and dinner was nearly ready to be announced. He went first to his mother, to apologise for his lateness, and found her chatting with Miss Ashford.

His mother simultaneously scolded and embraced him. Miss Ashford greeted him with her customary cool courtesy. He supposed he should be grateful that she acknowledged him at all, considering the escalating scandal surrounding his name. Indeed, he was grateful, he told himself sternly. He noticed that a few of the other young ladies his mother had invited for his benefit were not to be seen. Her very presence tonight was a testimony to Miss Ashford's loyalty and character. He resolved to devote himself to her this evening, and to firmly suppress the small part of him that wished to feel more than gratitude for his future bride.

Miss Ashford's father, however, requested a moment of his time, and Charles could not but agree. The baron drew him aside, and gestured to the long, crowded room full of glittering guests.

'A nice evening,' he said. 'Perfect mix of business and pleasure.'

'Thank you, sir. I hope you and your family will enjoy yourselves.'

'No doubt. Womenfolk are in alt planning that charity ball.'

Charles nodded his sympathy. Miss Ashford had indeed struck upon the idea of a charity ball, and showed more enthusiasm for it than anything he had yet seen in her. 'It is very good of your daughter to devote herself to such works.'

Lord Ashford gave an indulgent smile. 'She's a very good sort of girl, Dayle. Just what a lady ought to be.'

'I hope you are aware of my agreement on that score,' Charles said easily.

'Well, that's the subject I wished to discuss with you. I thought we had an understanding regarding your intentions, but now I find myself unsure.'

Startled into stupidity, Charles just gaped. 'Sir?'

'Rumours are one thing, Dayle. A man can't help what the tabbies will say about him, most especially if he possesses as chequered a past as your own.' He nodded his head in approval. 'You've had a rough spot recently, and I thought you were handling it well. Some kind of ruckus seemed inevitable, and I thought you might as well put your past to rest early in your career rather than later. Good for you too. Tempered steel is stronger, as they say.'

'I can honestly say, I never thought about it in that light.'

'But this broadsheet's another thing entirely. Takes it to another level, so to speak. Can't have my girl mixed up in such.'

'Surely you don't believe such rubbish, Lord Ashford?' said Charles, his temper starting to get the best of him.

'Don't matter what I believe, when it gets to this point. Matters what the rest of the world believes. I have a good bit of political weight. Meant to throw it behind you, if you and my girl found you suited. But I don't mean to hitch my girl to a runaway wagon, if you understand. Want what's best for her.'

'I comprehend your meaning, sir,' said Charles. And he did indeed understand the most salient point: his unseen opponent was gaining ground.

'Now, don't fret. You just keep your feet on the straight path and the situation will right itself.' He squeezed Charles's shoulder in a fatherly gesture.

'My girl rather fancies you, I believe. At least she likes you as well as she's ever liked anyone. If you need my help, you need only to ask.'

'You are most generous,' said Charles. It was a struggle to keep the bitterness from his voice.

The baron departed in search of his spouse, and Charles returned to Miss Ashford and his mother. Once there, however, he found it difficult to concentrate on the conversation. The events of this long and trying day were beginning to take their toll. He could swear the universe was conspiring against him. The harder he tried, it appeared, the heavier his burdens grew.

Suddenly the crowd in the parlour shifted. His gaze fell on Sophie, and the weight of his troubles was instantly forgotten. She was stunning. Her shining dark tresses were arranged in an elaborate coiffure that accented the length and slenderness of her neck. Her shimmering gown, dark blue over a white satin slip, had the same effect on her frame, without hiding her luscious curves. She was standing with Mrs Lowder and a blonde gentleman he had never seen before. A gentleman who had taken the opportunity of her turned head to run an appreciative gaze over her décolletage.

'Is that Mrs Lowder over there with Sophie?'

'Indeed it is,' his mother answered. 'Does she not

look divine this evening? I believe motherhood agrees with her.'

'I had a mind to speak to her husband. If you will excuse me, I believe I'll go and ask if he is here.'

Oh, Lord, but he was seven kinds of an idiot. He'd just spent a fortnight avoiding Sophie, trying to forget how she'd felt in his arms. He'd thought long on what to say to her tonight, and promised himself that he'd make sure he never found himself in that situation again. He'd just determined to spend the evening securing another woman's favour, and been warned by her father to keep his nose clean. Yet one glance had him abandoning all those good intentions, stifling the warning ringing in his head. He cursed himself for a fool all the way across the long, crowded parlour, but he didn't stop.

'Good evening,' he said when he reached them.

'Charles! You have finally come!' Sophie said, reaching out to him. Was that relief he heard in her voice? And was she relieved to see him or to be distracted from her companion? 'Please, allow me to present Mr Huxley? Mr Huxley, this is our host, Viscount Dayle.' They greeted each other and Sophie continued, 'And of course you are already acquainted with Mrs Lowder.'

'Of course. May I present my compliments? You look lovely this evening.'

Mrs Lowder thanked him with an amused look and a brow raised in Sophie's direction. Sophie, predictably, was not impressed.

'There, Emily, now you have experienced first hand a bit of Lord Dayle's famous charm! Come now, Charles, enough flattery, what we really wish to see is your hand.'

'My hand?'

'Oh, yes, my lord!' Mrs Lowder was smiling quite genuinely now. 'You see, Miss Westby and I were walking in the park today.'

'Which park?' asked Mr Huxley.

'Hyde Park, of course,' said Sophie, 'and we walked there via Brook Street to Park Lane.'

'I've always found Mount Street to be superior,' Huxley answered. 'Less traffic, you see.'

'In any case, we were introduced to a most impertinent young lady there. She knew we were acquainted with you, Charles.'

'But what does any of it have to do with my hand?' asked Charles.

'She wished to know if it were true that you were part-Selkie, Lord Dayle!' interjected Mrs Lowder. 'Can you imagine?'

Despite himself, Charles laughed. 'Unfortunately, I can imagine.' He shot Sophie a look of mock-severity. 'I can also imagine you telling the poor child it was true.'

'Well, I did assure her we would check for webbed fingers when next we saw you, but considering the light such a thing would cast upon Lady Dayle, I felt compelled to deny the charge. In any case, I told her, you most assuredly have your father's nose.'

Charles just shook his head. He didn't know which was more outrageous, the rumours or her method of dealing with them. 'I must thank you for defending my family's honour.' His mother, he could see, stood in whispered consultation with the butler, and was turning to leave the room. He turned to Mrs Lowder. 'I remember your skill on the pianoforte very well. I hope you will play for us all after dinner, but right now I must whisk Miss Westby away, as my mother has requested her assistance.'

'Of course, I would be honoured,' Emily answered with a smile.

'Mr Huxley, grand to have met you,' said Charles as he firmly grasped Sophie's elbow, ushering her away before she had a chance to protest. He led her out the door his mother had just exited, and stood a moment in the hall, debating. Likely, his mother had been called to the kitchens. The dining room, he knew, would be swarming with servants. As he hesitated, Sophie pulled her arm from his grasp.

'Where is your mother, Lord Dayle?'

'Soothing the cook, I imagine.'

'She doesn't need my assistance.'

'No, I do. We have to talk.'

Ah, the bookroom. He herded Sophie in and carefully left the door partially open. She looked around curiously, and then turned to him with a frown. 'How disappointing. Nary a radical nor a ladybird in sight.'

'Very amusing.' Charles grimaced.

'Well, I do have first-hand knowledge of what you get up to in empty rooms.'

'Stop it, Sophie, can we not talk seriously for a moment?'

She took a calming breath and threw back her shoulders. He wished she wouldn't—it strained both her neckline and his control. 'You've ignored my existence for a full fortnight, but you are compelled to talk now, in the middle of your dinner party?'

'My mother's dinner party, but yes.'

She waited; he stared, trying to gather his thoughts. What was there to say? There were at least a thousand thoughts crowding his brain, he had to tread carefully and choose just the right one.

'You'd been kissed before,' he said.

Her jaw dropped. He groaned and pushed a hand through his hair. That had not been the right one.

Her décolletage was heaving now, in perfect time

with his gut. 'I beg your pardon?' she gasped. 'That's what you dragged me in here to discuss? That's what you took away from our—encounter?'

Lord help him, but it was true. Though he hadn't articulated the thought to himself, it had been nagging at him, poking and prodding, making him squirm perhaps even more than his other troubles. 'You knew how to kiss. Someone had to teach you.'

True to form, Sophie laughed, but it was a desolate sound. Despairing. She turned and walked away.

Well, what did he expect? She would be well within her rights to leave the room and never speak to him again, but he couldn't stop himself, he had to know.

'Was it Sean Hill?'

'The blacksmith's boy?' Anger brought her back, and Sophie was angry indeed. Her dark eyes flashed, her cheeks flushed, and she advanced on him like Ney and d'Erlon into Wellington's centre line.

'You were gone, Charles. You left for school and never looked back. I didn't blame you. I knew how things were with your father.' She stopped before him, magnificent in her fury. 'But I was still there. I might be there still if not for Emily and your mother.'

She turned away again, and retreated to the far side of the room. 'Did you think because their mamas disapproved of me, the boys would steer clear of me? Foolish—don't you know that that made me even more interesting?' Her voice fell away to a whisper. 'I was alone, Charles.'

She rallied and shot him a look of defiance. 'Thank God for Emily. If we hadn't struck up a friendship, I might have done far worse than allow a boy to kiss me.' She gave an ironic snort. 'I might have run off to Gretna with the first man old enough to ask me, just for the conversation on the way. Had any of them paid me any serious attention, I think I might have done almost anything.'

Charles found himself barely able to respond. The picture she painted was devastating. 'I didn't know—I never thought…'

Undaunted by her own admission, she faced him squarely. 'You judge me if you wish, Charles Alden. But you remember that I never judged you. I cheered when the rest of the world reviled your exploits, and wished I could be kicking up rows right along with you. Nor did I judge you when you stayed away all those years, with never a word or a letter. You returned home for what—a mere two days—for Phillip's funeral? Less than that for your father's, but you never came to see me.'

Her anger seemed to have fled. It was disappointment he read in her eyes now. 'I didn't judge you, Charles. Even when you forgot me.'

Her skirt flared as she turned her back on him. This time she was the one to sweep out of the room without looking back.

Had he forgotten her? Charles sat through dinner ignoring his food, nodding as Miss Ashford talked—she had decided her ball must be a masquerade—and trying to answer that question.

He remembered the brash youth he had been, daring anything, risking everything, determined to force his father's displeasure, since nothing had ever earned his respect. He had indeed left for school, but he had always looked back—back to be sure his father was watching.

No, he hadn't forgotten Sophie. Unconsciously, he had held her memory close, sure as he raised every kind of hell he could imagine, that there was one person in the world who would forgive him. But he had held her static in his mind, never considering her growing older, becoming a young woman. She had always been his pig-tailed, adventurous partner in crime.

He hadn't forgotten her, but he had failed her.

That truth gnawed at him throughout the evening as he watched her. Another sin to shoulder responsibility for, another person who had suffered while he exercised his fertile imagination and frittered away his life. He wasn't sure his soul could bear another such burden.

Oddly enough, though, he found a measure of peace while he watched her. She had been hurt—perhaps only he knew how much—yet she had risen above it. Sophie had grown up, and Lord knew she had turned out to be unconventional, but she was also good natured, amusing, and intelligent. She was a beacon of light in the room, smiling and animated, and the people around her responded. She charmed her partners through dinner and was kept happily occupied in the drawing room afterwards. He noticed Mr Huxley was often at her side.

Watching her gave him hope. And that was only the top reason on a long list of them to stop.

Nevertheless, he was achingly aware of her as he circulated through the guests after dinner. There was excited talk of costumes for Miss Ashford's masquerade, and much animated gossip over the state of Prinny's health. The knot of young people about Sophie all seemed to be embroiled in a discussion on fashion, and of course, there was a good deal of political debate going on in pockets about the room.

At his request, his mother had invited a few members of the Board of Trade. Charles knew he should be courting them, but he was more worried about the young men courting Sophie. Was this the sort of attention she had craved? The thought had him contemplating mayhem, not party platforms.

But he knew his duty. Resolutely he turned his back and joined the men plotting the course of the nation.

He found his own situation to be nearly as dire as England's. Though the men here tonight supported him, there were others, they reported, who felt that his character was not steady. Charles sighed. Before all this he'd been at the top of the list to chair their new committee; now he'd be fortunate to be invited as a committee member.

Sir Harold commiserated with him, but advised him to be patient. 'Now is perhaps not your time, Dayle,' he said. 'Wait until this gossip dies down. There will be other committees, other paths to the ministry.' He sympathised with him on the simmering scandal broth as well. 'Still no idea who your enemy might be?'

'No.' Charles did not go into detail. 'Jack seems convinced that it is not Avery, however.'

'Hmm. His antipathy doesn't help your situation, for certain, but I tend to agree. Avery's style is to confront you directly, just as he has been doing. He's not the sort to sneak behind a man's back.'

Sir Harold was quiet a moment. 'I have the feeling that whoever is behind this is more powerful than we suspect. It won't be easy rooting him out.'

'I begin to wonder if the struggle is worth it,' Charles said. This setback disheartened him. He was tired, tired of fighting, tired of trying to prove himself to a world determined to see only the worst in him.

'Don't give up, Dayle. You've a great future ahead of you. Find the man behind all this and give him back a taste of his own misery. Once you've done that, take a little time for yourself. Concentrate on choosing one of these fine young ladies. Set up your nursery. Show the doubters that your judgment is sound, that you've finishing sowing oats and are ready to reap a more steady crop.' He gestured to the others, still energetically debating the latest Poor Relief Bill. 'We'll still be here for you.'

His mood low, Charles shook the man's hand and thanked him for his kindness. He stood alone a moment, wishing all his guests back to their own homes, himself to his favourite brooding chair, and his unseen enemy to the devil. He sighed. If wishes were horses, beggars would ride. The way Charles's luck was running, he'd likely be trampled instead. He would do better to seek out his brother.

He'd just spotted Jack in animated conversation with a crowd of young bucks when the sound of Sophie's name, spoken with derision, drew him up short. He glanced quickly around and saw a cluster of dandified gentlemen just off to his right.

'Impudent chit. I don't care if she is an earl's niece; she has spent her life buried in the country. What does she presume to know of fashion?'

Charles stared. Was that his cousin Theo rigged out in that hideous get-up of turquoise and buttercup yellow? Yes, he rather believed it was.

'Didn't like your waistcoat, old boy?' sniggered one of Theo's companions while gesturing to the elaborately embroidered disaster.

'Don't you dare laugh—this is the height of fashion, and cost me ten guineas! No, the chit betrayed her own ignorance when she said that not only should *I* not wear this colour combination, but no one in all England could pull it off.'

'Except for a jockey on the back of a deep chestnut bay!'

Peals of laughter rang out from the group, heightening Theo's colour, along with his temper, Charles surmised.

'Theo's right,' interjected a gentleman arrayed in silver and puce, 'the girl has no business giving fashion advice.'

'Well, you cannot deny her success, and certainly I've never seen her look anything less than smashingly gorgeous,' someone argued.

'True enough!' came a chorus of agreement.

'I wonder what her dowry is like?' someone

wondered out loud. 'I think I shall ask her to partner me in whist.'

'You shan't get a jump on the rest of us,' someone cried and as a group they moved off to seek out the lady's attention, leaving only Theo and the other malcontent still grumbling.

Moving forward, Charles decided to nip that little bud before it could bloom into a larger flower of disgruntlement.

'Good evening, Theo. It has been a while, has it not?'

'Dayle,' returned Theo, still in a pout over the attack on his sartorial splendour.

'My mother must be pleased to have you tonight, I know she wants all the family to meet her particular friend, Miss Westby.' As a warning it was not much, but it was all that was required. Mumbling his agreement, Theo and his friend took themselves off.

Charles watched them go. He was annoyed with Theo, but, oddly enough, the bulk of his irritation lay on Sophie's shoulders. Just once he wished she would hold her tongue and not say the first thing that leapt to mind. Yes, Theo was ridiculous, but must she point it out in such a public forum?

Who was he to conjure criticisms? His life was unravelling faster by the minute. He left in search of a drink.

He found one, but his mother also found him.

'Charles, dear,' she fussed, drawing him aside. 'Do you think you could influence Sophie and persuade her to allow me to make an announcement about her book?'

He lifted a questioning brow. 'Her book?'

'Yes, her book.' His mother sounded exasperated, but when she saw his puzzlement she relented. 'Do you mean she hasn't even told you? Oh, she must indeed be serious about keeping it quiet.'

'Explain, please, Mother.'

'Well, I suppose it's too late now, and I'm sure she doesn't mean to keep it from you. And at least I can break the news to you, if to no one else.'

'Mother…'

'Oh, yes. Well, isn't it the most wonderful thing?' She leaned in and lowered her voice. 'Sophie has written her very own design guide! And a very reputable publisher has agreed to take it on. The proceeds, of course, will be donated, but I know you can appreciate what such validation means to her.'

Indeed he could. Charles was sure that the accomplishment left Sophie feeling deeply satisfied. Unfortunately it left him feeling frustrated and strangely upset. He shook his head. Why should Sophie's good news make him furious? He murmured something to his mother about finding a drink and wandered off, quite forgetting the one he held in his hand.

The party broke up soon after, but far too late for Charles's peace of mind. He caught Sophie alone as her party was preparing to leave. In the dark corner of the hall he caught up her hand and held it, searching for something, anything, he could say to express the myriad of emotions that swamped him. It was all too much. He'd schooled himself to feel nothing save ambition for so many long months, and now Sophie had him twisted in ten different knots in one evening.

He couldn't just stand here, dumb as a doorknob. He opened his mouth to speak, but she stopped him with a shake of her head. Her hand lingered in his, however, and they stood together, silent, connected in a way that went beyond touch. The moment stretched on, but Sophie never looked up. Instead she kept her gaze locked on their clasped hands, until Emily Lowder cleared her throat, then Sophie recalled herself and her hand and swept away.

Somehow Charles got through the next hour. He bid goodbye to all the guests, kissed his mother goodnight, bade the servants to go on to bed and leave the mess for the morning. He took himself to the book room and shut the door. He poured a brandy, but didn't drink it. He stared long at the fire, without seeing it. He sat down in his favourite chair and slowly descended the slippery slope into insanity.

It must be what this was, insanity—or as close as he'd ever come to it. His mind was whirling, events and voices from the past weeks were haunting him. *Sacrifice anything...decide what you want...you forgot me.*

They were all slipping away, all the reasons that had given him purpose, allowed him to go on. If Viscount Dayle faltered, would there be enough left of Charles Alden to survive?

All of his hard work had been for naught. The progress he'd made in redefining his character, his potential—wiped clean. His committee position— gone. Even his social standing stood in jeopardy. He was a joke again, Wicked Lord Dayle who had played the greatest prank of his career on his peers.

He stood and leaned into the mantelpiece. It had been so hard, and now he must start again. But damn it, he would. He would. Just as soon as he could focus his thoughts, just as soon as he could deal with Sophie.

His heart began to pound, his hand, still holding a drink, to shake. He regarded the trembling amber liquid in a vague, detached way for a moment, wishing it contained the solace he needed. His goals were ripped out of his reach, his life was falling apart, and all he could think about was Sophie.

He stood abruptly and flung the glass into the fireplace, where it erupted into a flash of blue flame. He left the book room, grabbed a walking stick from the urn in the entry hall and strode past his startled footman into the night.

Damn her. Damn her for coming back into his life at the worst possible time and wreaking her own special brand of havoc. Damn her for being beautiful, and funny, and irresistible. Damn her for waking him up, making him laugh, making him *want*.

He walked far and long, but he could not escape his thoughts. The past had often haunted him, but now the future loomed troublesome as well. He didn't know which terrified him more—possibilities he feared might be closing to him, or the ones that he sensed might open.

Decide what you want. Perhaps Jack was right, perhaps it was time he faced the truth. It was simple and frightening at once. He wanted Sophie, passionate, beautiful, impossible Sophie.

She was intoxicating in a way that spoke directly to his soul. She comforted his battered spirit, captivated his wary mind, and tempted him with her exotic beauty.

For a dangerous moment he allowed himself to imagine what life might have been like if Phillip had never come to him on that fateful day. He might have reunited with Sophie a free man, unencumbered by grief and guilt. They could have met by chance in Dorsetshire or here in London— No, down that path lay madness. The nightmares were real. He would never be free.

Not even for her could he abandon the vows he'd made. There it was, plain and simple, the festering truth that had tormented him. He'd wanted her since she'd nearly knocked him down in the street. He'd known, almost since then, that to choose her would be to forsake everything he owed to his dead brother and father.

He'd told himself many times that Charles Alden had died right along with his brother. Viscount Dayle had sprung from the ashes of his former life, a shell of a man whose only purpose was payment of dark and deep debts.

Sophie had changed all that when she fell back into his life. Suddenly Charles Alden was alive again, resurrected by the laughter in her eyes, and torn between heart and mind, want and need.

He'd become a living cliché. A stone bench sat up ahead—he sank on to it and buried his head in his hands. It was an age-old dilemma. He supposed he was no worse off than a thousand poor devils before him. But who would have thought it would hurt so much?

A book. Charles could hardly believe she'd done it. He had given her her first design guide himself, to help her fill the imaginary rooms she created. His mother was right; he did know how much this meant to her, not just the book, but everything.

He felt a twinge of guilt. After a lifetime of censure, Sophie was finally enjoying what she longed for: welcome, acceptance. He should be happy for her, not begrudge her this first real triumph. But begrudge it he did, because her unconventional, meteoric success pushed her beyond his reach.

He was afraid for her too. Fickle society loved to force people on to pedestals, if only to watch them fall. Look at what had happened to Byron. Look at what had happened to *him.*

A cool breeze swept by, ruffling his hair and just possibly, bringing the idea with it. *Look at what had happened to him.* He lifted his head. It seemed so simple. Was it possible? Could both Charles Alden and Viscount Dayle have what they wished?

He looked about and found himself near the gates of the garden in Hanover Square. How long, he wondered, had he been here, across from the house where Sophie slept? A light came on in one of the upper windows, and Charles laughed softly. Perhaps Fate had finally taken pity on him and come to intervene on his behalf. There could be no other explanation. It must be Sophie up there, stirring long before anyone else would dream of doing so.

One way to find out. He searched out a few small stones, and, stifling a strong sense of *déjà vu,* launched them at the window.

Sophie had spent a restless night, but to no avail. Finally, just before first light, she gave it up as a bad business. She hadn't slept a wink, and still her thoughts were in a worse tangle than her sheets.

She had spent half the night fuming over Charles's perfidy. 'You'd been kissed' indeed! How dare he? When he'd spent years wenching his way through the female half of the population? He was no better than a child; he didn't want her, but he didn't want her playing with anyone else either.

Never would Sophie have imagined Charles indulging in such hypocrisy. She shook her head. But then, neither had she predicted the change in his temperament. And now his vacillation between hot and cold had taken on new and frightening dimensions.

She'd been so naïve! She had longed for the connection she'd felt with him so long ago, and had allowed her fantasies to run away with her. The understanding and intimacy that they had enjoyed had been so strong, so vital to her, that she'd assumed they would survive the years apart.

She sighed. There had been too many changes. He'd been correct, she didn't know the new Charles, but she was beginning to suspect that he didn't know himself either.

The thought led her back to Nell's attempt with the family's servants last night. Though Nell had enjoyed the idea of intrigue, she hadn't been very successful. The only thing of interest she'd heard was that old Lord Dayle had been furious when Phillip had accepted Lord Castlereagh's mission, and travelled with important papers to Wellington in Brussels. Sophie still wasn't sure just how he'd ended up at the battle at Waterloo, but she supposed it made no difference. Phillip had died, just as many thousands of other good and gallant men had.

Could she be making too much of the situation? Perhaps there was no mystery, only her own desires and the wish to fuel her own fantasies. There could be a simple explanation that she didn't wish to see. People changed. Or perhaps Charles's wish to mould himself into his brother's likeness had simply been the desire to impress his hard-to-please father?

Something kept her from embracing such an idea. She hoped it wasn't her own self-indulgence, but she couldn't shake the feeling that Charles was hiding something. There was a desperation about him that she could not explain. He seemed *driven* to succeed in politics, to impress the men in government with his solidity and responsibility. It must go deeper. Also, she thought, why wouldn't he have eased off after his father's death? And why the strange talk about old Lord Dayle's death? No, there was something more here she couldn't yet see.

Sophie shook her head and rang for Nell. She might suffocate if she stayed in this room any longer. She needed to get out, to breathe fresh air, to walk and clear her mind.

A small clattering sound, quite nearby, had her suddenly jumping back into her bed. Heart pounding, feet tucked safe away under her night rail, she inspected the floor. The noise came again, there by the window, but she could see no sign of a rodent invader. Once more, louder this time, and Sophie recognised the sound for what it was. Laughing despite herself, she climbed down, threw back the curtains and looked below.

Charles. He stood there on the pavement, wearing a grin and last night's clothes.

'Are you insane?' she called in a loud whisper. 'What are you doing?'

'Come down!'

'Now? Can't you pay a morning call like all the other gentlemen?'

'Where would be the excitement in that?' He

gestured to the burgeoning light in the east. 'It's morning. Come! We have to talk.'

Behind her a drowsy Nell scratched on the door and let herself in. She came wide-awake, however, when she took in the situation. 'Miss!' she gasped.

'I'll be down presently,' Sophie called to Charles. She turned to the maid. 'I know, Nell. Pray, don't look at me like that! Just fetch my wrapper, quickly.'

Oh, Lord, but she was a fool. She couldn't help it. This smacked of older, better times, and was nigh irresistible. She hurried into a heavy robe, allowed Nell to put her hair up loosely, and crept quickly down the stairs.

The night footman dozed in his chair. Nell put her mouth to Sophie's ear. 'It is Richard. He sleeps like a stone.'

Sophie held a silencing finger to her lips and slowly turned the lock on the front doors. With a sigh of relief she stepped out into the cool, early morning air. The street was deserted except for Charles, beckoning her from the gate to the square. Leaving Nell to quietly close the door again, Sophie ran lightly across the street.

'You imbecile! I thought it was your wish to stay out of the papers!' she scolded.

'I had to chance it. In any case, I knew it must be you waking. Anyone else would have been too cruel.'

Sophie drew back. 'Are you drunk, Charles?'

He grasped her hands tight in his. 'No, I'm just… Oh, I don't know. I feel as if I am waking from a long and terrible dream.'

She looked him over carefully and tried to calm the pounding of her heart. Her mind was racing almost as fast. What could it mean? She didn't know whether to dread what he had to say, or to long for it. The only thing she knew was that a rumpled and unshaven Charles was devilishly more handsome than the usually immaculate Charles. The image of her tangled sheets came to mind before Sophie could curb her wayward imagination. Blushing, she reined it in. 'Where is your coat, your hat? Heavens, but you are a mess!' She laughed. 'I've spent too much time with your mother. Never mind! What is it that you must say, that couldn't wait until a decent hour?'

'I had to apologise. The things you said tonight— they are burnt into my mind like a brand. I'm so sorry. I can't bear the thought that I added even a jot to your unhappiness.'

'No.' She bowed her head. 'I do beg your pardon for attacking you so unjustly. You owe me nothing, I shouldn't have implied that you do. You were, in fact, the one who taught me to be responsible for my own happiness. I'm sorry I failed to heed your perfectly correct advice.'

'You haven't failed.' He lifted her chin. 'Look at what you've done, Sophie. I saw you talking—cordially—with your uncle tonight. We thought such a thing would never come to pass! You've learned so much, and used your talents to make people happy. You should be proud of all that you've accomplished. I am. And I do owe you, for being such a good friend to my mother. But none of that is why I wished so desperately to speak with you.'

Sophie's eyes closed and she allowed a sigh of pleasure to escape her. She knew it was wrong, even dangerous, to allow his praise to warm her. But there was no fighting it. His understanding meant so much because only he knew how hard it had been for her to get to this place in her life, how much it had cost her. When she opened her eyes again, she knew her pleasure shone transparently, and probably more as well. 'Why then?' she asked.

'Miss!' Nell hissed from her position across the street. 'The baker's girl is coming up the street. We must go back in!'

Charles reached out and clutched both of her hands in his. 'Not yet,' he pleaded. He glanced about wildly. 'The servants' stairwell,' he exclaimed. 'Come, we can talk there.'

He pulled her across, to the stairwell at the front of the house. Sophie looked doubtfully down at the landing at the bottom, but she could not resist the imploring look on Charles's face.

'Please, Nell?' she asked. 'Just keep watch for us a bit longer.'

The maid did not look happy, but she nodded. Sophie turned and followed Charles down the stairs.

The temperature dropped several degrees as they descended. She shivered and pulled her wrapper more tightly about her. The light was murky down here; Sophie could only dimly see Charles's expression. He was gazing at her in a way that made her heart begin to trip.

'You are so incredibly beautiful,' he whispered.

'You brought me down here for a reason,' she reminded him tartly in a vain attempt to cover her reaction to him. She hoped it was too dark for him to see her flushed cheeks. 'You were going to tell me why you were so desperate to speak to me.'

'Because I couldn't let you go on thinking I had forgotten you,' he said, his voice rough with emotion.

'I don't, truly—'

He moved so quickly she did not see it; she only felt his closeness, and his warmth. He stopped her words with his hand on her lips, and desire burst past all her restraints. Swelled with new hope and old dreams, it coiled through her, igniting every dark recess of her body.

'You couldn't have known,' he whispered. 'I don't think I even knew, but you've always been with me. No matter what infamous prank I pulled, no matter how deep the grief, no matter how hard the task I faced, you were there. Tucked away in a safe corner of my heart, you were there, smiling at me, comforting me, forgiving me.'

His hand dragged slowly away, only to be replaced by his mouth, soft and sweet. From the moment his lips touched hers, she was lost. She'd known it the first time he'd kissed her, but she'd ignored it, hidden from the knowledge that might destroy her. This was home, where she belonged, in his arms. The lonely orphan inside her knew it and rejoiced, but there was still a coldly sane and logical bit of her that rang out a warning. *Be careful.*

She ignored it, let the heat of the moment wash over her, and allowed the kiss to deepen. His mouth was hot and demanding and she surrendered to it. Charles groaned and his own restraint fell before the onslaught of desire. She could feel his desperation as he pulled her tight against him, the rasp of his beard rough against her jaw, and down the length of her neck.

She held him tight, drew him closer, wordlessly asking for more. He gave it, burying his face in the smooth juncture of her shoulder and bringing his hand up to mould the weight of her breast.

Oh, yes, she thought. Or perhaps she said it out loud. She could not be sure; all she knew was that suddenly her back was pressed against the wall. She was trapped between the cold, hard brick and the throbbing heat of Charles's body, and she never wanted to be anywhere else. Ever.

Somehow her wrapper had come open and his clever fingers were making quick work of the tiny buttons of her night rail. His mouth, hot and wet, traced a fiery trail across the skin of her shoulder. The heat of it chased away the chill of the morning, rendered inconsequential the impropriety of what they were doing and where they were doing it.

His hand faltered a little, hung for a long moment over her breast. Her nipple was taut, thrusting against the thin linen of her gown, aching for his caress. She held her breath, waiting.

At last he gave her what she wanted. Suddenly impatient, he pushed the gown away, baring her body to the dim morning light. His fingers touched her, ever so softly circling, and then, finally, brushing over the hard, yearning peak.

Her breath slid out of her in a soft, satisfied sigh. It turned rapidly to a moan when he bent over and took her in his mouth.

His tongue worked magic. He licked and sucked and nipped and sent rivers of pleasure, of pure unadulterated *want* down to the spot where she pulsed with need for him, and down into the depths of her soul. Her passion only grew when his fingers found their way to her other breast. She moaned and clutched him to her, letting her head fall back against the wall.

Yet still that small voice inside of her tried to be heard, tried to clamour a warning. She ignored it, had no desire to listen. At long last Charles was in her arms and giving her her first true glimpse of passion. It was a victory of sorts. He had not wanted to want her; she knew it. But there was no mistaking the heat and tension and longing in him now.

She forgot to feel triumphant a moment later. She forgot everything as he raised the hem of her night rail. His bold touch on the naked flesh of her thighs sent a tingling sensation up to her very core.

He touched her, then, where no one else ever had before. He tangled his fingers in her curls and trailed them over her feminine folds. He made her ache, he made her gasp when his finger slipped inside of her.

The shock of it was sweet, but the sound of a loudly and repeated clearing throat was not.

'Nell,' Sophie gasped. 'Charles, we have to stop.'

He slid his hand away, and grasped both of her shoulders, breathing heavily and resting his forehead on hers.

'Miss!' Nell's voice was strident. 'We must go back in now! The sun is high and the maids are out to clear the steps.'

'We can be together, Sophie. I know we can manage it.' Charles's voice was as urgent as Nell's. He drew back a little and stared into her eyes, his face serious. 'Where do you go tonight? We must meet, I have to tell you.'

Sophie slumped a little. 'We cannot. I leave today with your mother, to Sevenoaks. There are things there that require our attention. We don't return until Saturday, for Miss Ashford's ball.'

His hands slid down her arms, finally grasping both of hers once again. 'Saturday, then. I have an idea. A plan, perhaps.' He smiled. 'I know it's a stretch, but just keep out of trouble until then. I'll find you at the ball.' He raised her hand and kissed it.

'Miss!' hissed Nell.

'Saturday!' Sophie smiled, and watched as Charles backed away, then turned and vaulted up the stairs, disappearing into the bright morning light.

Chapter Ten

The grinding of the carriage wheels, the creak of the harness, the *clop, clop* of the horses' hooves— the regular everyday racket of a slowing carriage was as nothing compared to the sound of her own pounding heart. Sophie bounced in her seat, impatient with waiting for the footman, and leaned forward to open the door herself. She found her hand stayed by Emily Lowder's.

As part of the evening's entertainment, Sophie and Emily had come early to the Argyll Rooms, the site of Miss Ashford's charity ball. 'I'm having second thoughts,' Emily said.

'About what?' Sophie asked. Finally the door opened and, without waiting for an answer, she eagerly alighted. The rooms were ablaze, but the spectacle couldn't compete with the glow of excitement in Sophie's breast. This was it. Tonight Charles would declare himself. She knew it.

Emily slowed once more as they crossed the threshold into the empty foyer. 'Perhaps we should reconsider this scheme. I'm afraid there might be some backlash. For you, Sophie.'

Sophie was flabbergasted. 'Emily Lowder, you've helped with every step of Miss Ashford's plans! What is it that is bothering you?'

'It's…well, it's your costume.'

She raised a brow in question. 'What objection could you possess? Nearly every square inch of me is covered. Far less of me shows in this than in the average ball gown.'

'I know!' Emily cried. 'That's why I thought it nothing more than a lark—but the overall effect— I couldn't have imagined.'

'Rubbish,' she said, tugging at the cords of her cloak. 'Come, let's find Miss Ashford. She herself condoned the idea, and you don't think she would countenance anything remotely scandalous tonight?'

'I don't think you should put your faith in Miss Ashford's judgement in this case.'

'Emily, I swear I don't know what has got into you. You could look the world over and not find anyone more closely acquainted with propriety than Miss Ashford.'

'Yes, but I see something in her eyes, occasionally, when she's watching you.'

'Shh. Here she is.' Sophie gestured as Miss Ashford, dressed in the flowing robes of the goddess Diana, entered the entrance hall with a gaggle of servants on her heels.

'Mrs Lowder, Sophie, dear!' she exclaimed upon sighting them. 'You are here at last. Do take their cloaks,' she said to one of the footmen. 'I'm so glad, I have been waiting to show you…' She faltered as Sophie's cloak came off.

'Not you, too,' Sophie groaned. She thought she looked rather well, especially for the role Miss Ashford had asked her to play. She wore *churidar,* or baggy silk trousers of deepest blue, an upper garment whose close-fitting bodice was of the same hue, with long, tight sleeves of white. Over this she had a tunic of pale blue, richly embroidered with silver and white, and reaching to her knees. Her hair hung loose in dark waves, adorned only by a plain corded band, with a single jewel—a sparkling tear-shaped sapphire—centered on her forehead. On her feet were velvet slippers of the same dark blue. A necklace of gold coins and bangles at her wrist and ankle completed the ensemble.

'Is this not what you described?' she asked. 'Don't I look like I could be Scheherazade's sister?'

'Indeed, it is what we discussed,' said Miss Ashford, 'and you do look very…erm…authentic.'

'You look like you walked straight out of a harem!' Emily said. 'Even when we assembled the pieces I could not object, and on me or Miss Ashford there would probably be no concern. I don't know how to say it, but somehow, on you, this outfit is very—' she lowered her voice to a whisper '—sensual.'

Sophie laughed. 'All well and good then, I should draw my share of donations.'

Instead of soliciting donations in a large bowl at the entrance of the ballroom as the guests entered, Miss Ashford had hit upon the charming scheme of offering entertainments in exchange for her guests' generosity. All of the young ladies on her committee were cooperating and she had struck upon the idea of Scheherazade's sister as a way of utilising Sophie's artistic talents.

Sophie's remark seemed to recall Miss Ashford to her senses. 'Yes, we must keep our goal in mind, after all. But come, you must see what we have prepared for you.'

They entered the ballroom and Sophie was transfixed. 'Oh, how delightful.' The galleries were draped with rich fabrics and musicians tuned their instruments on a dais in the back. Hundreds of candles and a forest of fresh blooms had transformed the room into a sparkling fantasy.

'It has turned out well, hasn't it?' Miss Ashford asked with a satisfied smile.

'The vignettes are darling,' Emily said.

Miss Ashford had set up separate areas around the room for each of her planned entertainments. The ladies who had agreed to perform were all present; they quickly gathered to exclaim over the new arrivals' costumes and to show off their own.

One young lady in an ephemeral white gown had a small stage with a grand floor harp. Another had a banner-draped corner with a small table and was dressed as a fetching gypsy girl. A painted backdrop set the stage for a charming girl in scarlet who meant to sing.

But none held a candle to Sophie's vignette. A shimmering ivory tent took up one corner of the ballroom. The flowing fabric was pulled wide, exposing an opulent scene straight out of *Arabian Nights*. Swathes of silk were everywhere, large pillows and rose petals covered the floor, and in the middle of this decadent Eastern scene sat a large easel and a pair of chairs.

'Miss Ashford,' Sophie said, trying to take it all in, 'you have been hiding a decided flair for the dramatic.'

'Indeed,' agreed Emily as they approached the tent. 'It is nothing less than awe inspiring. Sophie will fit right in. I am still worried, however, about the stir it might cause.' Her voice grew firm. 'I will not have her thought of as *fast.*'

'Nor would I,' agreed Miss Ashford. 'We must take care to see that all the proprieties are met. Would it suffice if we agreed that she shall have one of us as a chaperon at all times?'

'Well. Yes,' Emily said slowly. 'That should do. I shall take the first shift.' She turned to Sophie. 'You must promise to be on your best behaviour tonight, my dear. The costume alone is risky; we dare not give the gabble-grinders any further ammunition.'

'I do promise,' she agreed, stroking the rich fabric of the tent.

'Good, then I shall return when I find a chair to position at the entrance, for I will not recline on those pillows, even for a charitable cause.'

Sophie waved her off and turned around inside the tent. 'How wonderful! I feel positively transported.' She beckoned Miss Ashford in. 'Come along, as this was all your idea, you must be first to sample Dunyazade's talents.' Lowering her voice and attempting an Eastern accent she cajoled, 'Come, my dear, sit, make yourself comfortable. I shall draw you a picture of your fondest dreams.'

'No, no,' Miss Ashford protested. 'I still have much to do.'

'Nonsense. You have worked long.' She gestured to the glittering ballroom. 'All is set for a magical evening.' Sophie pulled her to the comfortable chair across from the easel. 'Sit back. Take a minute for yourself.' She took up Miss Ashford's hands and began to rub them, waiting for the tension to ease from her arms and shoulders.

'This is silly,' Miss Ashford protested weakly.

'Indeed, it is not. Close your eyes,' she directed softly.

Sophie took her seat. Paper was already tacked up, a box of coloured chalks sat at the ready. 'Now, bring your mind to your favourite place. Where would you most like to be? It needn't be a spot in the true world—perhaps it is where you have always dreamed yourself to be.'

She saw the moment when Miss Ashford gave in. She began to sketch quickly while her subject sat silent, still a moment. When she could see that Miss Ashford was absorbed in her own private world, she said quietly, 'Tell me what you see.'

'A garden. Full of blooms. The sky is very blue. It is lovely.' She sighed.

'Are you alone?' Sophie pitched her voice lower still as her fingers moved swiftly on the page.

'No. There are many people here. They are watching me.'

'Look down,' Sophie directed. 'What is in your hand?'

'More flowers. Lilies. I can almost smell them.'

'How do you feel in your beautiful garden?'

Miss Ashford was quiet a long moment. 'I feel… at peace. Appreciated.'

Sophie heaved a sigh. If this could work so well on practical, prudent Miss Ashford, then she could put away her last worry for the evening. She sketched in a few last details. 'You may open your eyes now, Miss Ashford, though I would not blame you should you wish to stay in your garden.'

Her eyes popped open and she blinked to focus. 'Oh. Yes. Well, I should run and check the kitchens.'

'Wait a moment,' Sophie called. She pulled the thick vellum from the easel and handed it over. 'Don't forget, a memento of your visit to Dunyazade.'

'Oh, my,' Miss Ashford whispered in awe. 'It is just as I imagined.'

'How lovely,' Emily said as she entered. She directed a servant to place the chair and peered over Miss Ashford's shoulder.

Sophie had drawn Miss Ashford in her garden, surrounded by a bower of fresh greens and pretty blooms. She wore a flowing white dress with tiny, capped sleeves, a wreath of flowers in her hair, and carried a group of vibrant lilies.

'I hope you have many happy moments there,' Sophie said, watching Miss Ashford's reaction. She looked on the verge of tears.

'Thank you,' she whispered again.

'Now then,' Sophie said, turning to Emily and giving Miss Ashford a chance to gather her wits, 'you must be my assistant as well as my duenna. Where are those ribbons we spoke of when we were planning this scheme? Ah, there in the basket. Let's tie up Miss Ashford's picture so that she may put it away until after her evening is done.'

'Yes, thank you,' said Miss Ashford, recovered now. 'I must be off. I see they still do not have the bookcase in place for Miss Harraday's poetry reading.' She strode away, the golden ribbons in her hair catching the light as she left the darker environs of the tent.

'Perhaps this will turn out well, after all,' Emily said.

'I do believe it will, at that,' Sophie agreed.

In fact, it turned out to be a very near thing. Before long the rooms began to fill. Milkmaids mixed with kings, pirates led medieval princesses onto the dance floor. Miss Ashford's young ladies began their performances and the silver bowls at each vignette began to fill.

Except at Sophie's tent. Lady Dayle sat for Dunyazade. The Duchess of Charmouth told Sophie to draw her in her new ballroom. No one else ventured close. People gawked, whispered, and walked repeatedly past, but no one entered.

'What is it, Lady Dayle?' Emily asked from her post at the entrance to the tent. 'Why aren't they coming in?'

'There's talk of Sophie's trousers, but even the highest sticklers cannot refute that she's more than decently covered,' the viscountess answered, her voice troubled. 'But there is another problem. Someone is spreading rumours, accusing Sophie of being difficult and temperamental, of trying to outshine the other young ladies.'

'I feared something would happen,' moaned Emily. 'What are we to do?'

In the end, they did not have to do anything. Charles's cousin, Theo Alden, of all people, saved the day.

He didn't mean to. He entered the lavish tent with malice, intending to take advantage of the wave of malicious gossip and take the impudent Westby chit down a notch or two. He settled in the chair with bad grace and pictured Sophie's downfall instead of his own piece of heaven.

Sophie gave it to him anyway. His jaw dropped and his heart swelled when she handed him his picture, effectively expelling all of his ugly intentions.

She'd drawn him strutting in the park, dressed to perfection in an elegant, only slightly showy ensemble, while jealous dandies and worshipful females looked on.

'The green of the coat exactly matches my eyes,' he exclaimed. 'The pleat in these pantaloons show-cases the length of my limbs.'

He tore his gaze from the drawing. 'I have wronged you, Miss Westby. You have the eye, the soul, of an artist. I will take this to my tailor tomorrow and have it exactly replicated.'

Sophie smiled. 'I'm glad you approve.'

'What shade of gold would you call this waistcoat?'

There were no more problems after that. Theo's set crowded in and soon there was a line waiting to sit in Dunyazade's chair. Sophie drew until she thought her fingers would fall off. The bowl outside her tent filled and had to be replaced. She hadn't had a rest or a dance all evening, but she barely noticed. Always she kept one eye on her latest subject and the other trained for any sign of Charles.

Charles swore as his valet struggled with the high boots of his costume. He was going to be late again.

Truly, though, it couldn't have been helped. He'd been closeted with the committee on farmland distress all day, and they had made significant progress. 'Sorry, must go and gather my costume for tonight's masquerade' wasn't an excuse that balanced against the fate of desperate English farmers.

His valet, Crocker, had done wonders without him, however. Now Charles stood and allowed him to drape the billowing black cape over his shoulders. There, he was the image of an eighteenth-century highwayman, lace collar, cuffs, and all. He had balked at donning the old-fashioned shirt, but Crocker had insisted. 'No,' his man had said in his usual raspy voice and blunt manner, 'my lord must be the romantic, noble thief of the last century, not the ill-bred, dirty, illiterate road agent one encounters these days.'

Charles had looked askance at the man and wondered briefly just what it was he did with his off days. He decided it was wiser not to know. He threw back his cape, strapped the light rapier to his side and bade Crocker not to wait up.

It was a sorry highwayman who rode through town in a carriage. Outside his groom waited with two restive mounts. They set off, and Charles chuckled, wondering whom he might startle in the streets of Mayfair tonight. It was a fitting disguise, for tonight he meant to defy both fate and his enemy and steal back his future.

His future with Sophie. Just the thought fired his

soul, filled him with a longing so intense it was almost frightening. His plan would work. It must. Sophie could do it—she could become the steady, respectable lady he needed. All this time he had fretted and worried that she might be a threat to his plans. It was the height of irony that she was now in the position where she might be the one to save them.

He needn't have worried about frightening anyone in the streets, for everyone in London was obviously at the charity ball. Impatience winning out over manners, Charles made his way through the multitude of revellers just waiting to get in. He stood in the entryway and marvelled at the crowd. Good heavens, but the modistes must have been burning the midnight oil for weeks. He saw mermaids, chevaliers, and Roman senators. If he was not mistaken, that was a member of the Royal Family dressed as old Boney himself. But nowhere did he see the smile he was looking for.

He did catch site of Miss Ashford as he entered the ballroom, dressed as one of the goddesses. Diana, judging by the purely decorative bow she had slung over one shoulder. She must be in alt at the success of her ball, and as heartily as Charles commended her, he most definitely did not wish to see her now. He ducked to one side of a bookcase as her gaze wandered his way.

Hold a moment. A bookcase? In the ballroom of the Argyll Rooms? He peeked out and noted a pretty young lady taking a stand on a carpet just in front of his hiding spot. A group was gathering politely before her. The young lady breathed deep.

> When Man, expell'd from Eden's bowers,
> A moment linger'd near the gate,
> Each scene recall'd the vanish'd hours,
> And bade him curse his future fate.

Not Byron, Charles moaned.

'I say,' a nearby satyr said to his companion, a robed wizard, 'had you heard the story of when Dayle dressed as Byron and visited the Mayfair Ladies Byron Appreciation Society to sign copies of the latest edition of his poetry?'

Charles dropped his head in his hands. At least this was a short selection. Soon the masked audience was applauding and depositing coins and tokens in the silver bowl on a nearby stand. Then, vaguely, Charles remembered Miss Ashford prattling about the performances at her ball.

A sudden, uneasy prickle tripped its way down his spine. He'd better find Sophie, fast.

His anxiety increased as he paced the length of the ballroom and noted each of the performers as he passed. Singer. Harpist. He shook his head. Sword dancer?

When he caught site of the tent, he knew. He knew, and his blood began to boil.

It nearly erupted out the top of his head when he grew close enough to see inside. Long, curling hair pulled back from her face, hanging loose to her waist. Smouldering, painted eyes. Long slim legs in *trousers,* though they were baggy, and a tight-fitting bodice exposed under the covering tunic as her arm lifted to the easel.

She was sex personified, igniting fantasies of long desert nights and secret Eastern skills. His heart contracted, his body tightened at the sight of her and he wanted to scream his rage—because he knew every other man here was having the same reaction.

Desperately trying to clamp a hold on his anger, he stalked to the tent.

Sophie was tiring a little of her role and wishing she could get up to see some of the ball. She brightened, however, when her uncle stepped into the tent, bringing someone with him.

'Uncle! How good of you to come. I'm sure Miss Ashford will be grateful.' She smiled. 'Shall Dunyazade draw your portrait? At least you have no mask to remove. Just have a seat and throw back the hood of your domino.'

'Your uncle is always ready to support a worthy cause, my dear. But see, here is the reason I've come tonight.' He motioned to the man accompanying him to step forward. 'I've brought you a surprise.'

Sophie smiled and studied the man as he drew closer. Tall and slender, he was dressed soberly, with a broad-brimmed black hat over dark curls. He seemed familiar, but she did not recall that they had met. 'Sir? Are you a Quaker, come to remind me of my old home?'

'Dressed as a Quaker, for expediency's sake, and definitely here to remind you of home,' he returned with a sparkling smile showcasing white teeth against dark skin. 'I do not expect you to recognise me, Miss Westby, but I would know you anywhere. You are the very image of your mother.'

'My mother?' Sophie stilled and cast a questioning glance to her uncle.

'It's been a long time,' her uncle said, 'but I'm sure you'll remember your cousin, Mr Cardea.'

A sudden vision flashed in her mind. A curly-haired boy, eyes alight with mischief, tugging her braids, chasing her through her home while she shrieked in glee. 'Mateo?' she whispered.

'Indeed, it is I!' He swept her up in an impulsive

embrace and twirled her around. Emily gasped from the entrance where she had once again taken up her post, and Mateo threw her a wink before he set Sophie down.

'But what brings you to London?' Sophie asked, smiling.

'Lord Cranbourne and I have business dealings. I was already contemplating coming to London, but when one of his letters mentioned you, my fate was sealed. I hopped aboard the first one of our ships leaving port, and here I am.'

'Here you are,' echoed Sophie. His blithe statement raised several questions in her mind. What sort of business dealings? And surely the timing was off, was it not? But before she could find a polite way to ask, some small, inarticulate sound made her turn to the wide opening of the tent. It was filled with a large figure in tight black clothes, long dark boots and a small black mask. Her heart began to pound.

'Charles!'

'Sophie,' he said abruptly. He advanced into the tent, changing the atmosphere with the dark menace of his assumed identity. Sophie swallowed and hoped it was only the costume. 'Lord Cranbourne. And?'

'Oh, Charles, please, allow me to introduce my cousin. Mateo, this is Lord Dayle. Charles, this is my cousin, Mr Cardea.'

Mateo flashed his charming smile and made a very credible bow. 'Delighted, Lord Dayle.'

'As am I, Mr Cardea.' He turned to her uncle. 'Congratulations, Cranbourne. I heard you had won the chairmanship for the Board of Trade's committee. I missed you at the preliminary meeting today, but I look forward to working with you.'

Cranbourne grinned. 'Thank you, Dayle. I'm sure we'll accomplish much.'

Charles nodded. 'I hope you will all forgive my rudeness, but Sophie is promised to me for this set.'

Sophie blushed with pleasure and laid a hand on his arm. 'Oh, that sounds lovely. I haven't had a dance all evening. Pray, do excuse us, Uncle, Mateo.'

His eyes warm with regard, her cousin pressed her free hand. 'We shall see each other again soon, I hope.'

Sophie could only nod as Charles stalked out, his hand tight on hers. She struggled to keep up with his long stride.

'The sets are forming this way, Charles.'

'We are not dancing,' he growled.

She swallowed her disappointment and surprise and looked at him in question. His eyes were cold and hard again, a study in opposites from the warm openness of her cousin's. 'What is it?' she asked.

He didn't answer. It appeared that he was looking for something. He stopped when his gaze fell on the galleries overhead and then he headed for the nearest stairway at the front of the room.

They had to manoeuvre through quite a crowd and by the time they reached the stairs, Sophie was tired of feeling like a toy on the end of a string. All of her happy anticipation was draining away. 'I'm not going a step further until you tell me what has upset you now.'

He paused part way up and threw a heated glance over his shoulder. 'We have to talk, and the things we must say to each other are not for other ears.'

She hesitated a moment. His walls were back and up and she was tired of trying to breach them. On the other hand, she'd heard of the cosy alcoves located above, and some of the things that were rumoured to go on in them. The thought of that early morning encounter and the way it had made her feel floated through her mind and sent a shiver of excitement through her. Before she could formulate another thought, her feet were mounting the steps right after Charles.

Oh, my. She'd come to the top and could see why the galleries were so well known, and masquerades so popular. Charles had passed by several alcoves, some with curtains drawn, some not. He drew her now towards a small room with a door, but Sophie's attention was caught by something else. 'Charles,' she whispered, 'is that shepherdess kissing the knight who I think she is?'

'Yes, but you are not to repeat a word of it,' he said in a harsh whisper.

'I wouldn't. I don't think her husband would approve, though.'

He pulled her into the room and shut the door. It was a subscription room, or something like. The walls were covered with shelves of books and periodicals, but Sophie barely noticed. 'Well,' she said, her mind still on what she had just witnessed, 'they shouldn't be able to get up to too much mischief. Just think of the noise, with all that armour.'

Charles laughed, the sound soft and bitter. Sophie looked at him in concern. She didn't wish to deal with one of his moods. In fact, she wanted him in another mood altogether. Like he'd been last time. Perhaps now she had a better idea on how to achieve that. 'Are you going to tell me what has upset you so?'

'I'm amazed that you must ask.'

'How could I know? You barely speak, you won't dance, you drag me up here like a toy you've found someone else playing with.' She was staring at his mouth while she spoke, unable to tear her gaze away. She bit her own lip in nervous agitation. 'You're certainly in a different temper from the last time we met.'

She sounded wistful even to her own ears. Edging closer, she saw the anger that had been haunting his eyes turn to wariness. And something else—desire. Slowly she raised her hand, placed it on his chest. Hard, like marble, but so warm. 'Perhaps we should just forget whatever's bothering you and pick up where we left off.'

He groaned, either in agony or amusement. Perhaps both. 'Sophie—you're driving me mad.' He reached out and wrapped her in his arms and she thought she'd gladly join him on the trip.

He smelled of sandalwood and leather and virile male. His vexation was apparent in the hard crush of his mouth on hers, but she didn't care. She opened her mouth, drank it in, and gave it back as hot, slick passion.

He shuddered and pulled her tighter, running his warm hands under her tunic. She gasped when he cupped the swell of her breasts. Then those large hands were moving, flowing around the curve of her waist and tracing the thinly disguised line of her buttocks. She pressed tighter to him and he kissed her deeper yet, while she savoured the heat and the strength and the taste of him.

Sophie was briefly bereft when his mouth abandoned hers, only to trail over the line of her jaw and down her throat. The rough cloth of his mask brushed her soft skin, arousing her almost as much as his searing kiss.

His hands came back up to her breasts, kneading her through the tight bodice. She felt her nipples swell, and her body arched, answering the rough caress with a pulsing throb that travelled from the point of his possessive caress to the coiling heat in her belly.

With a moan, Charles pushed a leg between her thighs. With no enveloping skirts in the way the contact was close and powerful. She could feel his full arousal against her most intimate spot, and she suddenly understood why a woman in trousers was so scandalous. She also understood for the first time what true passion was. Not restless longing and vague, unrelenting craving, but a powerful, lust-filled whirlwind that stole away all reason, crushed resistance and blew her inevitably toward her final destination.

Sophie couldn't summon the will to resist; she just clung to Charles and hung on, ready to follow the destructive vortex to the end. Charles, however, was made of sterner stuff. Eventually he wrenched his mouth from hers and pulled away.

Sophie breathed deep, desperate for air, for something to replace her abrupt loss. Charles was panting as well and glaring at her as if she had been the one to call a halt to the proceedings.

'Do you see?' he demanded. 'What you drive me to? What every man down there wishes to get a chance at?'

Sophie was shocked. 'Don't be ridiculous.'

'It's a far cry from being ridiculous, it's the truth. What was it I asked of you when we last parted? Just don't get into any trouble. But you take the first opportunity to make a grand spectacle of yourself.'

'A spectacle? It's a benefit. Other young ladies are performing as well.'

'None of the other ladies look like they sprang from a bordello's re-enactment of the *Arabian Nights!* You're wearing trousers! They'll have to destroy half the forests of England to print all that will be said of you in tomorrow's broadsides and papers.'

'You are overreacting. And in any case, what if they do?' she asked, tossing her hair. 'I told you once before—you cannot control what others think. I don't care what people say of me.' If she did, she'd have broken long ago.

'And I told you then—you should care.' He groaned and ripped off his mask. 'If you hold any hope of becoming my bride—you must.'

Sophie froze. All the elation she'd been feeling these past days began to wither. 'Pardon me?'

'You know my situation, what I've been doing this Season. I must find a bride of sterling character and reputation. People are watching me, judging me by the choices I make. I have to live down my past; I must show good judgement and an eye for the future when I wed.'

Sophie tried to breathe, but it seemed each word fed the pain that was building in her chest, cutting off her air, her blood, her belief in Charles and his in her. 'Choosing me would be a show of bad judgment?'

'I don't think so, but others will.'

'All this because of a masquerade costume?'

He took her hand, led her over to a little chair, then pulled up another close to her. 'It's not just the costume, Sophie. It's—it's more. I don't know. It's not always the things you do, it's the way you do them.'

She couldn't speak, couldn't force any words past the fist of agony inside her. All the taunts, all the rejections of her childhood—none of them had hurt so badly as this. It was *Charles* throwing these barbs at her now, and hitting her most vulnerable spot with devastating accuracy. She could only look at him with accusing eyes.

He misunderstood. 'No—it's more than your designs—because it's not *just* your designs. You don't just have an interest in décor—you publish a book. You trade fabric swatches with the Prince Regent, for God's sake!'

He took her hand, clasped it in his warm grasp.

'Please, just listen to me for a moment. We can make it work,' he said. 'I'm sure we can. But it will take some effort from you, Sophie.' He smiled, tried to rally her. 'It won't be so bad. Mother will help. I know you disapprove of Miss Ashford, but her reputation is spotless. We can use her as a model of sorts.' He smiled again. 'If I can go from England's worst profligate to a politician on the path to the ministry, then you'll have a much easier time.'

The air was cold in this little room, or perhaps it was just her frozen heart. She shook her head. He didn't even know that he was betraying her, killing the one belief that had given her hope, kept her sane. 'What you are saying—' her voice was dangerous '—is that we can be married, once I learn to behave?'

He heaved an exasperated sigh. 'Don't phrase it in such a way. You know the situation. We just have to change society's image of you.'

The cold was disappearing fast, fleeing before the heat of her rising fury. 'Oh, but why stop there?' she asked. 'For you surely did not. No—you changed their perception of you and then you continued on, changing your personality, your heart, and your soul. You've changed more than I suspected, to be able to say such things to me.' She turned, not wanting him to see the tears that she couldn't hold back.

He moved closer, until she could feel his breath

close to her ear. Before he could insult her any further, voices echoed in the hall, just outside the subscription room door.

'Do not look at them, Corinne,' someone commanded in a sharp, nasal tone. 'Oh, I shall shake the wretched girl. I do hope you are wrong, but we must look into it, I suppose.'

'I'm sure it is not what you might be thinking, Mama.' Miss Ashford's usually calm voice sounded almost smug.

The door opened and the two ladies peered in.

'Miss Westby!' Lady Ashford gasped. 'I am sure I did not believe the vile rumours that have been circulating about you tonight, but I see I have been proven wrong. And you, of all people, Lord Dayle!'

'It is perfectly all right, Mama, as I have tried to tell you,' Miss Ashford said. 'Lord Dayle and Miss Westby are old friends. They grew up together and regard each other more as brother and sister than anything else.' She ran an assessing eye down Sophie. 'No one who is familiar with them would suspect anything untoward. I am sure the situation is perfectly innocent.'

'Is my daughter correct, Lord Dayle?' Lady Ashford demanded.

He did not answer, did not even look her way. His gaze remained locked with Sophie's. She turned from him, avoided the questioning eyes of the Ashford ladies, and moved to brush past them.

'Please,' he said to her. 'I wish it were otherwise. Is it really too much to ask, when you consider what might be gained?'

She closed her eyes as the rage drained away. It left behind an empty husk in its wake, all too vulnerable to the pain that was quick to rush back. She turned to him, looked him in the eye. 'Yes,' she said simply. 'It is too much. If you knew me at all in the way that I thought you did, you wouldn't have to ask.'

She fled, fighting tears, running from the ache of despair. Her feet flew down the stairs as she struggled to rein in her emotions. She must get away. She absolutely could not break down in front of so many witnesses.

Her every resource was focused inward. She did not see the two men whispering together at the bottom of the stairs until she had run into them.

'I do beg your pardon,' she said thickly, without stopping.

'Sophie!' It was her uncle, and her cousin. 'Are you well? You look upset.'

'I am not feeling at all the thing, Uncle. Do excuse me.'

'Then of course you must go home at once.'

Sophie had to fight off a bitter comment about the extreme lateness of his solicitude.

'Mr Cardea will escort you, will you not, sir?'

Mateo bowed low. 'I shall be delighted.'

Sophie hadn't the energy to decline. She left a message for Lady Dayle and departed with her cousin.

She never felt the weight of two separate, but very satisfied, gazes as she went.

Chapter Eleven

The worst part was knowing that Charles was right. That he could breathe a sigh of relief with each new broadsheet posted across London, that he could thank his lucky stars that he was not involved, as each vile rumour grew worse with repeated whisperings.

Sophie had lived most of her life at the mercy of talebearers and scandalmongers. She had long ago learned to rise above such nonsense. But not this time. This time the whisperers had sharper tongues, wicked wit, and a broader audience. The tales circulating about her were outrageous. She'd worn trousers, she'd worn *transparent* trousers, she'd worn next to nothing at all. She'd danced a harem dance, she'd danced with the Prince Regent, she'd danced down the centre of the supper table. There was no end to the inventiveness.

Still, strange things had been said of her before,

and she had held her head high and taken the high road. She had even used her reputation as an eccentric to her advantage a time or two. It might have been the same with this, after enough time had passed, if this time, the scandal hadn't become the embodiment of her deepest insecurities. This time each fabricated account of her wickedness hit her like a blow, drumming the ugly truth deeper. *Not good enough. Not good enough.*

Oh, he hadn't said it in so many words, but the meaning was clear. She should know. She was an expert at being not good enough.

She'd been a disappointment to her uncle, a failure in reaching her aunt, a pariah to the people of Blackford Chase. Only Charles had ever made her feel truly appreciated just for being herself. The rest of London could go hang; it was the loss of that certainty, the sure knowledge of Charles's regard, that caused this pain, this blinding agony that only seemed to grow worse with each drawn breath.

She wandered the house, emotionally adrift. Only now was she coming to realise how deep her dependence had gone. She'd spent half her life on the wrong side of public opinion, but always she had clung to the rock of Charles's faith in her. Now she floundered. She hadn't felt this lost since the death of her parents.

She had to fight, to keep afloat, to flail blindly if need be, until she found something stronger to hold on to. But it was so hard. She couldn't think. It was all she could do to breathe, to ignore the hurt and make it to the next moment.

Emily's family was suffering as well. That first day her drawing room was a scene of frantic activity, as society came to sympathise, to gloat, or just to be in the centre of the scandal broth. Sophie stayed in her room and waited with a mixture of dread and anticipation for Charles to come. He didn't. And then neither did anyone else.

The number of visitors trickled, and then stopped. An air of dread inhabited the house. Deep silences, long faces, hushed voices. Sophie grew tired of mourning her reputation and heartily sick of waiting for Charles. Finally she could take no more. She packed her bags and went alone to Sevenoaks.

It was exactly what she needed. She threw herself into the dirtiest projects she could find. No job was too small to command her attention. Stripping paper, hanging fabric, and restoring plasterwork occupied her thoroughly. She concentrated on soothing the Italian *stuccatore*'s wounded vanity instead of nursing her own wounded heart. She spent her time curbing the hanger's passion for red-flock paper instead of dwelling on the passion that had flared so easily between her and Charles.

She worked almost unceasingly each day, falling into bed exhausted late each evening. As a plan for avoiding painful memories, it had merit. Unfortunately, it did not meet with success. In the quiet darkness her mind was too busy to allow her body to rest.

A thousand times during those lonely nights she changed her mind. Charles was right, he wasn't asking too much. Not if they could be together. Tired, heartsore, and more alone than she had ever felt in her life, she thought of marrying Charles, spending their lives together, and she knew she would do it. She would change. She would change into an elephant if he wished it.

Yet each morning found her back at work rather than on her way back to London. As much as she yearned for Charles in the night, in the clear, dawn light harsher memories returned. Cold eyes, hard words, high, strong walls keeping her out. She'd been exasperated by that side of Charles, but she could not deny that she had found him intriguing and irresistible in his own way.

Was that the sort of person he wished her to become? Even here, alone and covered in grime and plaster dust, she shook her head. Through years of loneliness and neglect she'd battled bitterness and despair. She'd refused to become closed and angry. She couldn't give in now, even for the sake of love.

That was the crux of it: love. Charles desired her, he wanted her, but he didn't love her. Love supports, love nurtures, it doesn't require you to change.

So, with stiffened resolve, Sophie laboured right along with the workmen, and slowly over the next few days the project drew close to the end. It was a bittersweet realisation.

The house had turned out to be even more beautiful than she had hoped, and now that it was nearly complete, she could picture Charles here all too easily. His image sprang to mind everywhere: in the library, in the hall, in the bedroom. He would spend many happy hours here. Without her.

Finally she had accepted the truth. She'd had time for a lot of relentless soul searching over the last days, and she wasn't sure she liked what she'd found.

No matter what she had told herself upon coming to London—regarding both her designs and her relationship with Charles—she had to admit now that some part of her had been hoping to have both. Well, she couldn't. He had changed, and so had she. And it was past time she changed again.

These days of grief and regret had been disturbingly similar to the days after her parents' deaths.

As a scared little girl, suddenly alone in the world, she'd put all her hopes and dreams into the image of a loving uncle, a man who would love and care for her the way her parents had. When that fantasy had died, she had focused all the love in her lonely little heart on the one person who had cared. Even after he'd left, she'd carried that dream in her heart.

No longer. She was a woman now, and it was time to finally recognise the difference between dreams and reality. Charles was a dream. But what was her reality?

This, she thought, gazing around her. No matter what society thought, no matter what Charles believed, she knew the kind of person she was. Not perfect by any means, but she did have talent, the ability to bring beauty to people's lives. More importantly, she could use that talent to accomplish something useful, to help those who had so much less than herself.

Society was closed to her now and she wouldn't give tuppence to have it back. But she had her designs. Her book. Mr Darvey and the workmen back at Blackford Chase. She could use her skills and accomplish some good at the same time. She would be content with that.

It was not long after reaching that conclusion that she stood in the drawing room, staring with a frown at the continued chimneypiece. She'd had the wood painted white to match all the moulding in the room and to complement the elegant plaster-work. But she could not decide on a painting to mount there. She had two candidates, but neither was quite right.

With the rest of the room she was more than sat-isfied. Here her ardent hanger had had his way, and the room was resplendent with red-flock paper. It contrasted beautifully with all the white. Here was a room a statesman could be proud of. Fit for enter-taining royalty, visiting dignitaries, or just close friends and loved ones. It was grand, impressive, yet somehow it also maintained the warmth of a home.

She could even think of it that way without regret. Almost.

As luck would have it, some sort of disturbance began at the front of the house and she was given no time to dwell on it. She had only just turned towards the door when it opened.

'Now that I see what occupies you so far from London, I must say it is worth the trip.'

'Mateo!' Sophie gasped.

'Indeed, it is I. You fled the city just after I arrived and I have chased you down, just as when we were children.' He smiled and entered the room to take her hands. 'The sight of you alone was worth the chase. This—' he waved his hand at the room '—is—what do the English call it—the cream.'

She laughed. 'How did you find me?'

'I have pestered the good viscountess day and night until she finally relented and allowed me to travel here with her. She will be in directly, she was delayed by the housekeeper, and I had the bad manners to come straight in here.'

'Well, I am glad you are here.' She surprised herself by meaning it.

'As am I.' He dropped her hands and began to circle the room. 'Lovely. Exquisite, in fact. If this is an indication of your work, then I can see why the Prince Regent adores you so.'

Sophie grimaced. 'I think you exaggerate.'

'Oho! So you have not been reading the papers here in your retreat?'

'No.' She could not keep the hard edge from her voice. 'And if you have, then you'll know why.'

Mateo tossed his head, setting his shining dark curls to bouncing, and laughed long. Sophie stared, filing the image away in her mind, knowing she would sketch it later. Young, handsome, confident, carefree, he was the very image of…something. Life, perhaps.

'Trust you, Sophie,' he crowed, 'to turn London upside down and not even realise it.'

'He's right, my dear.' Lady Dayle came in, and Sophie went straight into her embrace. She clung a little longer than she meant to, and when the viscountess finally set her back, she began, 'I'm so sorry, my lady—'

'No,' interjected Mateo. 'You do not apologise. It is these English. Such a fuss over such a small thing. They do not know how to enjoy life, Sophie. You have no wish to be like them.'

Despite herself, she smiled. 'You sound just like Nona Celeste. Nevertheless, I am sorry for any distress you have suffered, Lady Dayle.'

'Not at all, dear. You must listen to your cousin. The circumstances have changed since you left.' She looked around with pleasure at the room. 'How lovely it has turned out, Sophie. Let us sit while we speak.'

They all took seats, but Sophie could wait no longer. 'Circumstances have changed?' she prompted.

'Yes, they have realised that they have put their temper in a teacup,' Mateo said.

'Tempest in a teacup, Mr Cardea. In any case, Sophie, it is over.' The viscountess took her hands in hers and smiled.

'Over?' Sophie was perplexed.

'Over.' Lady Dayle said in a firm voice. 'After you left, the furore died down a bit. Only to be stirred up again every day or so with some new story or published account. Soon people began to notice that many of the articles printed about that night and your supposedly shocking behaviour were very similarly worded. As if it were one person behind all the stories, stirring the scandal broth, as they say.'

'But your defenders, they were legion!' her cousin said. 'The viscountess has stood your truest friend, and Mrs Lowder and many more.'

Sophie couldn't help the tears that rose. No one had ever defended her before. Except Charles. The stab of pain was acute, but she had to know. 'And Lord Dayle?'

'I haven't seen him since the masquerade,' Lady Dayle said, sounding troubled. 'Jack said he was locked up with his committee, but Sir Harold said they had adjourned several days ago to await a report from the north. No one seems to know where to find him. I thought perhaps he might have told you his plans?'

Mute, Sophie shook her head.

'You have no need of his aid, Sophie,' said Mateo. 'Your friend the Duchess declared she would cut dead anyone who spoke a wrong word of you. The cold one, Miss Ashford?' She nodded and he continued. 'Even she finally declared that the costume had been her idea and was unobjectionable. But the final blow to your detractors came when the Prince Regent spoke on your behalf.'

Sophie could only cover her mouth with her hand. 'He didn't,' she whispered.

'Indeed.' Lady Dayle smiled.

'He said that your talent is great and that the artistic temperament must be allowed more latitude than the average person's. He would be very displeased to hear anyone disparaging you. He may not be much of a ruler,' Mateo said with condescension, 'but he is a man who knows how to get the most out of life.'

They all laughed and Sophie began to feel a little better.

'The truly funny thing is that once Prinny made his pronouncement, everyone pulled out their drawings to prove him right and show their support. Now a Dunyazade original is quickly becoming the most fashionable object one can own.'

'Indeed, it is most unfair that I, your cousin, do not possess one.'

Sophie smiled. 'I'm afraid that Dunyazade is permanently retired, but I would dearly love to draw your portrait.'

Mateo's eyes lit up. 'Now?'

Sophie laughed. 'I'm sorry, but no. I have too much to do today. But perhaps tomorrow morning, when the light is best, we could begin some sketches. That is,' she said, turning to the viscountess, 'if you both mean to stay the night?'

'We do,' said Lady Dayle, 'and I really must get upstairs to help with the unpacking. Winston will not know which dress to leave out for dinner. By the way,' she said casually, 'I stopped at Emily's and brought Nell along, and the rest of your wardrobe.'

'Thank you. I have missed Nell. I hope you won't be disillusioned by my sad wardrobe while you're here, Mateo, but the work is hard on my gowns.'

'You would be divine in rags,' he professed. 'Business calls me back to London in a few days, but I intend to enjoy my time here with you, cousin.'

'I will see you both at dinner, then,' Lady Dayle said, rising to leave. She paused by the chimney-piece. 'The white is such an improvement! But do you mean to hang one of these here, dear?' She gestured to the two paintings propped against the marble hearth.

'I suppose so. Neither suits me exactly, but I haven't found anything else in the attics.'

'Then don't hang anything just yet. I have just the thing. I will send to Fordham—it should only take a few days to arrive.'

'Thank you, my lady. Now, Mateo, I hope you will excuse me.'

'Indeed I will not. I shall be one of your drudges, if you permit.' He chuckled. 'I suspect it is the only way to spend some time with you, cousin.'

Sophie accomplished much that day, even with Mateo's help. Actually he possessed a keen eye and a willingness to lend a hand to even the meanest task. He kept her laughing with his chatter and unflagging good spirits. She enjoyed the day, and later they all enjoyed a fine dinner, cosy in the breakfast room, as the dining room was not yet complete.

Afterwards, the three of them took tea in the less formal parlour at the back of the house. Sophie avoided the window where Charles had first kissed her.

Mateo did not. He stood right in the spot where Charles had and assessed the room. 'Sophie,' he said, 'this house will make your name.'

'If it does not, I shall set out a shingle as Madam Dunyazade,' she teased.

'Mateo is right,' Lady Dayle said, 'I cannot wait for everyone to see it.'

'You shall have to write and tell me how Lord Dayle's first entertainment is received.'

The viscountess set down her teacup and exchanged a glance with Mateo. 'I won't have to, dear,' she said.

'Why not?' Sophie looked from one guilty face to the other. 'What is it?'

'Charles's birthday, you know, is at the end of the week.'

'Yes.'

'I've invited some people here to celebrate. It is to be a house party.'

Sophie's jaw dropped. 'But, my lady! There is still so much to be done!'

'Nonsense. It is magnificent. What is left can easily be accomplished in time.'

Sophie was doing rapid calculations in her head. 'Perhaps.' She was quiet a moment. 'Yes, I believe we can manage it, but we must not delay. If we work very hard for the next few days, I should be able to be finished and out of the way in time.'

'Indeed, you will not. You will not be in the way and you will not be skulking off. You must be here.'

'I would rather not.'

'But you must, for they are your guests as well. I issued the invitation in both our names. It is to be a birthday celebration and an unveiling at once.'

Sophie sat very still. 'You…' She felt the urge to laugh, but was afraid it would turn into a sob. Charles. A house party. 'You do not play fair, Lady Dayle.'

The viscountess chuckled. 'True. All's fair in love and war…and decorating.'

'Ah, but the lady is right, Sophie. This is perfect.' Mateo's voice was intense. 'It shall be a triumph for you. After this you will be able to go anywhere, do anything you wish with your designs.'

'I agree. I have no doubt you will receive another commission when this is seen. In fact, I predict you will receive many offers.'

'Ah, but you are wasted on these rigid English.' Mateo was leaning forward in his chair, regarding her intently. 'I agree, you must receive due credit for this beautiful work, but then you must come home to Philadelphia with me. There you will be appreciated, revered. A lady designer with the ear of the English prince! They will be fighting over you like dogs in the street.'

'Such a charming picture.' Lady Dayle rolled her eyes. 'Sophie is well loved and appreciated right here. Surely the last few days have shown you that.'

'Yes, but here she will not be allowed the sort of success she could find elsewhere. In America, it is different.' He looked into Sophie's eyes, earnestness shining in his own. 'You think on it, eh?'

She would. After she found a way out of this house party.

Chapter Twelve

Charles was fifteen again, and finally going off to school. At last his father had relented, though he grumbled about throwing good blunt after bad and predicted his wayward second son would be sent back down before the quarter was out.

Charles didn't listen. He'd heard it all before. His father's grumblings couldn't touch him now, he was finally getting away and the world lay open before him. The only dark spot in his bright future was the interview immediately ahead. He had to say goodbye to Sophie.

He found her sitting on the lowest branch of the tree where they had first met. Her ebony hair curled down her back and silent tears streamed down her face. He sat down close beside her on the gnarled branch and her head fell to rest on his shoulder. They stayed—silent, beyond words—for a while.

Then he gave her a parting gift: a book. Thomas Hope's *Household Furniture and Interior Decoration*. She smiled her thanks and he said something to make her laugh.

Her laughter rang out in the quiet glade, fluid, almost tangible, then suddenly it *was* tangible, moving in sensuous tendrils, surrounding him. No, those were her arms sliding up his hard body, encircling him. They weren't children any longer. Sophie was a woman in his arms, hot and wanton, eager as she pressed herself against him, pressed her lips to his with a breathless sigh.

Charles moaned and buried his hands in her thick hair, clamped his hard and desperate mouth over hers and tightened his grip on her soft, writhing body.

In an abrupt change of mood that made him want to howl, she pushed him away. The forest had faded, she wiggled from his grasp and marched to his bedchamber door. Turning, she regarded him with a sneer, dark eyes flashing indignation and anger.

'No, Charles,' was all she said, then she slammed the door with a crash.

Bang! She slammed it again and the noise made his brainbox rattle.

Bang! Why was she still slamming the door? Somehow the racket had gotten inside his head and was set to explode out through his pounding temples.

'Don't you have a key?' Sophie said, still irritated. Wait, no. That was Jack's voice.

'He's got it in there with him,' someone answered.

Bang!

'Damnation!' Charles shouted, then clutched his head. 'Stop that bloody racket or I'll strangle you with my bare hands!' He lay back, bending over in agony. He wasn't going to kill anybody; he was going to cast up his accounts right in his own bed. Then he was going to die.

'At least he's alive,' his brother said, laughter and relief in his voice.

Bang!

The last great crash did kill him, or at least sent him spiralling past the pain and into a blessedly quiet, dark void.

He awoke to find his brother and his valet standing over him. Staring in horrified fascination.

'Any idea where he's been all this time?' Jack asked.

Crocker grunted a negative. 'Two gentlemen brought him in. Found him at Bellamy's. I don't know what he's been drinking, but he didn't get it there.' The valet's cragged face twisted in disgust. 'I left to brew some coffee and when I come back, the door was locked. Figured I needed to get in here, so I sent a man for you, sir, before I started taking the door down.'

'You did the right thing.'

Crocker wrinkled his nose. 'I'll fetch up a hot bath.'

Charles just moaned and rolled over.

'When I told you to decide what you wanted, I wasn't thinking of suicide as an option.' When he received no response, Jack continued. 'Well, come along, lay-a-bed! While you've been on a three-day binge, I've been a busy boy. I've brought a visitor for you.'

'Go away and let me die.'

'Not today, big brother. Come on, here's your man with some coffee.'

'Go. To. Hell,' Charles said succinctly.

Jack laughed. 'It looks as if Old Scratch has already ejected one Alden from his domain today, so I dare say I won't take you up on that.'

'Coffee, my lord,' Crocker said, holding a steaming cup and saucer under his nose. Charles tried manfully not to gag and waved him away. A regiment of footmen entered and the racket they made pouring his bath sent him diving back under the covers. But between them, Jack and Crocker got him into the steaming tub and the conviction that he was going to die out of his aching head. After half a pot of coffee he felt almost human again. Almost.

'I'm not even going to ask what precipitated this,'

Jack said once Charles was propped in a chair, wearing a robe.

'A woman,' Crocker said darkly as he cleaned away the shaving implements. He had the grace to flush when Charles eyed him with distaste, but stood firm. 'Nothing else brings a man so low.'

'Lord knows you're entitled to a binge, but we need to get back to business now,' said Jack. 'I meant it when I said I had brought you a visitor, and trust me, you'll want to hear what he has to say.'

Charles heaved a great sigh and allowed Crocker to brush back his wet hair. Lord, every strand on his head was a needle of fire piercing his scalp. 'Bad enough you expect me to be coherent, you shan't get me to dress. Unless I see him here, he'll have to wait.'

'I'll bring him up.'

When Jack came back he had a stripling lad with him. Charles grimaced at his brother and hoped the sight of such dissipation wouldn't ruin the boy.

'Charles, this is Mr Lionel Humbert, apprentice typesetter. Mr Humbert, Lord Dayle.'

The boy bobbed his head and wrung his hat in his hands. 'Good morning, my lord.'

'A debatable opinion, but I'm not up to arguing it, Mr Humbert.' He indicated a chair close by. 'Won't you sit down?'

The boy paled. 'No, thank you, my lord. I mean, I'll stand, my lord.'

'Do you care for coffee?' Charles tried to put the poor boy at ease.

'No. I mean, I do sir, but I better not drink it now. I'm too nervous, sir.'

At least they had gone from 'my lord' to 'sir'.

'Don't be nervous. I may look a fright, but I don't eat young men for breakfast. Tell me, what can I do for you this morning, Mr Humbert?'

The boy glanced at Jack, who nodded encouragingly. 'I think I'm to do something for you, sir. You see, I'm apprenticed to Mr Prescott, a printer.'

'One of Mr Prescott's accounts is with the *Oracle,* Charles,' said Jack.

'My sympathy is with you, for having to deal with the editor of that scandal rag.'

'Thank you, sir. Mr Griggs is a mite dicked in the nob, if you catch my meaning.'

'More than a mite, I would say,' Charles agreed gravely.

'Tell him about the man we discussed,' urged Jack.

'Well, a while back, I delivered the proofs to Mr Griggs, like always. It was about when they started hounding you in their paper, sir, if you'll forgive me. That's when I first saw the man that Mr Alden says you are looking for.'

'A short, dark, wiry man?' Charles asked, sitting up with interest.

'Aye, sir. An odd one, that. Moves quick and sharp, like a bird. That's what made me remember his name.'

'His name? What was his name, son?' Charles asked gently.

'Wren, sir. Wren, like a bird, see?'

'I do indeed. Smart boy,' Charles said with approval. 'Do you know what Wren was doing with Mr Griggs?'

The boy pursed his mouth and thought. 'Well, it looked summat like he was checking the paper and putting his stamp on it—like Mr Griggs usually does.'

'Hmm.'

'They looked at the articles about you, sir. They had a good laugh about 'em before giving me the go ahead to print.'

'You've indeed been a big help to me, Mr Humbert. Now I want you to think very carefully. Did Wren ever mention who *he* works for?'

The boy was silent a long moment. 'Nooo,' he said, and Charles slumped. 'But he did say once, "His lordship will be pleased."'

'Lordship?' Charles looked at Jack.

'Aye, but he said it funny—mean funny, you ken? Like he was mayhap making fun?'

Charles had a sudden thought. 'Does Wren still come around to look at the proofs?'

'No, sir. Since Griggs quit riggin' you in the paper, I haven't seen him back.'

'Thank you, Mr Humbert, you have been very helpful indeed.' He gestured to Crocker. 'Why don't you show our young friend down to the kitchens? I'm sure Cook has something for a growing lad. And give him something for being so co-operative.' Charles rose and shook the boy's hand. 'I hope we may do business together again someday.'

The boy, looking relieved, went off with Crocker. Charles sat down and looked at Jack.

'Thank you. It's more than we had before.' He sat silent a moment, before pounding his hand on his chair in frustration. 'It's still so little! Why can't we pin him down?'

'We have a few days. Perhaps we can find something else.'

'A few days?'

'Before your birthday.'

Charles rubbed his temples. Oh, Lord, this could not be good. He wondered what else he'd missed in the past week. 'My birthday?'

Jack looked at him in surprise and then laughed out loud. 'If you had been reading your mail instead of bending your elbow, dear brother, you would know that our dearest mother is planning a birthday bash for you.'

'How bad is it?'

'You really don't know? She's invited a slew of people to a house party this weekend.'

'A house party? All the way at Fordham?'

'No, Charles. At Sevenoaks. She means to unveil the new house at the same time.'

Charles slumped in his chair. His gut started roiling again, in time with the percussion in his head. Jack and Crocker had been wrong; he was going to die. He only hoped he could manage it before his birthday.

Chapter Thirteen

Of course, he didn't die. He didn't even get out of the house party. In the end, it wasn't worth it. It would have insulted his guests, hurt his mother, and given the score keepers one more black mark next to his name. He'd given them enough ammunition with this last trip below the mahogany, and they had revelled in it. He had a flock of reporters following him now, all poised with pencils and pads, waiting for him to speak in tongues or start fornicating in the streets, he assumed. He ignored them. He had other things to worry over.

When Sophie had walked out on him at that charity ball, he'd been shocked. As angry as he'd been, he'd thought they could come to an understanding. He'd still thought it an inspired solution to all their problems. He'd quickly moved from shocked to furious, and had spent the next couple of days cursing the inconstancy of women in general and Sophie's misplaced pride in particular.

And then, in the middle of a committee meeting, right in the midst of a report documenting bread riots in Birmingham, the realisation had struck him. How his brilliant idea might have sounded to Sophie. How it must have made her feel.

Gone were the disturbing details of protesting farm labourers refusing to work and harvests rotting in the field. Instead, images of Sophie began to flash in his mind. The hurt on her young face when her vague aunt forgot her name again. The defiant squaring of her shoulders when her birthday came with no acknowledgement except his own. Her reluctance to be drawn into the social whirl. Her grim pronouncement that she was a designer, not a débutante.

She put up such a brave front that even he—who knew what hurts lurked behind her bright vitality—had forgotten. He knew the frightened little girl who hid behind the beautiful woman. Yet he had been so wrapped up in maintaining his own façade, that he'd forgotten hers.

It was then that he'd realised the magnitude of what he'd done, how his callous words would have hurt her. It was then that he'd gone on his carouse. Lord Cranbourne—her uncle, no less—had shaken him back to reality when the meeting ended. Charles had thanked the man and left. Unable to bear the thought of the damage he'd inadvertently caused, he'd left Westminster, gone straight to the nearest grogshop, and washed away the agony brought on by his latest bout of selfishness with a river of cheap gin.

Unfortunately, one could only hide in an alcoholic haze for so long. Jack and Crocker had fished him out, and he'd tried to get on with his life. Only to find he could not. Politics, Miss Ashford's expectations, even the thought of the elusive Mr Wren— none of it could hold his interest. He'd wandered through the next few days numb, lost. He didn't know who he was any more. Not rakish, carefree Charles Alden, and no longer Viscount Dayle, young politician on the path to the ministry. Who was he then? He didn't know or care.

His only thought was that he must see Sophie. He burned to see her, with an aching desperation that obliterated all else. He had to know what they might salvage out of the mess he'd made. He had to tell her he finally understood how profoundly stupid he had been. He had to make amends.

He'd latched on to that thought like it was a lifeline. With his brother and his father there had been no opportunity for apologies, but with Sophie he had a chance to make everything right again. He didn't mean to waste it.

Thus he stood now, on the threshold of his newly redecorated house, and at a crossroads in his life. He breathed deeply and entered.

The entrance hall was bright with sun and welcoming with the gleam of polished wood and crisp, whitewashed stucco. Charles advanced, breathing in the homey, welcoming smells; beeswax and biscuits and the faint tang of new paint.

The dining room to the right stood empty, of both people and furniture. The paint smell was stronger here. He turned to the left and approached the entrance to the drawing room.

Sophie was there, with his mother. They were both bent headfirst into a packing crate. Bits of straw floated in the air above, and when his mother straightened, he could see it stuck in her hair as well. But it wasn't that that brought him up short. It was her face, alive with mischief and laughter. His mother, he realised, was happy.

Sophie stood then, laughing as well. She had a smudge on her cheek and a huge stain down one arm. Her dress was old and faded. Her dark tresses, once gathered simply at her nape, were a dishevelled mess. She was beautiful. Charles stood, absorbing the brightness of her smile, drinking the music of her laughter, and knew, with sudden clarity, what a colossal fool he was.

Sophie was a shining light in a world of dark indifference. She'd borne so much, and never broken. She might have become bitter and withdrawn; instead she gave of herself with every word, every smile. She didn't hide behind superficialities, or stifle her talent because it wasn't fashionable. No, she laid her true self before every person she encountered and she risked censure and disdain to make others happy.

Like his mother, who must endure one of life's worst hardships. Like Emily Lowder, who had faced the same sort of disappointment and heartache, yet emerged victorious. Like she might have done for him, had he been clever enough to recognise her for the treasure she was.

She might have shone her light into his darkness. He closed his eyes and imagined it. Gentle smiles, healing hands, forgiveness. He could have cherished her, pleasured her, buried his hurt in her lithe body and emerged clean, and nearly whole.

It was more than he deserved. He had disparaged her, lectured her, hurt her. She was open and generous, while he had secrets he could never share. But his yearning for her purity, her warmth, her love, was visceral and undeniable. He didn't deserve her, yet he wanted her with a desperation that was nearly palpable.

'Charles!' His eyes opened. His mother had noticed him in the archway. 'You're here!'

'Yes,' he said, trying to hide his need, his confusion. 'I thought I should be here when the guests begin to arrive tomorrow.'

Sophie stood silent. His mother was fluttering, placing the top back on the crate and signalling the footman who had appeared behind Charles to take charge of it. 'I'm so glad you've come, dear. We are nearly ready. I do need to see Mrs Hepple about the dinner tomorrow, though, so I'll let Sophie give you the tour of the house.' She gave him an affectionate peck on her way out. 'I shall see you a little later, hmm?' and then she was gone.

He advanced cautiously into the room, his mind awhirl with so many regrets. She dropped her eyes when he grew close. He stopped. 'Sophie.'

'I didn't expect you until tomorrow,' was all she said.

'I wanted to see you. I thought it might be awkward were we to meet again in company.'

She risked a fleeting glance. 'Yes, it might have been awkward.' A flash of a quick smile gave him hope. 'But so is this.'

He grinned back, with relief. 'Yes, but at least there are no witnesses.'

Her face fell and he cursed himself for a fool. 'I didn't mean it like that.' He took a step closer, fighting to keep from just taking her in his arms. He wanted to kiss her, softly, until the wounded look in her eyes was gone. 'Every time I try to hold a conversation with you, I'm suddenly a gawky boy again.' He waited but she gave no response. 'I have to tell you how sorry I am. It finally penetrated my feeble brain just how my idiotic ramblings might have hurt you. I never meant to, though. It nearly killed me when I realised it.'

She drew a ragged breath and he stopped. 'Please. I accept your apology.'

Charles sighed his relief. 'Thank you.' He couldn't help himself then; he reached out and took one of her hands. Stained and callused, with ragged nails, it was a physical representation of all that she'd endured, of the generosity of mind, spirit and talent that set her apart. Ridiculous as it might seem, the touch of that worn little hand was more beautiful, more dear, more arousing to him than the boldest caress from any other woman in the world.

'I know I've been selfish, blind, and testier than William the Goat—' there, almost a smile '—but I also know that my feelings for you are real and abiding. Can't we salvage something from the wreck I've made of our friendship?'

The smile disappeared and she pulled her hand from his. 'No, Charles. You were right all along. We can't go back. I was foolish to think we might.'

Charles's breath caught. 'But, Sophie, there's so much I want to tell you—'

There was panic in her face now. She stopped him with a sharp motion of her hand. 'I'm sorry. No. I cannot have this discussion with you now. This house party is going to be very difficult for me. If I am going to get through it with any semblance of dignity, then I have to ask you to wait.'

'Wait?'

'Yes. All the…things we need to discuss will still be there later. Perhaps they will come easier then, too.'

'I understand.' Charles thought a moment. 'I don't want to make this more difficult for you. Shall I go then, make an excuse for abandoning the party?'

'No.' Her reply was instantaneous. 'It means so much to your mother.'

He should have expected her reaction. He was truly a fool. 'Perhaps, then, we can try something new. Grant each other a clean slate. Spend these days as new acquaintances.'

Her look was speculative. 'Yes, I think perhaps I should like that.'

'Good. Well, then, Miss Westby, as a new acquaintance who also happens to be my designer,
will you escort me on a tour of the house?'

They were both able to relax a little as he inspected the renovated rooms. It was easy to show
his approval of her work. She'd turned a musty old
house into a vibrant, welcoming home.

He was especially pleased with the library. The
old pair of windows, tall and narrow with a padded
seat at each base, had been ripped out, along with
the entire wall between them. In their place stood
an entire bank of windows, turning a gloomy room
into a warm and sunny retreat. Outside the lawns
stretched in a gorgeous, gradual slope down to the
lake. Dappled sunlight danced on the water's
surface and reflected back from something shiny on
the far side.

'What is that, across the lake?'

'A folly, a very beautiful one in the classical style.
Your mother specifically requested it and has overseen
its installation. She walks out there most mornings.'

'Shall we go out and inspect that as well?'

'Perhaps later.' She smiled. 'The reflection is from
the copper cupola. The effect won't last, though.
Once it weathers a bit it won't bother you.'

'It doesn't bother me now.' Charles strode about

the library, admiring the new bookcases, the tasteful refurbishings, the elegant carpet. 'Is this new?'

Sophie's smile was genuine now. 'No, we only cleaned the old one. I don't think it had been done in years.'

'It's beautiful.' He trailed a finger over the immaculately shining, nearly empty desk. 'I see my correspondence hasn't caught up with me.'

Sophie winced and Charles chuckled. 'Yes, I can well imagine the tone of your own correspondence of late.' He grew more serious and looked her in the eye. 'I'll only mention it this once, until you are ready to talk, but I want you to know that I am glad you emerged from that situation unscathed. For your sake,' he emphasised.

Her face was pale, and she only said, 'Thank you.'

He lightened his tone a bit. 'There's something you might have missed, if you've been neglecting your post.'

She raised a brow in question.

'Lady Avery has returned.'

That did capture her interest. 'Has she?'

'Indeed. She ran out of money and the valet ran off with the jewels. She's returned to London.'

'And what of Lord Avery?'

'By all accounts, he's taken her back.'

'Oh, but I am so proud of him! How he must have

missed her. I hope they can find happiness in each other, now.'

'I do as well, for he's little chance of finding it elsewhere.'

Her brow furrowed. 'What do you mean?'

'I mean the poor man's a laughing stock—even more so than before.'

'Because he loves his wife?' She looked indignant.

'Because he looks a besotted fool, and men are…well, men. Society will shun them. They may establish their own circle, as Lord and Lady Holland eventually managed, but Lord Avery's political influence will falter as his supporters scurry away.' Much like his own, Charles thought with some irony. 'Like rats before a fire.'

The dismay on her face both touched him and ignited a twinge of exasperation. 'Have you learned nothing from my situation over the last months? From your own dip in the scandal broth?'

'Yes,' she shot back. 'I've learned that London is full of hypocrites, people who won't hesitate to criticise others even while perpetrating worse behind closed doors.'

'Exactly!' Charles said. 'Then you've learned the most valuable lesson regarding the *ton.* You can get away with almost any evil if you are discreet. The only unforgivable sin is to get caught.'

She was ablaze with anger now. 'Token sancti-mony. It is ridiculous! How can you so calmly accept such a gross injustice?'

Lord, but she was beautiful when she was in a passion. Charles shook his head as the import of her question sunk in. 'Because I've already tried to fight it, and lost. Can you have forgotten my misspent youth? I broke every one of society's rules and flaunted each misdeed. I flung their hy-pocrisy into their faces—and what did I reap? Ruination and destruction.'

'Destruction?'

He'd said too much. The warning was in the arrested look on her face. 'Yes,' he hedged, 'even now, after so much time, it is destroying my politi-cal career. I fashioned my detractor's most lethal weapon myself.'

She didn't look entirely convinced that's what he had meant. 'Lord and Lady Avery know this, Sophie,' he said, trying to get her back on to the thread of the conversation. 'I'm sure they've accepted it. They'll be happy in their private life, even if they must give up their public one.'

'They should have both. They've harmed no one but themselves. If they can forgive and embrace each other still, what can anyone else say of it?'

Her anger faded, and the look in her eye became

thoughtful, crafty. Charles sucked in a breath. He'd seen that look enough to know that trouble followed.

'All that is required is a little help.'

'Help?' he asked.

'Yes, someone to show their acceptance and support.'

Charles considered. 'You may be right. Some of Avery's cronies are very well placed. He might muddle through with their assistance.'

'I hope so.' She sighed. 'Have you seen them?'

'Me?' Charles snorted. 'I have no doubt that mine is the last face either of them wish to see.'

'On that score I would guess you are wrong. Lord Avery strikes me as a very honourable man.' She lifted her chin, looking him direct in the eye. 'They would both be easier if given the opportunity to apologise to you, I imagine. At the very least you might let them know you hold no grudge. Your good wishes would probably hold more weight than anyone else's.'

Charles closed his eyes and rubbed his brow. He had always hated it when she was right. 'No doubt you are correct. I shall call on them.'

'Good.' Now that she had won her point, she grew brisk, businesslike. 'I hope you enjoyed the tour and approve of the house,' she said, turning to the window as if unsure of his answer.

'You know I do. It is lovely.' *Like you,* he wanted to say.

'I'm so glad you like it.' She turned back. 'It's time I changed for dinner, and I must speak with your mother first. We have been dining early. I hope it will be acceptable? It's a bit late to ask Cook to put it back.'

He nodded and she continued. 'Shall I see you in the drawing room around six, then?'

'Six,' he affirmed. He watched her go, and then sank into the chair behind the desk. His head was spinning. He stared out of the window, the glinting light catching his eye again, and decided what he needed was a walk. Time to think, to sort all the conflicting loyalties that beset him, to decide what it was he wanted. Of Sophie, of his life. Perhaps he would have it all solved by dinner.

He would not care to wager on it.

Chapter Fourteen

Sophie sat before her mirror as Nell brushed the plaster dust from her hair and wrestled it into a semblance of decorum. She'd waited too long for a bath, but she'd had to speak with Lady Dayle. Lord Avery and his wife were in need of aid. She knew she was right about their situation. It could be brought about, with just a little nudge. It was fortunate indeed that Lady Dayle agreed; it would be so much easier with her help.

She had a plan, but it was risky. It would also provide the definitive answer to her lingering questions about Charles's character. Would he prove himself to be her Charles or Miss Ashford's? It was time he made a decision, so they could all get on with their lives.

Her Charles. How beautiful it sounded. She'd thought she'd been ready for his arrival, armed against him with logic, determination, and a healthy dose of fear for how easy it had been for him to hurt her. She'd meant to take this opportunity to begin the process of withdrawal, to begin to unravel the ties that bound them. It hadn't been easy when, instead of resentful and angry, he'd been apologetic and sincere. Yet she had held firm.

Until she heard Lord and Lady Avery's story. Now she wavered. Sophie had felt for the couple since she'd first heard of their strange relationship. She had wanted to help them, would have helped them in any case. To see love triumph over anger, hurt and betrayal was a worthy cause on its own. But now she had an ulterior motive.

The situations were not exact, but similar enough. Surely if Charles saw Lord Avery survive such a scandal with social acceptance and political influence intact…

'Would you hand me the comb, miss? The one with the pearl inlay?' Nell broke into Sophie's scheming.

'Thank you, almost done.' When the maid spoke again, she sounded hesitant. 'I know we haven't spoken of it for some time, but I thought you might like to know that the servants here are a good bit freer with their gossip than the viscount's London help.'

Sophie started to turn, but stopped at Nell's cry of dismay. 'Sorry, Nell. Have you heard something of interest?'

'Something small, but I thought you would want to know.'

Sophie nodded encouragingly.

'There's talk of old Lord Dayle's death, like we'd heard before.' Their eyes met in the mirror. 'There's also a footman here who says that old Lord Dayle was furious with his lordship at the time.'

Sophie snorted. 'That's nothing, Nell. They didn't get on at all. The old gentleman was angry at Charles for half of his life, at the very least.'

'Not just angry, John says, but furious.' Nell insisted. 'Wouldn't talk to his lordship after the bad news of his brother came, wouldn't be in the same room with him. Not even for the funeral.'

'That does sound excessive. And hurtful.' Sophie sighed. 'Poor Charles, I wonder what was going on between them?' It would explain a few things too. If Charles's father died before they made up the quarrel, then it was no wonder he was sensitive about the subject.

'It's led to some pert talk about his lordship below stairs, miss.'

Sophie sent her a sharp glance. 'I hope you set that right?'

'You can be sure of it, miss,' Nell said with firm satisfaction. 'It won't be happening again.'

'Thank you, Nell. I'm sure his lordship would thank you for your loyalty as well.'

'I do my duty.'

Sophie turned and clasped the girl's hand. 'You do so much more than that, and I hope you know I appreciate it.'

She was still coming to grips with this latest piece of the puzzle as she made her way to the drawing room a little later. Charles and his father had a turbulent history, it was true, but surely such a breach was extreme, even in a time of grief. She wondered if she dared to ask Charles about it. She would gauge his mood before she considered it.

It didn't look promising. Charles was already in the drawing room when she entered, frowning up at a painting hung in the formerly blank spot on the chimneypiece.

'Oh,' Sophie exclaimed. 'Lady Dayle has had the portrait hung!' She stepped up next to Charles to examine the effect.

It was all that she could have asked for. The colours blended well with the room and the subject matter was both appropriate and heart-warming. It was a lovely painting of Lady Dayle, clad in a crimson gown of the old, panniered style, her arm around two of her young sons, and the youngest seated on the floor at her feet. Phillip, the eldest, stood at her side, staring forward with a serious mien. Charles stood next to his brother, with an armful of squirming puppy and an eager look on his face as he looked up at his elder sibling. Jack, still a toddler, sat on the floor surrounded by blocks and more puppies.

'I like it there very much,' Sophie said. 'What do you think, Charles?'

She could see what he thought on his face. His expression was pained, haunted. 'Are you all right?' she asked with concern.

'Yes.'

His voice sounded strained. Sophie could see that his colour was pale as well.

'Do you think that it is formal enough for this room?' he answered at last. 'The family has more than its share of masterpieces, I'm sure we could find something more appropriate.'

'It's a Reynolds,' she said simply. 'I find it charming.'

He stood, silent. Sophie pursed her lips and decided to say what was in her heart. 'I think that it is a matter of significance that your mother chose it. After all the pain she's endured in the last two years, don't you think it is a sign of healing that she can look on this with pleasure?'

Charles flinched as if her words had actually hurt him. Still he did not respond. His eyes were closed now, as if he couldn't bear to look at it any more.

'Charles?'

He started and opened his eyes. Sophie began to be concerned.

'Shall I remove it?' she asked.

'No.' He sighed. 'I can endure it, for my mother's sake.' He turned then and went to pour himself a drink.

She watched him down his drink and pour another. She thought of what Nell had told her earlier, remembered the accusation she had flung at Charles in anger, in this very house. *Do you think to turn yourself into your brother?*

'What happened to Phillip, Charles?' she asked softly.

'What?' His head snapped toward her and he nearly dropped his glass.

'What happened to Phillip? Everyone in Blackford Chase knows he died at Waterloo, but no one is sure just why he was there. It's something of a mystery.'

Charles's gaze burned into hers. He didn't want to answer, she could tell. Though his face was rigidly set, emotion churned in his eyes. For a moment she feared he would walk out, rather than answer.

Eventually, though, resignation replaced the stiff

wariness. He set down his drink and moved away from her, away from the painting. His eyes, when he finally began to talk, were focused on the fancy scrollwork before him, but Sophie guessed that what he saw in his mind's eye was very far away indeed.

'Phillip was very interested—obsessed, almost—with the war.' His voice was distant, unconnected, as if he was merely repeating a story. 'From the beginning, when we were younger, he would read every article, every dispatch printed. He longed to purchase a commission, to serve as an officer. I think he would have if it hadn't been for…'

'His duty?' prompted Sophie.

'Yes, duty.' He made it sound like a dirty word. 'And Father. You can imagine his feelings on the subject.'

Sophie grimaced. 'Yes. I think I can.'

'Though he couldn't follow his inclination, Phillip became involved in the war effort here at home. He worked with the Foreign Office. He was very busy, and happy, I thought.' Charles fell silent a moment. When he continued, he spoke low, and Sophie had to strain to hear him. 'Until Napoleon escaped and returned to France.'

'What changed then?'

'Phillip did. He was in a frenzy. So was everybody, if you remember, so I didn't place too much importance on it. Until it was too late.'

Silent, Sophie waited.

'You would have thought that Boney's sole purpose was to give Phillip a second chance at him. He was wild to go to Brussels, along with much of society. Father, of course, would not hear of it. But when Castlereagh himself asked Phillip to carry important messages to Wellington, Phillip agreed.'

She was in complete sympathy with Charles's brother. She knew how difficult it was to yearn, with no hope. She could well imagine what had happened next. 'He got there, and he stayed, didn't he?'

Charles glanced askance at her. 'Yes, he did.'

She understood about Phillip, then, but not about the level of pain in Charles's voice. It was not just the pain of loss. There was something more here.

'Yes. I'm sure he was useful, and wildly happy,' Charles continued. 'Wellington's staff was swelled with all manner of people who didn't belong there by the time they engaged the French, but Phillip made himself valuable.'

'And he fell at Waterloo, along with so many other good men,' Sophie mused.

'No.' The single word was harsh, as if ripped from Charles's soul.

'No? But the lists, I'm sure—' Sophie stopped, horrified by the look on Charles's face as he turned around.

'Yes, that's what everyone believes.' Charles spoke in a rush now, as if in a hurry to spit the story out and be done with it. 'The truth is that Phillip died before the battle even began. Wellington went out riding that morning, inspecting the area and the troops. Phillip numbered among the men with him. There was a battalion positioned on the edge of the Hougoumont fields, close to the French. They lost nerve and broke position, turned to flee long before even a shot was fired. The Duke saw them, rode them down and rallied them.' Charles stopped and drew a deep breath. 'But as he rode back, a few of the disaffected men fired shots after him. None hit him, as you would know,' his voice was but a whisper when he finished, 'but one killed my brother.'

'My God,' Sophie said, sinking into a sofa.

'It was remarked how history might have changed, had those men been better shots.' His voice was bitter. 'I can't help thinking I might be tempted to exchange history for my brother's life.'

'Oh, Charles, I am so sorry. Such a waste of a fine man.' It was tragic, even more so for the reckless stupidity associated with it. 'No wonder your father was inconsolable.'

Charles winced and paled even further. Sophie stared as he visibly gathered himself back under control. 'Wellington himself came to give my parents the story and to express his sorrow.'

'A fine consolation that was to your grieving mother, I'm sure,' Sophie said, just as bitterly.

'It did help my father. A bit.'

'Thank you for telling me.' She could see what it had cost him.

'It's time you knew. But I would ask you not to mention it to my mother. She's so improved.' His look was intense. 'I know I have you to thank for that.'

'She's a lovely woman, I love her very much.'

He didn't reply, but he took a step towards her, eyes fastened on her face. Sophie drew a deep breath.

'Such serious expressions!' Lady Dayle had arrived. 'Charles, you are not forcing Sophie to talk of dismal economics, are you?'

'No, nothing so bad as that, Mother.'

Sophie watched as he summoned a smile from somewhere and returned his mother's embrace.

'Good, you'll have plenty of time for that later. I want to know what you think of the house!'

Chapter Fifteen

The tragedy of Phillip's death was still echoing in Sophie's head the next day, as she rearranged yet another group of fresh flowers and tried to calm her nerves. The guests would be arriving soon, but that was only one of her worries. Her thoughts were in a whirl, and she couldn't choose one to focus on for very long. So many fragmentary troubles, and they seemed to be converging on her now.

Phillip's story, though horrifying enough, still didn't seem to explain the depth of Charles's pain. No, depth seemed the wrong word. Was there a *timbre* of something like pain? It also failed to explain the strain between Charles and his father. Sophie remained convinced that there was still a piece of the puzzle missing.

On top of that mystery, she was going to have to deal with Mateo, whose hints had been growing broader and more insistent, and, she was very much afraid, were leading to a proposal of marriage.

Lord and Lady Avery's situation still troubled her, as did her uncertainty about her own future. And then there was her biggest problem of all…poking his head around the dining-room door.

'Ah, Sophie,' Charles said, entering with a paper in hand. Obviously ready to greet his guests, he was immaculately handsome in high boots, buckskin breeches, and a form-fitting coat of soft brown. 'Here's a note from your uncle, saying he cannot join us until tomorrow. Mr Cardea, however, will be coming in today as planned.'

'Thank you.' She took a deep breath. Charles was not the problem so much as her undisciplined reactions to him. 'I'll be sure to tell your mother. It will throw off her seating at dinner.'

Sophie wondered if Charles knew why her uncle was delayed. If he didn't, she didn't wish to be the one to tell him. Mateo had written to her with the news.

'It appears we must congratulate him when he arrives.' Charles spoke with studied casualness. 'He's to be appointed Treasurer of the Board of Trade.'

She spoke carefully. 'I know it must be difficult for you to see him succeed further. After he won the position you had hoped for, I mean.'

'I'm not so shallow as that. I'm pleased for the man. I'm sure he'll perform splendidly.'

'Of course. Thank you for sharing the news.' She turned back to her arrangement, but he didn't leave. She could feel his presence hovering in the doorway.

'Didn't I see you arranging those flowers earlier this morning?' he asked.

She laughed and tucked the last bit of foliage back in among the blooms. 'Yes, I suppose I'm trying to entice the butterflies in my stomach to abandon me for greener pastures.'

'You're mixing your metaphors,' Charles said with a quick smile. 'You are nervous.' He came into the room, all solicitous concern. 'You cannot be worried about the house—it's superb. Everyone who sees it will fall in love.'

Sophie took a step back. She exercised her woman's prerogative and changed her mind—Charles was indeed the problem. There was something seductively different about him since he'd come back to Sevenoaks. His eyes were less guarded; he spoke to her more easily and openly. He'd shared the story of his brother's death.

Her reaction was confusing and convoluted. Part of her rejoiced. *At last.* At last he was accessible, approachable, sharing himself with her. The other part of her didn't trust it. She kept waiting for the walls to slam back up, for his eyes to turn cold and for him to shut her out. It was nerve-racking, especially when she thought of the invitation that had gone to London this morning. 'No, I'm satisfied with the house. It has turned out to be more beautiful than even I had hoped.'

'What is it, then?'

She shook her head.

He rounded the corner of the dining-room table and paused. 'Never tell me you are worried over your own reception?' He raised a brow and his voice grew slightly mocking. 'What happened to the Sophie who didn't care what others thought of her, who didn't need anyone?'

She met his eye with an unwavering gaze. 'I've learned the danger of needing people in a hard school, haven't I?' She didn't add that the blow he had dealt her had been the hardest lesson of all.

He blanched. She might not have accused him outright, but he understood.

'Perhaps you have taught me something after all,' she continued. 'I've grown up a little. I may not enjoy depending on the goodwill of others, but I can see that it is sometimes a necessity.'

He acknowledged her barb with a nod. 'Truly, though, you have no need to fear. You, at least, have champions and they have defended you well. When you are ready, you will be speedily accepted back into society.'

'I have no wish to go back into society,' she said firmly. 'I only wish to be free to continue my work.' She folded her arms in front of her and shot him a defiant look. 'It's quite ironic, isn't it? In Blackford Chase they abhorred me because I was different. But it is those very differences that titillate the *ton,* my eccentricities that distract them from their deadly *ennui,* and win their acclaim.'

'But don't you see,' he pleaded harshly, 'that is the very type of notoriety that will have them turning on you in the end. The acclaim won't last. That's why I—'

'I don't care,' she interrupted. She couldn't bear to hear it all again. 'I don't wish to be a darling of the *beau monde.* As long as I can use my momentary popularity as a springboard for my design work, I shall be happy.'

'And if you cannot?'

'Then there are plenty of wealthy cits who need furniture too. Or perhaps I will heed Mateo's advice and pursue my career in America.'

'What?' His shock was genuine. He moved away from the table and towards her. 'That is the most ridiculous thing I have ever heard. Absolutely not.'

Her anger was genuine too. Was it the same old reaction? Indignation at the thought of someone else using his plaything? Or perhaps worse. Perhaps he didn't believe she could succeed there either. 'I beg your pardon?' He was nearly upon her now. He was coming too close. 'You have no right—'

He silenced her with his kiss, deep and dark with instant desire. His arms encircled her, crushed her to him.

No, this is wrong, she thought, even as she melted into his arms. She needed to be free of him, of her frightening dependence on him, because she didn't know yet if she could trust him. But the orphan inside of her refused to listen. *Home,* that voice said, revelling in the taste and scent of him, relishing the warmth and security of his embrace.

It's an illusion, her logical self insisted, *not real.* But logic was soon silenced by sensation, drowned in desire. Instead of pushing him away, her hands were wrapping about him, pulling him close, curling through his hair.

No, she wasn't fighting him. She was opening wider, inviting him in. He tasted of coffee, and rich, bittersweet sin. She was meeting him stroke for stroke, entwining her tongue with his in a thrilling, languorous dance.

Charles groaned in response, further drowning any voice of protest. His hand was low on her back, urging her against him. She went willingly and allowed her own hands to roam, to trace a restless path over the muscles of his back and then lower. He returned the favour, cupping her bottom and pressing her closer still.

It was lovely, it was intoxicating, it was dangerous. Slowly, fear began to succeed where logic had not. He had hurt her, badly. How much worse would it be if she let this go too far? She was a woman grown, a lonely little girl no longer. She dug deep, summoned her strength and her hard-won wisdom, and broke away.

He protested and reached for her again, but she stepped back. 'No, Charles.' Her anxiety threatened to spill out of her in a heartrending sob, but she forced herself to stand firm.

'Nothing has changed,' she said. 'Yes, we still have this between us—' she made a vague, encompassing gesture '—but so do we still have all the problems.'

'Then let us face them together,' he said.

'I—' She couldn't say the words out loud. *I'm afraid.* So she took the coward's way out. 'I'm sorry.' She kissed him softly, and then she turned, fighting tears, and slowly climbed the stairs.

* * *

It was only a little later, after Sophie had had a chance to gather her wits and her resolve, when Nell came to her room.

'Mrs Hepple's having a tussle with the drapery in the blue guest room,' the maid said with a grin. 'She asks if you would lend a hand?'

'Of course,' but it was with a heavy heart and a slow stride that she entered the hall and headed for the blue room. Lady Dayle, climbing the staircase, list in hand, hailed her as she passed.

'Nearly time, now. Are you dressed and ready, my dear?'

'Yes, my lady.'

'Oh, my darling, what is it? You look positively blue-devilled!' The viscountess bustled over and, a hand on each shoulder, looked searchingly into her face. Clucking to herself, she took Sophie's hand. She glanced about the empty hall then shrugged, and perched herself on the first shining oak step, patting the spot beside her invitingly. 'Come now, sit, and I'll soothe your nerves.'

She was so warm and motherly, Sophie couldn't resist. She chuckled and sat down. 'I can't stay, Mrs Hepple needs me, and what would she say if she came out and found you like this?'

'Pish! If she caught a look at your face, she'd

hustle off to bring you a dish of tea, then she'd likely perch on your other side.'

Sophie laughed.

'That's better. Now, what is it that has brought you so low?'

She sighed. The truth wasn't an option. But her troubles with Charles were only a part of it, in any case. 'I'm not certain, exactly. Did you ever have the notion that you've arrived at a short time in your life that will affect all the rest of your years? It's ridiculous, really, since I suppose one could say that about nearly any moment.'

Lady Dayle smiled. 'Not ridiculous. I understand that feeling. It's wonderful and terrifying at once, isn't it?'

Sophie could only nod. To her horror, she felt tears gathering again.

The viscountess took her hand and sandwiched it between her own. 'Let me tell you what it is that I admire most about you.' She brushed a wayward curl off Sophie's face and continued, 'You've faced a great many challenges in your young life.'

Sophie tried to protest, but Lady Dayle shook her head and went on. 'I know, we all encounter our own obstacles in life's path. Sometimes they appear so large they blot out the sun, the other side, and it seems, any possibility of happiness, ever again.'

She took Sophie's chin in her hand and smiled into her eyes. 'But you never let those obstacles stop you. Oh, I've heard you rail in shockingly unladylike language, when things don't go your way.' She let Sophie go and grinned. 'And sometimes it feels as if you're doing nothing but pounding your head against it in frustration, but you are strong. Always, you pick yourself up and find a way to scramble over.'

'Or chisel through,' Sophie said softly.

'Or chisel through,' the viscountess agreed. 'I've never seen you give up, Sophie Westby, and that is a rare thing in this world.'

Lady Dayle dropped her chin and put her arm around her. Sophie leaned gratefully into her comforting embrace. 'The bright side, I've found,' the viscountess continued, 'is that once you make it past the hard spots, there always seems to be something good on the other side.'

'Like you,' said Sophie, a single tear sliding down her cheek.

'No, it's you who has been a blessing to me, dear child. And I promise, even if we hit some obstacles in the next few days, there will be better things to come.'

They sat then, arms around each other, drawing strength, until the jingle of harness outside announced the first guests.

'I'll wager you a bolt of fine sarcenet that it's Emily who's here first.' Lady Dayle grinned.

'I'm not fool enough to take that bet.' Sophie laughed.

Arm in arm, they went down to greet their guests.

Chapter Sixteen

The afternoon had been taken up with the greeting of guests and with showing off the splendours of the newly refurbished house. It had been hectic and chaotic, leaving Charles no time to consider what he'd done with Sophie in this very room this morning. Now, however, he found himself seated at the head of a happy, boisterous group, the recipient of enough birthday toasts to float a fleet on, and in possession of plenty of time for reflection.

Ignoring his guests was a bad idea, though, and useless besides. Only one thought continually emerged from his self-absorption. He wanted Sophie, needed to have her in his life. Whether he should, or could, have her were two very separate issues that he still had no answer for, but on that one point, he was firm.

It was with some trepidation, therefore, that he

had welcomed the Ashfords to his home. They must suspect that their inclusion in this gathering meant more than it did. In truth, what it meant was that his mother's vaunted perception must be a little slow in this instance. Now he must find a way to communicate the change in his intentions without insulting them.

It seemed an easy feat compared to the Herculean task of keeping his temper around Mr Cardea. The man's charming manner, his easy smile, and, above all, his constant, adoring attendance on his cousin infuriated Charles, as did the suspicion that Sophie's uncle might be promoting a match between them. He resolved to watch the man carefully once he arrived.

Another toast was proposed, this time by Sir Harold, and echoed by Mr Chambers, the young nephew who had accompanied him. Charles smiled, drank, and tried not to gauge just how far down Sophie's décolletage Mr Cardea, seated next to her, could see.

At last the final cover was removed. Charles relaxed a little as his mother led the ladies away.

Too soon.

'Another ridiculous English custom,' Mr Cardea announced in ringing tones. 'In Italy we know that it is the ladies who make such gatherings interesting.' He stood and Charles gaped as he saluted the astonished men and followed in the ladies' footsteps.

Silence reigned a long moment as the port was brought out. Yet soon a strange, creaking sound echoed in the room. It was the protest of Lord Ashford's corset, as he wheezed with laughter. Soon all the men were howling along with him. Even Charles chuckled a bit and raised a glass in salute to a brilliant manoeuvre.

He found he was not alone in his disgruntlement, however, when the gentlemen did rise to join the females in the drawing room, only to find them clustered around the pianoforte, listening, enraptured, to Mr Cardea's pleasing baritone.

'I can see what the man's about,' complained Mr Huxley. 'There's no doubt the ladies adore him, but his attention to Miss Westby is too marked. I shall mention it to the lady's uncle myself, for I can't approve of such close cousins as a match.'

'Why ever not?' asked Mr Chambers. 'It's done all the time.'

'Useful means of keeping property in the family,' added Mr Lowder.

'I believe the ancient Egyptians actually married their siblings for just that reason,' Jack said helpfully.

'I still think the relationship too close. I just cannot like it,' said Mr Huxley, and he went to extricate Sophie from her cousin by means of an argument over the superiority of English versus American roads.

For once Charles found himself in sympathy with the man, but not for the professed reasons. Watching the others squabble over Sophie made him insane. It roused some hidden primitive instinct that made him want to snatch her away, warn them off, and shout 'Mine!' to every male in the vicinity.

But he had no right to do so. Worse, he didn't know if he should.

He eased his way through the room, stopping to laugh at a ribald joke told by the lively Mr Chambers, exchanging a few comments with Sir Harold, but gnawing on that thought all the while.

He must own up to the truth. Much as he might wish it, perhaps he wasn't the man for Sophie. All the harsh words he'd spoken to her haunted him. The stark memories of her sweet offers of friendship and his own emotional retreats mocked him. He'd been horribly unfair to her. No doubt she would be better off with someone else.

He distinguished her throaty chuckle of delight from across the room. It triggered the image of her radiant smile and shining eyes. She'd brought laughter back into his life, and companionship and passion.

He watched her, studying the lovely angles of her face, and recalled how her eyes looked when heavy with desire, how ripe and full her mouth appeared when she'd been kissed. He remembered how she felt in his arms, all curves and tangible need. And he knew. Without further doubt. No, she wasn't better off with any of these milksops. She was his. He would find a way to make it so.

He would begin this very moment, he pledged, as he saw a pained expression cross her face, by rescuing her from Miss Ashford and her mama.

His mother, he found, was there before him. 'I think that Hannah More is a very fine person,' Lady Dayle was saying.

'Yes,' agreed Miss Ashford, 'Mama is a great admirer of hers.'

'But in this time of post-war distress, I think there are very many other charitable institutions you might consider,' Emily Lowder said with conviction.

'Mama and I have agreed to donate the money to the Society for the Suppression of Vice. Mama has had the fortune to meet both Mr Wilberforce and Mrs More, and has high hopes of being mentioned in that great lady's next edifying book.'

Charles was standing behind Mrs Lowder and heard her mutter something under her breath about not seeing Lady Ashford's performance at the ball.

'Indeed,' said Lady Ashford, 'Hannah More is a saint. She does so much for the unfortunate, all the while encouraging them to become honest, industrious and accepting of their lowly path, which was, of course, assigned to them by the hand of God.'

Charles decided it was time to interrupt. 'May I join you, ladies?' he asked.

'Please, sit down, dear,' his mother replied, moving over and indicating the bench she was sitting on. 'This is sturdy enough to hold two.'

Charles sat, admiring the bench as he did. It was a clever piece; the scrollwork was a mirror image of the moulding on the wall behind it. 'This is one of my favourite changes in the room,' he said with a nod to Sophie.

'Indeed, I am very proud of you, Sophie,' said Mrs Lowder. 'The whole house is quite transformed. It's hard to believe how much you've accomplished since we picnicked here.'

'It was clever of you to design the features in the room to match the furniture,' conceded Lady Ashford.

'Actually, it was the other way around. I designed the furniture to match the lovely plasterwork done in the last century,' Sophie replied in a pleasant tone.

'Ah, I'd forgotten that you dabble in furniture design as well.' Charles thought Miss Ashford sounded sour.

'Now here is an example of a worthy charity for you, my dear,' his mother said.

Sophie made a sound of protest, but his mother

did not heed her. 'Please, Sophie, this is exactly the sort of effort that Miss Ashford might not be familiar with.' She turned back to the ladies. 'Sophie founded the workshop that makes her furniture with her own funds. Her foreman, Mr Darvey, was in the Corps of Royal Engineers. He lost a leg in the march on Toulouse, unfortunately, and was sent home with no pension, a broken man.'

Charles did not miss the look of distaste that passed over Lady Ashford's face, but his mother seemed oblivious. 'Sophie found him selling exquisite little carvings in the street, just trying to survive. Now he has a respectable position and recognition as a talented artisan.' She beamed proudly at Sophie. 'They have provided work for local men as well as taking on quite a number of veterans with no place to go.' She gestured to the room at large. 'You can see the quality of the work they have done.'

Charles did not hear the Ashford ladies' responses. He had been seized by a flash of memory. Sophie, leaning down from Jack's cabriolet, talking earnestly with a man in a ragged regimental jacket. He remembered the slip of paper and the look of bemused hope on the man's face.

He remembered the thick portfolio she'd had the first day they had met again in London. He remembered his mother mentioning to someone that the proceeds from Sophie's book were to be donated to a veterans' charity.

He'd just spent over a year toadying, courting the goodwill of influential, but inflexible, men. All for the greater good, he'd told himself. Once he had achieved his goals, he could be of use; help his fellow man, help his country through the time of transition that lay ahead.

And all the while he had been making grand plans, telling himself and others how many issues they faced, how many people stood in need of their support and assistance, Sophie, this little slip of a girl, had been out there providing it.

His thoughts flew back over the months. He'd dragged himself out from his dark and dank hiding hole of grief, talked fustian with narrow-minded fools, listened to self-serving rationalisation, smiled when his heart was breaking, danced when he wished nothing more than to lie down and die. And what did he have to show for it?

Nothing. An anonymous enemy, a shattered reputation, a stalled political career. He lifted his gaze, stared at Sophie's embarrassed countenance. Thwarted love.

He knew then, with an excruciating pang, that she'd been right all along. They had never really known each other.

Sophie was no flighty, capricious girl. She was an incredible woman, more beautiful on the inside than the out. And he, he was a hopeless fool.

He could stand it no longer. He had to get away. He rose, took his leave of the ladies, excused himself to the gentlemen, then left the drawing room, went out the back and set out for the lake.

Sophie watched Charles leave the room. The look he had given her before he stood to go had been disturbing, unfathomable.

She couldn't blame him if he was disgusted with her. She was ashamed of herself. Today, for the first time in her life, she had acted the coward and let fear rule her.

The question was, was she going to continue to allow it?

'Wherever has Lord Dayle gone to?' Lady Ashford asked after a little while had passed. 'I can't approve of a host who deserts his party without a word.' She looked at her daughter with displeasure, as if it were her fault.

'I notice that Sir Harold has also absented himself,' Lady Dayle answered. 'No doubt some vastly important political matter is detaining them in the library.'

'Oh, I'm sure you are right,' the baroness said,

somewhat mollified. 'Do you believe they will return soon?'

'Hard to predict. Sometimes these political conversations can take hours,' Lady Dayle said with a shrug of her shoulders. 'Would you care for more tea? Miss Ashford, if you feel up to it, I shall bring out the backgammon board.'

'Thank you, but no,' Lady Ashford said, getting to her feet. 'Travelling always tires me. I believe we shall retire. Come, darling, a little extra beauty rest shall not harm us.'

It shan't harm any of us either, Sophie thought uncharitably as the ever-obedient Miss Ashford rose and followed her mother out. She was glad to escape the tiresome pair. Neither seemed inclined to forgive her for bringing the taint of scandal to their ball.

Their exit appeared to be a signal to the rest of the party. Most of the ladies followed suit and retired upstairs. Some of the gentlemen did as well, while others settled down to a game of cards. Sophie rose and made to bid Lady Dayle goodnight.

The viscountess had seated herself at the escritoire, and was scribbling out a note. 'Sophie, dear, before you go up, would you mind leaving this note in the kitchen for cook? I wish for her to see it first thing.' She lowered her voice and leaned in close. 'Grant me a favour, dear, and make sure the kitchen door is unlocked?' she said. 'Cabot said that Charles has gone out walking. I wouldn't wish for him to be locked out.' She stood. 'I always sleep so well in the country, do not you?' She blew Sophie a kiss and started up the stairs.

The kitchen was quiet and dark, the servants gone to their rest. Sophie placed the note square in the middle of the scrubbed oak table and then checked the door that led outside. Locked. She drew back the bolt and stood with her hand on the knob.

Lady Dayle's words today had greatly affected her. This time the obstacle she must overcome lurked within her own heart. Would she continue to allow fear to rule her? There was only one way to find out. She turned the latch and slipped outside.

It was a gorgeous night. The air was fresh and clear, free of the tension that had lingered in the drawing room. A heavy, nearly full moon hung low over the lake, making magic of the ordinary park.

She stepped away from the door, made her way past the kitchen garden, and set out across the lawn. She knew what she was doing. There was only one reason, after everything that had passed between her and Charles, to seek him out like this.

The risk was huge and potentially disastrous. The heartache would be far worse, if he left her, than the pain that had already scared her so. Yet still she walked, her feet heading unerringly to where the moonlight beckoned her, winking off the waters of the lake, calling to her from the copper cupola of Lady Dayle's folly.

She knew that's where he would be, and she was right. The effect of the moonlight on the Doric columns turned the place into a study of light and shadow. Charles sat in the dark, in one of the comfortable chairs Lady Dayle had had placed here, his head hung in his hands.

She spoke softly into the gloom. 'Charles.'

He raised his head, no hint of a surprise in his face. 'I should have guessed,' he said, no discernible emotion in his voice.

Sophie entered and took a seat near to him. They sat in silence a bit. 'What's wrong?' she finally asked.

'Me. You. The whole damned world. Take your pick.'

She sighed. 'I'm sure it's a tangled combination of the three.' But no problem, however convoluted, stood a chance against his strength of character, his determination to do the right thing. 'I'm also sure that, however problematic, you'll be able to fix it.'

He snorted. 'Now that's where you're wrong. Oh, I might have been arrogant enough to think so, just a few months ago. But you've changed all that.'

She was horrified. 'I have?'

With a muffled oath he stood, banging the chair back against the stone floor. 'Sophie, you don't even know what you've done to me! Before you came back, I was firm in my goals, sure that my redemption was possible, if only I worked hard enough, long enough.'

He strode away from her, striding between the columns with the sinewy grace of a cat. 'Then you slammed into my life like cannon shot, and tempted me.' He glanced back at her, his face twisted. 'So beautiful, so full of life and laughter. I resisted, though, for, as much as I might regret losing you, I knew that there were other things that would haunt me even more.'

She sensed a hint of the answers she had been looking for. She sat up straighter, started to ask, but he continued on, unaware of her reaction. 'Now I see what you have done—with just your stubborn will and your generous heart—and I am ashamed. All my great and lofty goals, all my hard work, and nothing to show for it.'

He turned to face her then, and she thought her heart would break at the grief and chagrin and tenderness she saw in his face. 'You put your talent and your determination to good use. You're the one who has made a difference, in a concrete, human way that I never gave a thought to.'

'I did what I could, based on my circumstances, but you are different. You have a chance to help thousands, to change the course of so many lives.'

'Perhaps once, but my chance seems to be slipping through my fingers. Worse, I don't even know if I want to hold on. Oh, God—' he groaned '—what if I've been wrong all along? I don't know what to think, what to feel. All I know is that I'm tired of pretending.' He turned, propped a hand on the nearest column and stared out again at the lake. 'I don't suppose you know what I mean, do you? You don't pretend, you throw yourself out to the world with no thought of what you might suffer. You put others before yourself and they love you for it.'

'Stop it, Charles. I'm not a saint. Look at all the times you've railed at me for my behaviour, and don't make me out to be something I'm not.'

He laughed, a harsh, ironic sound, and spun abruptly around. Slowly he began to stalk toward her, the moonlight alternately lighting his face and casting it into shadow. 'Sophie,' he said, his voice low, seductive, 'I'd be the last one to call you a saint.' The deep timbre of his voice somehow echoed in the pit of her belly.

'Do you know what you are?' He lifted his hand and tenderly cupped her jaw. 'You're a terror.' His thumb caressed her chin, then brushed her bottom lip, gently, sweetly. 'A beautiful, exasperating, un-selfish, great-hearted monster.'

Her every nerve ending was focused on his touch, on the promise of more implicit in his voice. She allowed him to pull her closer, into the shadows as well. 'Thank you,' she said, her voice husky.

He laughed, and this time it was genuine and a little rueful. 'Ah, Sophie, you've turned my world upside down.' He dipped his head to brush her lips with his. Sophie's head swam. A stab of fear tried to surface, but she closed it away, opened instead the door to her longing and let it flood over her.

'You've been the only thing keeping my world right side up,' she whispered.

Her words seemed to snap his restraint. He kissed her again, deeply, surging inside her mouth with quick, possessive strokes, claiming her, marking her as his.

She surrendered to it. Passion flared, hot and low in her belly. A sense of recklessness made her bold and she answered him in kind, entwining her tongue with his with hot, silky strokes.

So long had she dreamed of this. So many nights imagining the tenderness of his touch, the sweetness of his kiss. How often in life are we granted what we want most? And this might be all she ever got. She had no idea how he would react when he discovered her latest scheme. She felt like a thief, stealing these few minutes of happiness when their future was so uncertain, but she didn't care. If the worst happened, she would accept the pain, in exchange for the rare wonder of a dream come true.

Her hunger grew as she gave herself up to the moment, and she slid urgent hands up and over the expanse of his chest, to the barrier of his neckcloth. She tugged experimentally. It loosened a bit, but Charles gave a sudden growl, then quickly unwound the thing and flung it away.

She smiled and he buried his face in the crook of her neck, nipping and kissing. Her chuckle turned to a gasp and then a low moan as his fingers sought the hidden fastenings of her gown.

Suddenly he stopped. 'Wait,' he said. Her breath caught, as effortlessly he took her in his arms and carried her the few steps to the *chaise* that Lady Dayle had placed facing the lake. Crouching down beside her, he smiled up into her eyes and slowly raised her skirts, stopping when they had just topped her knees.

'Ahh,' he said, tracing reverent fingers up one leg and turning it to explore the dark birthmark on the inside of her knee. 'There it is.' He leaned down and pressed a warm kiss on it. Heat flared and travelled the short distance straight up, to where she pulsed with need for him.

He flashed his devil's grin at her. 'Do you know how many times you flaunted that at me when we were children? Every time you ran fast or climbed a tree or hiked your skirts to wade. I never thought a thing of it, then. But I watched you dancing, that first night at Lady Edgeware's ball, and I suddenly remembered. The thought of it has driven me mad ever since.'

She smiled down at him. 'Now it's yours.'

His eyes darkened and he surged up against her. She clutched his shirt, pulled him down to her, kissing him deeply. Quickly then, they tugged, and pulled and tossed clothing aside, neither heeding anything except the next exposed spot to touch, caress and kiss.

When at last Sophie lay in naked splendour before him, Charles could only gaze in awe. He'd been right, she was a terror, but she was also a miracle. She'd forced him to rediscover his heart, an organ he'd done his best to forget. She'd forced him to realise that pain was not the only thing he could feel. He was alive again and free to experience pleasure, and passion.

Neither of which adequately described how he felt looking at her now. He stared, wanting to imprint this image, never to forget. She lay reclined on the *chaise,* a glorious vision of ebony tresses and creamy curves. The moonlight caressed her, flowing over her high and heavy breasts, kissing their taut peaks.

He bent to do the same. His breath flowed hot over her skin, making her gasp in anticipation. He smiled up at her, detoured to place a soft kiss on her mouth, then leaned down and drew her breast into his mouth. Her shoulders slammed back, lifting her breasts higher in a wordless plea. He answered it with hot and languid kisses until she began to squirm in pleasure.

He lifted his head. She cried out, and reached for him. 'You are the most beautiful thing I have ever seen,' he said, his voice rough with emotion.

He turned his attention to her other breast, loving her that way for long moments, while his hand travelled the length of her, exploring and teasing. She tensed a little when his hand strayed lower, but he kissed her worries away. He cupped her, teasing her with strokes as light as a feather, until she relaxed. Then he bent to her breast again, sucking hard and nipping as his fingers spread her, delved deep and drew forth the hot, slick evidence of her desire.

'Oh, my,' she said, sounding breathless with surprise. He found the tender nub at the heart of her, and began a slow, enticing stroke that had her twisting and turning, clutching him like he was her anchor in a storm of passion.

'Charles,' she gasped, 'I want to touch you.'

Already hard as a pike, his shaft stood ramrod straight at the mere thought. With a wordless moan of assent he rolled over, taking up her former position as he reclined back against the scrolled arm of the *chaise*.

Sophie leaned on one elbow, her dark hair spilling down and caressing his chest. Her fingers followed, touching him with the endearing curiosity of innocence, and raining soft little kisses on his neck. He reached for her breast, tracing a slow path around her nipple, but she gave a little shake of her head and pushed his hand away. Deliberately she looked down the length of his body. His manhood stood at attention, pleased with her look of awe.

At her questioning glance he nodded and her hand skimmed downward, grazing him with soft fingertips.

Slowly she slid up and over him, testing the weight of his shaft, eventually wrapping her fingers around the throbbing length. Without thought he placed his hand over hers, showed her how to stroke him and drive him mad. She was a quick learner. Within seconds he was ready to explode.

'Stop,' he rasped, stilling her hand.

She released him as if his heat had scalded her. 'Did I do it wrong?' she asked, frowning.

'No—just right, too right. Any more right and I won't be able to stop.'

Her brow cleared and she leaned down, her breath hot against his mouth. 'Don't stop,' she said, before pressing her mouth to his in a devouring kiss.

He let loose a helpless sound, somewhere between a choke and a sob, and pushed her over and down. Her thighs fell apart and he wedged a knee in between them.

Eyes shining, she gazed up at him, reflecting moonlight and trust. 'Show me what to do,' she whispered.

'Are you sure? We don't have to—' He stopped, praying she said yes.

'Yes.'

He parted her with his fingers once more, feeling a surge of power at her wet, inviting warmth. Her nub was swollen, and he teased it again, softly, then harder, until she was wild again beneath him. He replaced his finger with the head of his rod, rubbing and groaning out loud at the feel of her, wet and slick.

Need hit him like lightning, but he had to go slow. He must. Gently he probed her swollen flesh. Her innocent, uncontrolled movements pulled him in deeper and he groaned. Ever so slowly he tilted his pelvis, stretching her, giving her time to accommodate him. And then he reached her barrier.

He bent and kissed her. 'Hold on,' he whispered, and surged into her, burying himself deep in her sweet flesh.

She gasped and froze. He stilled, sweating and fighting to wait while she grew accustomed to his invasion.

'All right?' he asked quietly.

She nodded and with a heartfelt moan he began to move.

Oh, Lord, but she was tight. She began to move with him and he surrendered to her warm, wet welcome. He lost himself in her, set free from his burdens by the sweetness of her flesh, and the warmth of her spirit.

He thrust hard, settling into a sweet, rocking rhythm. This was going too fast, he was already on the edge, and she couldn't keep up. He eased a hand between them, gently rubbed.

She clutched him, her eyes opening in surprise as sensation overcame her. Her breath came in quick, panting gasps now. Charles kept his rhythm steady and suddenly she moaned into the night. Deep within her, he felt her passage tremble, convulse, pull him even deeper.

It was too much. The pleasure was unbearable. Harder he thrust, deeper, every fibre of his being focused on the hot, sweet feel of her, until, with a shout, he shattered. Pieces of his soul scattered, leaving his heart free to soar in the healing darkness of peace.

* * *

They came back to earth together, leaving a trail of tender sighs, soft whispers and gentle laughter. Sophie regretted nothing, was happier, in fact, than she had ever been in her life. This, this was what she had been longing for: this utter contentment, complete acceptance, pure happiness that only grew with each touch.

Anxieties tried to crowd in, but she forced all doubts, all fears from her mind. She breathed deeply, determined to absorb everything while she could. The alien planes of his body, hard and flat where hers was soft and curved, the weight of his limbs entangled with hers, his easy laughter and smooth brow, the pleasure in his eyes when he looked at her; they were a gift to her. These were the things she would remember.

Eventually, of course, reality intruded. But it was with soft laughter and unhurried movements that they dressed and prepared to go back to the house. They took their time, enjoying each other and absorbing the peace of the night. When they reached the low wall that surrounded the kitchen garden, Charles sat down upon it, pulled her on to his lap and wrapped her in his embrace. They stayed and watched as the moon began to sink behind the temple, reminiscing, and talking of inconsequential things, each avoiding any mention of the future.

'Jack mentioned that you have made some progress towards finding your secret enemy,' she said, just to put off their leave-taking a little longer.

'Very little.' Charles sighed. 'It's naught but a wild goose chase. Almost literally.' He made a face and asked, 'You haven't seen any small, wiry men skulking about here, have you? Especially one who moves like a bird?'

Sophie laughed. 'No, none that I've noticed. If he wasn't a plasterer or a carpenter, then I probably wouldn't take notice of him, in any case.' They sat quietly a moment. After a moment's reflection she said, 'I did know a man like that once, though. He even had the name of a bird.'

She felt Charles stiffen behind her. 'You did? What was his name?'

'Mr Wren. He worked for my uncle. It's strange that I remember him, I haven't seen him in years.' She reconsidered her words. 'Well, perhaps not so strange.'

'Why do you say that?' Still wrapped in Charles's arms, she could still feel the tension growing in his frame.

'Oh, I don't know, it's silly, I suppose. I didn't like him. He was the one that always came in my uncle's stead when there was business to be done with our steward. He carried messages and bank drafts and such, and communicated my uncle's wishes.' She paused. 'I used to dread his visits.'

'Why?' The question was low, dangerous.

She considered her words. 'I was young. He was a visual reminder of my uncle's neglect. And not only to me, I think. Whenever he stayed with us, the talk in the village always seemed to start up again. You know what I mean—talk of my uncle's estrangement from my aunt and me, of my father's disgrace, of my unsuitability. All the usual gossip.'

His grip on her tightened. He held her close for a long minute, and then kissed her softly. 'I am so very sorry,' he said.

She twisted in his embrace and smiled into his eyes. 'It's long over. We've come a long way since then, haven't we?'

He kissed her forehead and pulled her close again. 'And this is only the beginning. We'll go on together.'

Sophie wanted it to be true. A little *frisson* of panic seized her at the thought that it might not be so. She sank into the warmth of him, seeking again that feeling of content abandonment. It escaped her, perhaps because Charles's focus suddenly seemed to be far away.

'Charles, what did you mean tonight when you spoke of your redemption?' She regretted the words almost as soon as they were out of her mouth. But perhaps it was for the best, she thought a little desperately, to know where they stood right now.

He said nothing for a long moment, yet his stillness held a different quality now. Wariness? Regret? She wasn't to know.

'It didn't mean anything. It's not important.' He dropped his head, breathed deep in the crook of her neck. 'Let's just enjoy each other tonight.'

The spark of hope born inside her tonight flickered and died away. Her eyes closed. So much lay between them, but not enough. Charles had shared much with her, but he still couldn't open his heart, gift her with his trust.

This was it, then. This time, stolen away from the real world, was to be all they had. She clutched him tightly, determined to wring every drop of happiness she could, to help her survive the cold and lonely years ahead.

'The sky is starting to lighten,' he said, his breath hot against her skin.

She glanced over at the house. 'We should go in separately, don't you think?'

'Yes.' He turned her and kissed her once more, his eyes intense. 'Everything is going to be fine, do you understand?'

She nodded, even though she didn't believe him.

'You go on,' he said. 'I'll stay out here for a bit, then follow you in.'

She went, wrapping tonight about her like a blanket, refusing to think of tomorrow.

Chapter Seventeen

Charles was inside waking his brother before the eastern sky had fully lightened. He was on the road to London before the sun had fully crested the horizon. He still couldn't quite grasp the truth. But he had had it from Sophie's own lips.

Lord Cranbourne was his unknown enemy? It seemed absurd. All this time he'd assumed it would turn out to be someone he had wronged in the past. A cuckolded husband, a woman scorned, a victim of some mindless prank. He could think of nothing he'd ever done to Sophie's uncle.

But perhaps it was the future that concerned Lord Cranbourne? He'd always been involved in politics, always been known to be influential, but in a quiet way, in the background, so to speak. Until recently. He'd won the chairmanship that Charles had wanted, hadn't he? And it had led to even higher placement in the Board of Trade. The ministry was the next logical step. It was working out for Cranbourne just as Charles had hoped for himself. Perhaps that was it? Perhaps it was the talk of Charles's potential that had represented a threat?

His horse was fresh and almost as eager as Charles. The miles sped by quickly, but could not match the fast pace of his churning thoughts. He might not know precisely what Cranbourne's motivation might be, but he meant to find out. And then what? He might expose the man and clear his name. He could have his political future back.

But what would that do to Sophie? One thing Charles knew beyond the shadow of a doubt. He would do nothing that might harm Sophie, not ever again. He had caused her enough pain—it was time he put her happiness first.

What of his own happiness? For so long he had been convinced that such a thing did not exist, that his only path led inexorably toward a future in the government.

Except that path was truly Phillip's. It was Phillip who had paved the way for him, Phillip who had lived for it, who had been talked of as a potential Prime Minister. Charles knew now that his own reach would likely never be as lofty. His past would always block the way to such a future.

For so long he'd been certain, sure that to follow Phillip's dream was the only way to redeem his mistakes. He would take the place of the brother who should have lived. But, just perhaps, there might be other ways to help, other ways he could give back. Sophie had shown him that.

Sophie. Just the thought of her calmed him, gave him hope. They'd exchanged no promises, but last night had changed everything. He knew now that she cared for him as he did for her. Somehow he would sort out this mess, and then they would plan the future, together.

It was mid-morning when he reached London. The streets were bustling and Charles was tired and hungry. He considered stopping at his own house first, but there was no time to waste. He went straight to Green Street.

'Yes?' Lord Cranbourne's butler was cordial, but clearly not impressed with the grubby viscount on his steps.

Charles was in no mood to deal with the snobbery of an upper servant. 'Has Cranbourne set out yet?'

The man looked him up and down a moment, as if deciding whether to answer or not. 'Yes, sir. Not half an hour past.'

A sudden notion hit him. 'Let me see Mr Wren, then.'

The servant looked startled, but recovered quickly. 'I'm sorry, but I don't know who you mean, sir.'

'Do you know who I am?' Charles barked.

'Yes, sir.' There was a wealth of contempt in the simple words.

'Then you know that I have personal as well as political dealings with your master. He's on his way to my house as we speak. Now tell me where I can find Mr Wren.'

The autocratic tone had the desired effect. The butler let down his guard enough for Charles to see his genuine bewilderment. 'But I can't tell you, sir. Wren comes and goes as he pleases, at every hour, but he does not bide here.'

'And you don't know where he lodges?'

'No.' The impudent blighter actually cocked a brow at him. 'I'm sure Lord Cranbourne has that information.'

'Fine, now listen closely. If you see Mr Wren, you be very sure to tell him that his lordship has need of him in Sevenoaks. He is to get himself there, straight away.'

'Yes, sir.' The man watched as Charles began to search his coat pockets. 'I'm to see Cranbourne's solicitor next, but I've lost the direction on the trip.'

When he withdrew his hand there was a glint of gold in his palm. 'What was the name, again?'

After a long moment of consideration, the butler answered at last. 'Bridewell, sir, of Bridewell and Locke.'

'Thank you.' Charles tossed the coin and didn't wait to see if the man caught it. He mounted, and then paused to think. After a moment's reflection he turned the horse's head towards St James's Street.

His instincts had been good. Just a quick question to a porter at White's and he had the solicitor's address. A scant few minutes later he was being ushered into the comfortable offices of Bridewell and Locke.

'Good morning, my lord.' The young man rising from behind the formidable desk was definitely not either of the portly gentlemen whose portraits hung in the reception area.

'Good morning. I am Dayle. I'm here to see Mr Bridewell.'

'Alas, Mr Bridewell passed on last year. I am Mr Locke.' At Charles's sceptical glance he added, 'Mr Locke, the younger. My father's health is unfortunately tenuous as well. He has been forced—and I mean that almost literally—to hand the reins over to me.'

'Including the affairs of Lord Cranbourne?'

'Most of them,' Mr Locke said with a cheerful grin.

'Then you may congratulate me, for I am to wed Cranbourne's niece.'

'Indeed, I do offer my felicitations. Are you here, then, to discuss the settlements?'

'Only briefly. We must save the meat of it for a time when Cranbourne and my own man are available. I only wished to inform you so that you may begin to draw up the papers.'

'I don't blame your impatience, when such a sum is involved. You understand, though, that there is little I may do for you until I have word from Lord Cranbourne himself?'

'I see.' Charles spent a fleeting moment wondering if a flash of gold would work as well on Cranbourne's solicitor as it had on his butler. His instincts said not.

'But may I ask you to pass along my best wishes to Lord Cranbourne,' Mr Locke continued, 'and, of course, to your intended?'

'I shall be sure to do so.' Charles began to rise. It seemed useless to question this young man. He doubted he could tell him anything, in any case.

'Thank you,' Mr Locke continued. 'Though it may be a blow to his purse, I'm sure Lord Cranbourne is thrilled to see his niece happily settled at last.'

Charles sat back down and fixed an eye on the man. 'A blow to his purse?'

'Yes. The lady's fortune has been held in trust for her, but it is meant to be a marriage settlement.' Mr Locke returned the same sort of measuring stare Charles had just given him. 'May I ask how long you have been acquainted with the lady?'

'For ever.' Charles smiled, but he could see that the man was serious. 'Since she came to England as a child.' He hesitated, then said, 'I care for her very much.'

Mr Locke smiled. 'I am glad to hear it. Every young lady needs someone who is looking out for her best interests.' His smile faded and he was quiet a moment. 'I shall tell you something that I likely should not. Someone else should know, I think.' He met Charles's eye. 'There is a stipulation in her father's will. If Miss Westby does not marry by the age of five and twenty, her annual stipend will increase a bit, but the bulk of her fortune will pass to the trustee.'

'And the trustee is—?' Charles knew the answer already; he would stake his life on it. But he wanted to hear the words.

'Lord Cranbourne, of course.'

'I see.' And he did. Indeed, suddenly so many things were becoming clear.

'May you put it to good use, sir. Many things can be accomplished with eighty thousand pounds.' He leaned forward, catching Charles's eye again and said in a level voice, 'Many things might be done to gain such a vast sum.'

The man was trying to warn him. It wasn't necessary. His eyes were wide open, now. Charles stood and gripped his hand. 'Thank you for your help, Mr Locke.'

'Congratulations again, my lord.'

Charles vaulted to his horse, his mind awhirl. It was growing late and he still had a long ride ahead of him. Cranbourne might even be at Sevenoaks by now. So much deceit, and over so many years. By God, the coming confrontation was going to be ugly, but the old fraud had much to answer for. Charles's only regret was the thought of what this would do to Sophie.

He turned south, then paused, seized by a sudden thought. Coming to an abrupt decision, he changed direction, heading for Mayfair. He had one more call to make before he returned.

Sophie came late to the breakfast parlour that morning, and had to endure some good-natured teasing from Jack Alden about being the last to rise.

'But she is not the last,' Lady Ashford said, pointedly looking at the empty chair at the head of the table.

'Ah, but she is,' said Mr Alden. 'Charles was

actually the first to rise this morning. An urgent matter in town had him gone at first light.'

Lady Ashford had much to say at that news, but Sophie heard none of it. Charles was gone? And at first light. He must have set out just after she left him. Her eggs grew cold as she was beset by a surge of conflicting emotions. She didn't know what to think, to feel. Her insecurities told her that this development could not bode well. Yet she could not help but feel a reluctant relief at the thought of not having to dissemble in front of everyone. How could she pretend not to be affected by his presence after all that they had done to each other last night?

But neither of those reactions was the one that cut most deeply. Without a doubt her overwhelming response was an abiding sense of loss. One night only? It hardly seemed fair. Her appetite fled along with her hope of extending their idyll a little longer. So few moments together—she'd hoped for just a few days more, a few more memories to carry with her once he was gone.

The sound of Charles's name broke into her reverie. 'I'm going to agree with Lady Ashford this time,' Mr Huxley was saying. 'It's raggedy manners indeed to leave us all in the lurch. Wouldn't you agree, Miss Westby?'

'No, I would not,' Sophie said firmly. 'Lord

Dayle's work is important. I'm sure he had a good reason for leaving.'

'Indeed,' Mr Alden agreed, casting an approving glance her way. 'Nor are you left in the lurch, or even to your own devices. Charles has asked me to act as host for him today, and he fully expects to be back with us by this evening.'

'Given the state of the country,' said Emily with a quelling glance at Lady Ashford, 'I would say we can forgive Lord Dayle one day.'

'We shan't miss him a bit,' Lady Dayle put in. 'I have a full day planned, and for this evening, a truly splendid surprise.'

Mr Alden set his cup down and stood. 'Miss Westby, if you have finished, will you join me on a walk along the lake path?' He looked over the crowded table. 'Anyone who wishes may join us, of course.'

Nearly the whole party decided to go along, and in the end, Sophie was kept so busy she did not have time for reflection. It was a very good thing too, for last night had provided plenty of fodder for her unruly mind to dwell on. The rest of the group might exclaim over thrilling vistas and picturesque views, but Sophie was preoccupied with the memory of Charles's hands on her body, the musky scent of his skin and the feel of him under her own roving touch.

Such thoughts had to be banished, however, as the

party had gathered at the small dock. Sophie fanned her hot cheeks and hoped the sun was bright enough to account for her flush. She watched as the guests separated into groups of two and four and set out in the boats for a leisurely row. Mateo tried to coax her into his boat, but she smilingly declined and urged Miss Ashford to take her place. As the awkward pair attempted to paddle together, she retired to a bench in the shade with Emily.

'You are singularly quiet today, Sophie,' Emily said. 'Are you feeling well?'

'I am fine, thank you.' Sophie summoned a smile for her friend. 'Actually, I was going to make the very same remark to you.'

Emily sighed. 'It's little Edward. He's teething and not sleeping well. I relieved the nurse for a bit last night, and did not get much rest at all.' She glanced about at the few people left on shore. 'In fact, perhaps I shall take this opportunity to go in and check on him.' She grinned. 'If my husband notices I am gone, tell him I may also take the opportunity to take a nap.'

'I shall do so,' Sophie agreed. She sighed as Emily set out for the house and she was left alone on the bench. She was tired as well, albeit for a much more wicked—and more pleasurable—reason. Her thoughts wandered back to the first day they had picnicked here; it seemed so long ago. That day Charles had rowed Miss Ashford on the lake. But then he had come to her, and shocked her with that heady, passionate kiss. Her eyes drifted closed at the memory. Then he had kissed her in self-defence, trying to distract her from probing into his wounded past. Had last night been the same?

She didn't believe so. He'd been open with his feelings last night. They had, at last, come together with all barriers down, and it had been as exquisite as she had dared to dream. Charles had, in fact, already shared the secret he'd been trying to protect that long ago day, or at least a part of it. He'd trusted her with the truth about his brother's death.

And yet, Sophie was not fool enough to believe that Phillip's secret was all that Charles was hiding. She knew instinctively that he hadn't shared everything, and she suspected that whatever the problem was, it was all mixed up with his feelings about his father, his brother, and his political career.

She sighed again, mourning the brevity of the time she'd had in Charles's arms, missing the sense of peace and security that came with his embrace. Already she was back to the familiar realm of doubt, anxiety, and uncertainty.

'Would you, Miss Westby?'

She opened her eyes with a start. 'Excuse me?'

The boats had come back to shore. The little beach was a milling mass of bodies as the gentlemen helped the ladies to dry land and others to their places in the boats. Mr Huxley was standing before her looking earnest. 'I asked,' he said with exaggerated patience, 'if you would pardon me for speaking out of turn this morning. I didn't mean to disparage our host, but I am moved by his neglect of Miss Ashford.'

'Miss Ashford is a guest in Lord Dayle's home, as are we all,' she replied, rather more sharply than she had intended. 'I know of no reason she should feel more slighted than any one of the rest of us.'

He looked a little hurt at the sharpness of her tone. 'I know nothing has been officially announced, but I feel sure there is some understanding, or at least some sort of expectation, between the two of them.'

'Between the two of who?' Mateo asked as he dropped into the seat beside Sophie.

Mr Huxley looked definitely disgruntled by her cousin's lack of formality. 'Between Lord Dayle and Miss Ashford, if you must know,' he answered.

'Mateo, show some manners,' chided Sophie.

'I am sorry. It has been too long since I have actually rowed a boat and it has tired me. I am too much accustomed to standing at the wheel and shouting orders.' He turned to Mr Huxley. 'I do beg your pardon for interrupting. To make amends I shall give you a piece of advice. If nothing has been announced, my friend, then I would not be so quick to allow Lord Dayle to cut you out. Miss Ashford's dowry, I hear, is formidable indeed.'

'I am surprised you do not pursue the lady yourself, then,' Mr Huxley said stiffly.

'Not I! These English girls are not for me.' Mateo grinned and raised a brow in Sophie's direction. 'I prefer a woman with some fire in her blood.'

'But Miss Ashford is no wilting flower,' Sophie protested. 'She tells me she has travelled extensively. I understand she has been to Bath, and even, I believe, has journeyed to visit family in Wales.'

'Indeed?' Mr Huxley did seem impressed. 'Perhaps I will just take this opportunity to ask her about the state of the Welsh toll roads.' He bowed to Sophie, cast a distasteful look in Mateo's direction and went to Miss Ashford's side.

Sophie exchanged a grin with Mateo. 'Yesterday I asked you to cease baiting the man,' she said, 'and what do you do today but dangle Miss Ashford in front of him like a worm on a hook.'

'Yes, but it was you who gave it that enticing little wiggle.'

They both laughed.

'I suppose we should be ashamed of ourselves,' Sophie said eventually.

'I refuse. In any case, they will hopefully keep each other occupied for a bit.'

'Oh, look, an added benefit.' Sophie gestured to Lady Ashford, who was heading in a determined fashion to the spot where her daughter stood in conversation with Mr Huxley. 'Perhaps Lady Ashford will find a new target for her sniping.' She smiled at her cousin. 'For that I bless you.'

Mateo took her hand. All the laughter had died out of his face. 'I am happy to hear it.' He spoke in the most serious tone she had yet heard from him. 'You give me hope where I begin to fear there is none.' He met her gaze with wistful eyes. 'Perhaps you will bless me in other ways as well?'

Sophie could not mistake his meaning. Indeed, somehow she had known this moment was approaching. Gently she withdrew her hand from his. 'Mateo. I'm sorry, but I cannot. I care for you a great deal though, my cousin, and am so happy to finally have a family again. I hope we can remain so?'

Something dark swam in his eyes, just for a moment. Sophie caught her breath. Then he was Mateo again, shrugging in nonchalance. 'Ah, well.' He reclaimed her hand and pressed an ardent kiss upon it. 'I had to try, did I not? And yes, rest assured, we shall for ever be family.' He smiled. 'Now that

I have found you again, you will find it difficult to shake off your cousin Mateo.'

'Miss Westby!' A shout hailed them from the water's edge. Mr Alden waved from one of the boats. 'We've room for one or two more!'

Sophie returned Mateo's smile, pressed his hand, then turned and waved back at the pair in the boat. 'Yes, I'm ready!'

Chapter Eighteen

Charles had still not returned as the dinner hour approached and Sophie's nerves had worked themselves into a frazzled snarl. Bad enough that she had no idea what his absence meant for the two of them, but she was certain that it spelled disaster for the scheme that she and Lady Dayle had already set into motion.

She tried to distract herself by spending a bit of time with her uncle, who had arrived this afternoon. He was in good spirits and eager to talk about his new position. She listened, happy that things were moving smoothly for someone, but after a few minutes Sophie noticed that he was repeatedly rubbing his left arm.

'Are you well, Uncle?' she asked, with a nod towards his arm.

'What? Oh, yes, fine, fine. An old complaint, no

need to worry.' He pulled his watch from his waist-coat pocket. 'You'll have to be dressing for dinner soon, girl, so send your cousin in to me on your way out, will you? We've business to discuss.'

Thus dismissed, Sophie did go up to prepare for the evening's festivities. She dressed carefully, but for once Nell's chatter did not help to ease her ner-vousness. Heart fluttering in anticipation, she met the rest of the party in the drawing room, only to find that she had not been included in all of Lady Dayle's scheming. She gaped in wonder along with the rest when the viscountess led them, not to the dining room, but outside, to a magical twilight picnic.

Surely the old gods must have conspired with the viscountess, for the evening was idyllic, full of soft light with just a touch of a fresh breeze blowing off the lake. On the other side the folly gleamed in the late sun, rivalling the nearer display of sparkling silver and crystal. The tables stood in readiness, as did an array of servants, ready to serve a lavish feast fit for the Regent himself. A trio of musicians played soft dinner music, adding a final touch of elegance.

The guests were enchanted. Moods were light and conversation flowed as easily as the wine through-out dinner. But all talk ceased as the evening faded and darkness set in. To a man they watched, en-tranced, as the full moon rose over the lake. Only

Sophie closed her eyes against the beautiful sight. In the face of all her uncertainties, she could not bear to look. It was too painful to be reminded of what had transpired under that moon last night.

The sound of wheels in the drive had her snapping to attention, though. She looked to Lady Dayle, but the viscountess had heard it as well. She directed a nod towards Sophie and set out for the house. Sophie saw her whisper something to the staff on the way, and a few moments later the guests' attention was diverted. Everyone gasped as tiny lights began to wink on in the trees. Even Sophie was awed. The effect was magical, a bit of the vast heavens come to earth for their delight.

The last lantern had only just been lit when the shadowy figure of Lady Dayle could be seen, returning on the arm of a gentleman.

'Oh, good,' Lady Ashford said. 'Lord Dayle must have come back at last.'

Sophie knew better. She clutched the table as the viscountess stepped into the island of light with an older gentleman on her arm. They stood a moment and Lady Dayle cleared her throat and loudly asked for everyone's attention.

'My very dear friends, I ask you to welcome some distinguished new guests to our party. Of course, most of you are already acquainted with Lord

Avery.' The gentleman bowed, and a woman stepped from behind them into the light. 'And of course you will remember Lady Avery as well.'

A moment of silence met her pronouncement, broken only by a gasp of outrage from Lady Ashford. Sophie's knuckles grew white as she waited, then she could stand it no longer. Into the breach she stepped. She stood, and dipped a curtsy. 'Welcome to Sevenoaks, my lord, my lady. I'm afraid you've missed dinner, but there is still a sweet course to be served.'

She breathed a sigh of relief as Emily rose then, as well. 'Indeed, come and be welcome. There is a pair of empty seats here next to my husband and I.'

Lady Avery went to her with a grateful look, while Lord Avery stopped to shake hands with Sir Harold. 'Beg pardon, didn't mean to be so dreadfully late,' he was saying, 'one of the horses threw a shoe and we were forced to wait with the carriage while another nag was found.'

Sophie was ready to collapse under the weight of her relief. She and Lady Dayle had taken a definite risk tonight. It had taken courage for Lord and Lady Avery to agree to come, as well. For a moment, she'd thought that, without Charles's influence, their scheme was doomed. But the first step had been taken. Perhaps it was going to come about all right on its own.

But suddenly Lady Ashford was on her feet. 'I will not,' she flung at her husband, before turning to glare at Lady Dayle. 'The effrontery of this is beyond belief! First we are abandoned by our host, then we are subjected to—this!' She waved a hand in Lady Avery's direction. The poor woman kept hold of her dignity and kept her chin in the air.

Lady Ashford grabbed her daughter's hand and hauled her to her feet. Her husband merely hung his head. 'My daughter is an innocent. She is not to be exposed to such—persons. Come, Corinne.' She stalked past the tables, nose held high, and paused to sniff at Lady Dayle. 'We will be packed and gone by morning.'

'That is well—' it was Charles's voice, ringing out of the darkness. Sophie was not the only one startled. She could see several of the ladies in the company clutching their dinner partners '—because I will not tolerate such rudeness to a guest in my home,' he finished.

Everyone watched, spellbound, as Charles stepped forth into the light. Sophie sighed. He was rigged out in full evening garb, all in black and gleaming white. He looked as starkly beautiful as the night sky, but his expression was as formidable as the darkest thundercloud.

Lady Ashford merely continued past him,

dragging her daughter behind her. Sophie noticed that Miss Ashford kept her gaze down and did not look in Charles's direction. Lord Ashford rose slowly from his chair, murmured a soft apology to the company at large and stopped to shake hands with Charles. 'Not the outcome we hoped for, eh?' he said with resignation. 'Ah, well.' He trailed after his family.

Another moment of silence hung in the air, but not for long. The sound of a clearing throat brought all attention to Mr Huxley, who had, in his turn, risen to his feet. 'I am sorry to say it, but Lady Ashford's right in this case,' he said, shaking his head. 'Unmarried girl and all, it ain't proper.' He cast a look at Sophie and followed the others towards the house.

'If anyone else is of the same opinion, I suggest we hear of it now.' Charles's tone said clearly that he would not welcome an answer. He cast a stern glance over the group.

After a moment, when he received no response, Charles continued. 'Well, then, let us make our new guests welcome, shall we?' He chuckled and went to shake Lord Avery's hand. 'I would suppose this explains why you were not at home when I stopped today to call on you, on my way out of London.'

Lord Avery shook Charles's hand heartily.

'Come, Avery,' Sir Harold said, 'Tell me what

the blasted Whigs have been up to in Parliament since we left.'

'Come and sit with me, Annalise,' Lady Dayle cajoled the still-silent Lady Avery, 'Charles's cook has prepared these marvelous *petite souffléts au chocolat.* I give you my word, it is like tasting a cloud.'

At last Sophie could relax. A bit. The remaining guests erupted into enthusiastic chatter. Lord and Lady Avery were accepted into the group with a graciousness that was clearly meant to outshine the bad grace of those who had gone. Sophie saw them exchange an emotionally charged look across the crowd. Lady Dayle trailed past and paused to share a glance of warm accomplishment with her.

It was a start. Lady Avery might never be welcomed by society's highest sticklers, but she had a foot in the door now. They could claim acquaintance with Viscount Dayle and his family, at least. And it might lead to more, thanks to Lady Dayle, and Emily and the other kind souls here, wise enough to embrace forgiveness and eschew judgments. But first and foremost it was thanks to Charles.

Sophie looked for him, praying he could forgive her meddling and find hope for their own tangled situation in the older couple's success. He was mixing with his guests, making sure that Lord and Lady Avery were settled and going out of his way to stop and chat with every member of the party. Except for her. Never once did he look her way. She unabashedly watched him, however. She noticed that he looked earnest as he spoke, and Sophie guessed he was apologising for his absence today. She hoped he was also thanking them all for their generous acceptance of his new guests.

Gradually, as was inevitable, the excitement began to wear down. Mr Chambers hid a yawn behind his hand and suddenly everyone realised the lateness of the hour. Lord and Lady Avery were persuaded to spend the night and were bustled off to their rooms. Reluctantly, people began to drift towards the house and their beds. Sophie couldn't blame them. It had been an amazing evening.

Any hint of fatigue fled, however, when she saw Charles at last making his way towards her. She smiled a nervous welcome as he drew near. 'Did you really call at Lord Avery's today?' she asked.

He didn't return the smile. His brow was drawn, his face serious as he took her hand. 'Sophie, I must ask you to join me in the library.'

She searched his eyes for some hint of what could be wrong. Had her meddling upset him further than she had expected? She could find nothing hidden in his expression except for grim concern.

'Please, my mother and your uncle will be there as well.'

'Of course.'

In silence the small group gathered in the library. Sophie had seen Jack Alden start to follow, but some signal from his brother had stopped him. Mr Alden had turned back to the party and asked the musicians to play a waltz, so that the remaining guests could dance under the stars.

Sophie sent a questioning glance at Lady Dayle, but the viscountess only shrugged, clearly as mystified as she. Only her uncle appeared to have an inkling as to what was afoot. He wore a strange grin as he watched Charles close the door behind them.

Charles did not look his way. Instead he came and sat by Sophie. She started when he took her hand and cast a guilty glance over at Lady Dayle.

'I discovered, several days ago, the name of the man who had been feeding stories of my past to the papers,' Charles said, 'However, it appeared clear that he was a lackey only, working at the behest of someone else.'

Lady Dayle sent a dark glance towards Sophie's uncle. 'Pray, don't keep us in suspense, Charles. Who was it?'

It was that look that did it; that finally connected

all the pieces of the puzzle in Sophie's mind. The comforting smell of old leather faded away, the tense faces about her were forgotten. She was transported, sitting once again in the night air, feeling the relaxed comfort of Charles's embrace turn to a hard wall of tension. She heard the strain in his voice as he asked, *What was his name?*

'It was Mr Wren,' she said aloud, wondering. 'Was it not?' she whispered, coming back to the reality of the library and looking to Charles. She saw the confirmation and concern in his face, and turned hard eyes to her uncle.

He sat, apparently relaxed and unconcerned, but Sophie noticed that he was massaging the palm of his left hand with his right.

'I don't understand,' said Lady Dayle. 'Who is Mr Wren?'

'He is Cranbourne's man,' Charles answered.

Her uncle had at last decided to speak. 'Ridiculous. What would make you say such a thing, Dayle?' he asked, shaking his head. 'I know it sticks in your craw that I am heading the Board of Trade committee, but this is going beyond even your reputation for tomfoolery.'

'It is over, Cranbourne. It is time to tell the truth. It has been you all along. You arranged for that first piece in the *Oracle,* to discredit both Avery and I, and take us out of consideration for the post that you wanted. It worked well, too, did it not?'

'I do not know what you are talking about,' her uncle said. But Sophie saw the truth in his eyes, and something else too. Pain, perhaps, and fear. Good, she thought, letting her shock and fury have full head. He had been hurting her for years—but to find that he had been behind all the attacks on Charles? She hoped the truth did hurt him. It was time he reaped a little of what he had sowed.

'It is too late to deny it,' Charles told him. 'You made a mistake. You should have stopped with the one story. I probably never would have found you out, and you would still most likely have had your chairmanship. But you didn't stop. You kept grinding the axe, seeking to destroy me. I wonder why?'

Sophie was aghast. She tried to catch Charles's gaze, to somehow communicate how incredibly sorry she felt.

'Of course I deny it. I have never heard such foolishness.' He stood. 'Lady Ashford is correct. You are a rag-mannered young fool.' His face twisted, and he teetered forward a step, but he recovered himself and sent a look of loathing towards Charles. 'You have no idea what you have done. You will pay for this night's work.' He stretched an imperious hand towards Sophie. 'Come, niece. I think it would be best if you and I departed along with the Ashfords.'

But Charles was on his feet as well. 'Do you think I will allow you near her? I don't think you understand, Lord Cranbourne. I know what you are. More snake than man. Cold-hearted and manipulative. Do you think I will see her future ruined for your own selfish ends?' His voice was cold, full of fury and disdain. 'These are people you meddle with, you miserable worm, not puppets on a string. We will dance for your pleasure no longer.' He pointed towards the door. 'You are correct, you will leave, but you will leave without Sophie. I will expose your treachery to the world if you even think to come near her again.'

'Just who do you think will be believed, boy? Whose word is better? And it would come to that, for you can prove nothing,' her uncle snarled. His face was pale and he looked to be sweating profusely.

'I have ample proof. Several damning witnesses, even confirmation from your own household. It should be simple enough to lay it all out before a magistrate.'

'No,' Cranbourne rasped. He was cradling his left arm. He took a step towards the door, but listed to one side and fell back.

'My tonic,' he pleaded. 'In my room.'

'Mother,' Charles said, the fury fading from his face, but Lady Dayle was already ringing for help.

Chapter Nineteen

A part of Sophie wanted to watch, to stand implacable in the face of her uncle's pain, exactly as he had done to her for years. She could not do it. She turned away, unable to look at him any longer, as Charles arranged for help, and sent for a doctor. She refused to watch as he was carried out by a brace of footmen. She acknowledged Lady Dayle's quick embrace, but did not turn from the bank of windows as the viscountess bustled off to see to the sick old man.

Beyond this room, the house was in an uproar. Guests clamoured to know what had gone wrong. The village doctor arrived and was ushered upstairs. Footmen and maids scurried back and forth with linen and water and simples from the stillroom.

Through it all, Sophie stood waiting. She waited to hear whether her uncle was going to live or to die.

She waited for her wildly conflicting feelings to settle enough for her to know which of those outcomes would be more welcome.

Eventually the house grew quiet once more. Sophie heard the doctor leave the house. She did not hear Lady Dayle approach until the viscountess was almost upon her.

'Sophie, darling,' she said quietly. 'Are you all right?'

'Is he…?' Sophie could not finish the sentence.

'No, dear. He is weak, but resting comfortably now.' She paused, and then laid a hand on Sophie's shoulder. 'The doctor says he cannot be certain, but he doubts whether Cranbourne has much time left. It could be a matter of weeks, he says, or months.'

Sophie did not answer. She could not sort through the myriad of emotions besetting her.

'He is asking to see you, dear,' Lady Dayle said gently.

'No,' Sophie said at once. Of one thing she was certain, and that was that she was not ready to face him yet.

'I fear you must. No matter what he has done, he deserves the chance to confess, to at least try to right some of the wrongs he has perpetrated. Before it is too late.'

Sophie shook her head.

'I think you need to hear it as much as he needs to tell it,' Lady Dayle insisted. 'And if you will not do it for him, or for yourself, then do it for Charles. I will send for him as well.'

Against her will and better judgment, Sophie allowed herself to be persuaded. She entered the room where her uncle had been taken, hesitantly, on Lady Dayle's arm.

He lay, looking thin and pathetic in the large bed. His skin tone had faded almost to the colour of the bed sheets. She could hear the rattle of his breath from across the room.

Charles and his brother entered the room behind her. They both looked as comfortable as she felt. Lady Dayle drew Sophie to the chair situated close to the bed and called her uncle's name.

His eyes fluttered open. He looked at once into Sophie's face and sighed at what he saw there. His gaze flickered to Charles, standing by the door, then returned to Sophie.

'Niece,' he said. She could barely hear him, his voice was so frail.

'Uncle,' she returned. For some reason it made him smile.

'Dayle is right,' he said. Sophie lowered her head. 'I just wanted you to hear why.'

Sophie was instantly angry. 'Do you look for forgiveness? This is not the theatre, where the villain is excused all on his deathbed just because he makes a pretty speech of contrition. These are real people, not actors, whose lives you have tampered with.'

'Not forgiveness,' he said quietly. 'I just want the truth to be known.' He paused for several breaths, gathering strength.

'Then why?' Sophie asked. 'Just tell us why.'

'I'm old,' he said simply. 'I've worked long and hard for this country, done the things that had to be done. The hard and dirty jobs,' he rasped, 'the sorts of things that are not celebrated in society's parlours. But it has all been clandestine, behind the veil, as they say.' He shrugged, a pitifully small gesture in the vastness of the bed. 'For a long time I was satisfied with that, happy even. Then I began to become aware that my time on earth is limited, and I suddenly realised that no one knew my name. Only a handful of people would ever know what I had done.' He looked at Sophie intently, clearly wishing for her understanding. 'I want them to know my name. Before I shuffle off this mortal coil I want to be acknowledged. I want my name in the history books, too.'

'But what has any of this to do with Charles?' Jack Alden demanded from his position at the door.

'Nothing at first.' Her uncle spared a glance for

Charles, who had moved into the room and now stood implacably at the foot of the bed. 'Rapscallion turned politician—I didn't take him seriously. No one did. But he kept his nose to the grindstone, proved himself on small issues, until he began to be noticed, praised, held up as a bright future for the Party.' He was silent a long moment and only the sound of his laboured breathing filled the room.

'Your name came up too often, and then it came up for the appointment I wanted. You're young. You'll recover, despite your tendency to side with the ones with no power or influence.'

'But all those stories, the statue of King Alfred, the jockey at the Hampstead races, even I had never heard of half those pranks that Charles had played,' Sophie said. 'How could you have known?'

'He kept a file on me,' Charles said quietly. 'Going back for years. What I want to know is why?'

Cranbourne creaked with laughter. The sound made Sophie cringe. 'Good Lord, son, I've got files on everyone. If there is a dirty little secret in London, then I have it at my fingertips. But why you?' He cast a feeble grin. 'Because of a letter I received from an impudent pup years ago. Do you not recall?' He smiled at Charles's blank look, but it faded as his gaze drifted to Sophie. 'A letter from a sprout of a boy, telling me how a gentleman treats his family.'

'Oh my God.' Charles gave half a laugh himself. He turned to Sophie, something unreadable in his eyes. 'I had forgotten. I wrote, chiding him for his neglect of you. He never answered.'

'Neither did I forget,' Cranbourne answered with something of his old energy. 'I had a feeling you might be trouble. Kept an eye on you.' He nodded towards Sophie. 'It's like I told the girl, knowledge is power. How do you think we beat old Boney? Wellington might have whipped him on the battlefield, but it was behind the scenes that the real work was done. We whipped him there, too.' He finished with pride.

'It sounds like an expensive undertaking,' Charles said.

Cranbourne closed his eyes and nodded. 'A sight more expensive than you might think.' He stopped suddenly and his eyes opened again. Sophie did not understand the arrested look on his face. He stared for a long moment at Charles. 'I give you credit, Dayle. Never expected you to figure that out, too.'

It was all becoming too much for Sophie. All the pain, all the embarrassment Charles had suffered these last months. Her fault. She was reeling. Lady Dayle was softly crying. But Charles wasn't through yet.

'Sophie,' he said softly, trying to get her attention.

She shook her head, tried to gather her thoughts. 'I'm so sorry,' she whispered.

'No, I'm sorry, sweet, for there is more.'

More? God, how could there be more?

Charles looked at Cranbourne. 'Tell her,' he said harshly.

Her uncle looked away, refused to meet her eyes. Sophie shivered. It must be bad. 'What is it?' she asked Charles.

'I think he's stolen all of your money,' he answered grimly.

'What money?' She glared at her uncle. 'What is he talking about?'

Cranbourne's head tossed back and forth upon the pillows. She stared, fixing on the motion, not the face of the man who had hurt them all so callously. 'Not all of it,' was all he said.

'Your parents left you money,' Charles broke in. 'It was to be a marriage settlement.'

Sophie was almost relieved. 'No, there was no updated will. I wasn't mentioned. Their estate went to the family shipping company. I, however, was given their shares in the company. I receive the dividends each quarter.'

'I don't know the specifics, but there was a large dowry. Eighty thousand pounds. If you do not marry before you are five and twenty, it goes to him.' He waved at her uncle. 'However, I suspect he's stolen it.'

'Not stolen,' Cranbourne whispered. 'Spent. Put

to good use, for the good of the country. Do you think that bribes to the people close to Napoleon came cheap?' His voice was harsh, his breathing rattled louder now.

Eighty thousand pounds. Sophie thought of what she might have done with such an amount. Hospitals, schools. She thought of the difference it might have made to Mr Darvey, and all the men at the workshop back home. But then the words registered. Marriage settlement. It had never been hers, in any case.

'I don't need it,' she said with conviction. 'I've done well enough with what I have.'

'Yes, you have done marvellously well, dear,' Lady Dayle whispered through her tears, taking her hand. Sophie clung to her, drawing strength.

'Unfortunately he's robbed you of something more valuable than money,' Charles said grimly.

Sophie did not want to hear any more.

'Recall how he campaigned against me, here in town? Not just the papers, but the rumours, the whispers, the innuendo?' He met Sophie's eye. 'Do you remember what you told me about the aftermath of Mr Wren's visits? I think he's waged a similar war on you, in Blackford Chase. To make you unmarriageable.'

Surely not. Not even her uncle could have been

so cruel. All the taunts, the rejection, the anguish of always being on the outside looking in. She couldn't ask, couldn't speak. She only stared at him, unspeaking.

'I don't regret it,' he rasped. 'It was the making of her. Look at her! The girl has spirit, strength.' His face contorted.

Lady Dayle stood, at last putting an end to this torture. 'That is enough, now,' she said. 'I will fetch your medicine, Lord Cranbourne. The rest of you, we will speak more of this later.'

Sophie left the room in a hurry, not stopping to wait for Charles. How could she face him, knowing what their friendship had cost him?

She did not return to her room. She could not bear the thought of being confined. The enormity of her distress forbade it. She had to be out, in the fresh air, where perhaps some of her emotional turmoil could leak away, bleed into the black heavens and leave her less burdened.

The kitchen door was locked again. She slid open the lock and stepped out into the night, aware of the vast emotional distance between those same simple acts last night and this.

She walked through the night, annoyed that the beauty of the evening had not faded, resenting the fact that everything could look so unchanged, when her life had been shattered so completely.

Unerringly her feet carried her the long distance to Lady Dayle's folly. The tears came as she stepped in. She stumbled to the nearest column and leaned against the cool marble. She gripped it while she sobbed, as if the force of her anger and grief might tear her away, and when the storm of crying abated she stayed, letting the beauty and serenity of it support and calm her.

She heard Charles's footsteps long before he arrived. But then he was close behind her. His body loomed over hers, so large and warmly masculine. He wrapped her in his arms, and she was safe in the warmth of his embrace again. She leaned back into it. All she wanted to do was forget. Forget it all, and stay here, secure in his arms forever.

'I am so very sorry,' he whispered.

She sighed. He'd held her in just this same way last night. The difference was, this time she knew how short the moment would last. He would leave. She would be left hurting. It was a pattern in her life that was becoming entirely too apparent. She straightened, stepped away, and put a little distance between them.

'What do you have to be sorry for, Charles? Nothing, except for the fact that you ever met me.

It is I who am sorry. It seems I've been nothing but trouble since the beginning.'

'Don't think of it like that,' he said. 'Let's just be happy that it's over. We know the worst now, and can go on from here.'

'Over?' Her voice sounded strained, strange, like it belonged to someone else. 'It is hardly over. You can have your life back now. Reveal what he's done to you. Do it with my blessing.'

She stopped, cursing the devastating irony of the situation. The discovery of her uncle's perfidy was the answer to Charles's prayers, and the end to hers. For once scandal was going to work in Charles's favour, but it was going to tear her down along with her uncle, placing her for ever out of Charles's reach.

She tried to sound pleased for him, but even she could hear the hollow echo of her words. 'You'll be back on the path to the ministry in a matter of weeks, once the truth is known.' And back to the search for the perfect political hostess.

The tears were gathering force once more, she could feel them building up from the bottom of her soul. She turned away. 'Please, I need to be alone.'

'No, you don't.' He was coming toward her again, the image of tender concern. 'You don't have to face this alone.'

'I am asking you not to make this more difficult for me.'

'I'm trying to help, not make it more difficult. I know how you must feel. Let me help you.'

She felt a fleeting moment of anger. How could he even begin to know her feelings? Then she remembered—she wasn't the only one who had been betrayed.

But he had seen and understood her flash of emotion. 'No, you are right. There is no comparison to what he's done to you, and with such callous disregard. I could kill the man myself.' He drew close and this time she let him. 'I don't know how you feel. Tell me.'

She wrapped her arms around herself. 'I feel naked. Vulnerable.'

She could feel him smile against her hair. 'No, yesterday we were both vulnerable and alone. Then we came together, here in this very spot, and today we are together and strong.'

'How I wish that were true,' she whispered.

'It is true.' He took both her hands in his. 'As far as I'm concerned, last night's events are all that matter. We may have cleared up a lot of mysteries tonight, but when you cart away the rubble, it changes nothing.'

She gaped at him. 'Are you daft? It changes everything! It changes my past, and both our futures.'

'What's past is just that.' He dropped one of her hands and cupped her cheek. 'I've known your uncle was evil since the first day I saw you come crying down that forest path. Today isn't any different. The future is ours to shape.'

Ours. It had to be the most beautiful word in any language. She leaned into his caress. He gathered her close, pulling her in for a kiss. A soft, sweet, decadent kiss, full of visions of the future, full of promises. For a long moment she lost herself in it, let the heat and the lethal longing he stirred in her sweep away reality.

He broke the kiss and buried his face in her hair. His breath burned against her ear, sending a shiver down the length of her, igniting a slow burn of desire. 'No one has to know, if you don't wish it. We don't have to tell anyone what he's done.'

A splash of cold water could not have quenched her fire more thoroughly. Is that what he wished for? More secrets? More lies?

'No,' she said sharply. 'That is not an option we can consider.' She pushed away from him. 'Haven't you learned that lesson yet? I have seen what the weight of your secrets has done to you. Do you think I would add to that? Would you ask me to carry a similar burden?'

He stiffened, the oh-so-familiar mask dropped into place. 'I don't know what you mean.'

Sophie was growing more furious by the minute. 'You spout the words like you actually believe them. "What's past is past." Should I follow your words or your deeds, Charles?'

He didn't answer.

'You see, even now you shut me out. My life, my soul is bared before you, and still you close yourself to me. Even after all of this…' she waved an encompassing hand '…you still do not trust me.'

'You speak in absurdities. How can you say such a thing?' Now he was growing angry. 'You dare to speak of trust? When you went off half-cocked and pulled that stunt with Lord Avery and his wife?'

'I was trying to help them.'

'Yes, after *we* spoke of helping them. I said I would call on them, and I did, at the first opportunity. But it wasn't enough, was it, you interfering little minx? Did *you* trust *me* to handle it? No—you brewed up another of your hare-brained schemes and you came close to ruining them both for ever!'

'You know what I was trying to accomplish—for them and for us, too. But I'm not going to debate it with you now. This is just another distraction to keep me from the real topic. You are just building another wall to keep me out.'

'Stop it.' Now the anger in his voice was tempered with exasperation. 'You are just being fanciful.'

'Am I? No secrets, have you? Then explain it to me, Charles. Tell me just how you have come to believe that you killed your brother?'

Charles had once had the wind knocked out of him by a champion pugilist at Gentleman Jackson's. He had lain gasping like a fish out of water for a good fifteen minutes. But even that blow had not held the power of Sophie's words. He gaped at her, unable to accept that the truth had been uttered out loud.

'That is it—is it not? The truth you have laboured to hide? Or rather, that's the load of nonsense you have accepted as the truth.'

He stood, unmoving. He'd become accustomed to the swirling, unruly mess that replaced orderly thought and emotion whenever he stood in Sophie's presence, but this, this was reaching a new depth of chaos. He couldn't think, couldn't formulate a coherent response. He could only stand and wait for the surge of adrenalin to ebb, for panic and fear to recede.

'You don't know what you are talking about,' was all the response he could manage.

'Oh, but I think I do. I can scarcely believe it took me this long to unravel. It explains so much: the guilt, your talk of redemption, and the way you cringe every time Phillip's name is mentioned. Once, at this very house, I asked if you wanted to turn yourself into your brother, when all along the truth is that you think you must replace him.' She moved and took up a position between him and the house, as if she expected him to run. 'I want to hear the reason why.'

Charles couldn't bear to look at her. He turned away, and swept both hands through his hair. He wished he could cover both his ears to block her out, the way he had done to irritate Phillip when they were small. Oh, God, Phillip. He missed him so damned much.

But Phillip was not going to rescue him from this situation, or any other, ever again. He breathed deep and reached for courage. He only hoped he had some.

'Fine,' he finally said. 'Only you could take this hellish night and wish to make it worse. I can see that you will not be satisfied until I am naked and vulnerable too.'

He began to pace. He couldn't hold still, couldn't believe he was admitting the ugly truth.

'You want to know why? Because it *is* the truth. Phillip came to me after Castlereagh offered him the assignment. He hadn't accepted it yet, and didn't know if he would.'

'And you encouraged him?' she asked softly.

'No—I taunted him. It was obvious he was wild to do it. He was actually thrilled that Napoleon had come back, because it gave him one last chance to get in the action. But Father had forbidden him to go. I laughed at him. Mocked him. Asked him if he meant to live under our father's thumb for ever.' Charles couldn't believe how much it hurt to say it, to remember it. He stopped at the far edge of the folly and stared out at the lake. 'He was so angry.'

'And you think that was the reason he decided to go?'

'The next time I saw him, he was preparing to leave. He came to say goodbye. If only I had known…' Grief choked off his words.

Sophie was behind him now. Her hands, so strong and capable for a woman, touched his shoulders, and slid around to embrace him. She laid her soft cheek in the middle of his back. 'Phillip was a good man. He did his duty, but he knew his own mind. He was only human. He chose to go because it was what he wanted, not because his little brother goaded him into it.'

'If you had seen his face. You can't know how it haunts me.'

'I know he would have been in his element. I imagine he was supremely happy in the time he was there.'

'I don't care—he shouldn't have been there at all. He shouldn't have died. He was the good one, the useful one, the one who would have become a great man.' He hung his head. 'It should have been me who died, not him.'

She circled around until she stood before him, her face aghast. 'How can you say such a thing?'

'I didn't. I didn't have to. My father said it for me.'

'Oh, Charles.' Her face crumpled, her lip trembled. Tears welled in her eyes. Charles felt like the biggest ass in the kingdom. She'd been through so much tonight and now here she was, grieving for him.

'How horrible. I wish I could give him a piece of my mind.' She wiped her eyes; he could see she was trying to pull herself together. 'I'm sure he regretted saying such a hateful thing.'

'The only thing he regretted was losing Phillip. He had been so proud of him. I don't think he could conceive of living in a world where his eldest son was no more. He didn't want to. When he contracted the lung fever, he didn't even try to get well. He just let it take him.' Charles did not want to remember the horror of those days, or his mother's frantic worry. 'He never forgave me.'

She stepped forward until their bodies were in contact. Her warmth and softness were a comfort. So was the hand that she slowly stroked through his hair.

'My poor Charles,' she breathed.

'That's not even the worst of it,' he whispered.

'When I heard the news about Phillip, I thought that I would die too. But do you know how I felt when my father died?' He took her by the arms, to be sure she looked him in the face, to be sure she saw the stark horror of the truth. 'Relieved,' he said harshly. 'I was relieved, almost glad, that I wouldn't have to see the bitter disappointment in his eyes every time he looked at me.'

He let her go. He felt empty, drained. 'There you have it. Now you know the worst, all the monumental failings of my life. But do you know, Sophie, as much as women value talking and sharing, I think there can be a point when two people know too much about each other.'

Now he was the one to draw away, to create a physical distance to represent the emotional room that he needed. 'We know the worst about each other now. You are afraid you will be hurt yet again, and I am just the selfish idiot to do it.'

There was sympathy and understanding in her eyes. He didn't want to see it.

'You are being too hard on yourself. You have been letting this gnaw on you for so long. Now that you have faced your demons, you can begin to heal. You must learn to make peace with yourself, Charles. Only then will you be able to move past this.'

'No. The only people whose forgiveness I need are dead.'

'Charles, please.'

'You'll never look at me in the same way again. I couldn't bear it.' He turned away. 'I can scarcely look at you now, knowing that you know.'

He was afraid she would press him. She didn't. For several long minutes, she stood silent. Then she squared her shoulders and breathed deep. 'You are wrong, Charles. There is only one person whose forgiveness you require. Your own.'

She came to him and laid her head on his chest. 'Tonight has been very difficult for both of us. I think we each have some serious decisions to make.' Her arms were around him, embracing him tightly. 'Let us both take some time and try to absorb all of this.'

She looked at him again, her face weary, her eyes serious. 'If you reach the point where you are ready to let go of the past and look to the future, then come to me.' Her voice dropped to a whisper. 'I will be waiting.'

She pressed a quick kiss to his lips and was gone.

Chapter Twenty

In the morning, the Ashford family was gone. So was Sophie. Mr Huxley was preparing to depart. And although, in Charles's view, Lord Cranbourne deserved nothing more than to be preparing to depart the earth for ever, the doctor declared him a little stronger today.

It was, perforce, a small group that gathered for breakfast. Charles forced himself to join them. Vaguely he wondered where the Averys were. He was in no shape to handle anyone else's difficulties. His own were stretching every resource he possessed. He got up and left the table before he ended up venting his despair.

By unspoken consensus the remaining guests began to prepare to return to town. They would all dine out for years on the story of this botched house party, Charles thought bitterly. He stayed out of their way and left them to their packing. Then he haunted the stables so he could stop Mr Mateo Cardea before he mounted up and left.

It worked. Charles stood in the bright sun and held the horse's bridle while Cardea lashed his small portmanteau behind the saddle.

'I want to know what sort of hold he had over you,' Charles said.

Cardea did not pretend to misunderstand. 'He knew some dangerous details from my rash youth. Back then I thought privateering to be more glamorous than hauling cargo.' The man actually winked at him. Charles's snort echoed the horse's.

'Let us just say it was information that I do not wish a few of the people I do business with today to discover.' He shrugged. 'It was no hardship to go along with the old man. Besides keeping his information to himself, he offered me a handsome settlement. And who would not wish to be married to the beautiful Sophie?'

Charles clenched his teeth, but Cardea grew serious as he reached to shake his hand. 'You watch how you treat her. I have promised her that we will be a close family once again.' His grip grew stronger. 'I still know a few dirty tricks from the old days.'

Charles did not respond. He watched as the man mounted up and rode off.

* * *

Later in the afternoon, Charles stood at the library windows when Lord Avery entered the room.

'My wife and I are heading back into town, Dayle. We wished to thank you for your generosity. It's a sight more than I showed you.'

Charles would have spoken, but the man stopped him. 'You've given us a start. No doubt it is more than I deserve, but I thank you for it. We'll take it from here. I don't know how far we will get, but we'll make the journey together, and that's what matters.' He clapped Charles on the back. 'See you in Westminster.'

At last everyone had gone. Only Charles and his mother, and Cranbourne, still upstairs in his sick room, were left. Charles wandered the empty house, seeing Sophie in every corner, and knew how wrong he had been, about so many things.

He set off in search of his mother, and found her at last in the red drawing room. A bench had been pulled over and placed in front of the chimneypiece. She sat there, silently contemplating the portrait above the mantel.

Charles directed a wan smile at her and motioned for her to make room. Sitting next to her, he stared at the past and resolved to fix the future.

With a little sigh his mother let her head lean on his shoulder. Charles breathed deep, took her hand, and told her. He confessed it all. Everything about Phillip and his father and his vain attempts to make amends.

She cried. Each tear cracked Charles's heart open a little further. Then, being his mother, she scolded him, comforted him, and ultimately, forgave him.

Evening had come on. The servants, perhaps sensing that they were best left alone, had not come in to build up the fire. Charles did it himself, and then he leaned on the mantel and watched the snap and crackle of the flames.

'There is something else,' he said.

He told his mother about Sophie. From their childhood, to their more recent tempestuous relationship, to how he had allowed his guilt and self-loathing to spur him into pushing her away. Before he had done, he was the one with the tears in his eyes. He looked for her reaction.

She stared at him in fond exasperation. 'I would never have expected you to be such a nodcock, Charles. I swear, I will take back all my words of forgiveness if you do not get yourself after that girl,' she threatened.

'I will. I promise. But there is one place I have to go before I do.'

* * *

Charles went home. He had not been back to Fordham for more than a few hours since the day he had left, at fifteen. But, at last, he was home.

On the first day he visited Phillip's grave. He stood for a long time, just staring at the marker, then he sat down with his back against it and he talked with his brother. He laughed as he recalled the times of their childhood. He cried as he begged for his forgiveness. He told him all about Sophie and the muddle he had made of things, of his life. When the sun started to sink in the sky and the air grew chill, he stood, and he promised to visit again.

The next marker was his father's. Very gently he laid a lily at the base of the stone. His father had had a fondness for lilies. Maybe more than for his wayward second son. But Charles had to learn to let go of that resentment. 'Perhaps some day,' he whispered into the still evening air, 'I'll be able to do it.'

On the second morning he went straight to the forest after breakfast, to the tree where he and Sophie had first met. Charles stood at the base of the massive old monument and looked up into a maze of leafy green and gnarled brown. He took off his coat and grasped a branch.

It was not as easy as he had expected it to be, given

the additional height he had gained over the years, but he made it almost to the top. It was the additional weight that kept him from getting as high as he used to do. He settled himself into the crook of a sturdy branch and he looked out over the green landscape of the forest.

Just the smell of the place brought back so many memories. He breathed deeply, absorbing the smell of loam and life, and remembered the surprise on Sophie's tear-stained face that first time they had met, when she had climbed up and found him here before her. He had climbed up here in a temper, he recalled, resentful of the increasing time his older brother was required to spend learning the workings of the estate. But he'd found the very best possible distraction for his sorrow. He smiled to recall that funny little face, the braids, and the pinafore she had left on the ground below.

He climbed down then, and revisited all their old haunts. There had been so much laughter, a few tears, and a bone deep trust. It had been a rich friendship, a balm to the soul of two lonely children. Looking back now, he could hardly believe he had left it behind when he had finally left home. He should have recognised the value of what they had shared.

The truly horrendous thought was that fate had given him a second chance at it and he had nearly made the same mistake. For a long time he sat in the gazebo where the pair of them had spent so many hours, and let the wind ruffle his hair.

Unbidden, his own words came back to him. He could hear them as clearly as if they floated past on the breeze. *He would sacrifice anything, do anything, to prevail.* That vow still held true, but it held a wealth of new meaning. He knew, now, what he must do.

Sophie had been right. He had needed this. He was ready now to move forward, to accomplish something with his life. With her.

Fate had given him a second chance. Charles only hoped Sophie would as well.

Chapter Twenty-One

The brush had drifted off the edge of the page. Sophie failed to notice for several long minutes, until her listless strokes resulted in a Prussian blue smudge on the edge of her draughting table.

'Ohh…' She tossed her brush away in disgust and began to search for the solvent.

A brisk knock sounded at her chamber door and Nell entered, carrying a tray. She set it down. 'Not again.' The maid sighed. 'Beggin' your pardon, miss, but p'raps you should concentrate on eating something before you try to work again. Else your table is going to look like little Edward has been at it.'

'Thank you, Nell. You may be right.' Sophie sat when Nell held out a chair, but she did not eat. She couldn't eat, she couldn't work, and she couldn't pull herself together enough to receive visitors or pay any calls. All she had accomplished since returning to Emily's London house, in fact, was sitting at her desk, staring out the window, and wondering if Charles was ever going to come to his senses.

She rubbed her temples. It was beginning to look as if he would not. She rubbed her eyes next. She refused to cry; she had done enough of that since leaving Sevenoaks. She refused to doubt herself too. The fact that Charles had not come to her was proof enough that she had been right.

'Miss?' Nell was standing before her, looking concerned. It was a nearly constant expression these past days. 'Will you let me pour you a dish of tea?'

'Yes, of course.' Sophie tried to smile. She accepted the cup, but forgot to drink from it. She must begin to make some plans for her future. She had received several flattering offers for design commissions. She could choose one of those. Mateo had reiterated his offer to take her home to Philadelphia. As a cousin only, he had said with a wink. She ought to at least consider it.

The tea had grown cold in her hand when Nell returned to the room a while later. Shaking her head, the maid took the cup from her and set it down. 'There is a visitor downstairs. For you, miss.'

'Oh, no. I'm not prepared to receive anyone, Nell. Please, just tell whoever it is that I'm not at home.'

Nell took her hand and pulled her to her feet. She began to tuck in her hair and straighten her gown. 'Oh, this one you will want to see, miss. Trust me.'

Bemused, Sophie went down. She knew by Nell's manner that it could not be Charles. Granted, she was not sure if the maid was more likely to be happy, if and when he did appear, or to be ready to knock him about the head with a chamber pot, but she definitely would not have remained so calm.

A strange man sat alone in Emily's drawing room. He stood as Sophie entered and executed a nervous bow.

'Miss Westby,' he said.

'Sir.' She made her curtsy. 'I am afraid you have the advantage of me.'

'I'm Mills, ma'am. I am editor of a paper, the *Augur*. Perhaps you will have heard of it?'

'Indeed I have.' She raised a brow. Surely this man had not come begging for a story? No, the staff would not let her be so harassed.

'Ah, good. Well, then you will be aware that I have had some dealings with Lord Dayle?'

Sophie's breath caught, but she merely said, 'No. I was not aware.'

'Oh. Well, I have had dealings with him, and he has asked me to deliver this.' He passed over a folded issue of his paper.

She glanced at it. The screaming headline took up half of the page.

Lord Dayle's Political Career at an End

Sophie gasped and looked up to question the man, but he had already gone. She unfolded the thing to read further.

It is rumoured that the much beleaguered Charles Alden, Viscount Dayle, has had his fill of scandalous slander and scurrilous attacks.
A source close to him reveals that he intends to eschew town life, desert his party, and his seat in the Lords. He will retire to his country seat, it is said, where he will raise bog berries and produce goat cheese, with the help of the multitudinous progeny of William the Goat.

Sophie laughed out loud. She snapped open the paper to read more, but found the remaining pages were blank. However, something did drop and land at her feet. She bent over to retrieve it. It was a sprig of lilac, and a sealed note. She broke the seal and spread the paper out.

You told me once that you knew all the pranks that I had played in my nefarious career. Prove

it. Come now to the spot where I cavorted with Cyprian mermaids.

Cyprian mermaids? Ah, she knew the story it meant. Charles and the famous courtesans, swimming naked in the Serpentine.

'Nell!' she called, striding to the door. 'Fetch our wraps. We are going to the Park!'

'I just happened to have them right here,' Nell said, popping in from the hall and holding out Sophie's favourite pelisse.

Sophie laughed. 'You are a wretch, but I love you. Let's go.'

They set out. The sun hung high and a brisk wind blew threw the city streets again today. Sophie smiled and buried her nose in the fragrant lilac. She didn't notice the pair of heads peaking from the doorway behind her, watching her leave.

Sophie doubted whether she had ever walked faster in her life. They reached the Park in record time. She hurried toward the Serpentine. As she drew near she could see a lone gentleman standing on the banks of the pond. She left the path, lifted her skirts and began to run. He turned around…

And she skidded to a stop. It was Theo Alden. He was grinning from ear to ear and striking a dramatic pose. She stared, uncomprehending, until two facts simultaneously became clear: he was holding a sprig of lilac, and he was dressed exactly as Madame Dunyazade had drawn him. Sophie dropped her skirts and started to laugh.

'I am your vision brought to life,' he crowed. 'Magnificent, isn't it? All my friends are ragingly jealous.' He pointed and Sophie turned to see a crowd of Theo's dandified friends looking on. She waggled her fingers at them and they all waved back.

'Here you are,' Theo said. He handed her the lilac and pulled another thick sheet from his waistcoat. 'When you are a member of the family,' he said a little plaintively, 'will you design something else for me?'

Sophie was too busy breaking the seal to answer. Again there was just a short note.

I knew that one was too easy. Here is your next clue: Brew in the shoe.

She immediately knew what that one referenced: the tavern brawl at the Lady's Slipper. It had always been one of her favourites. She looked up at Theo with a grin.

'I'll design you an entire wardrobe if you will find me a hackney as fast as you can.'

He was off like a shot, running towards the corner gate. In a matter of minutes she and Nell were ensconced in a hired carriage and heading for the Strand. They clasped hands and grinned like fools at each other. But Nell dropped her hand and let out a little scream as there came a repeated thumping from the back of the vehicle, right behind her head. She recovered herself and put her head out of the window and looked back. When she ducked back in, her smile was back in place. She gestured for Sophie to do the same.

Several of Theo's cronies were hanging on to the platform on the back of the old carriage. Evidently above hitching a ride, Theo himself was right behind them in another hackney, his own head out the window just like hers. He was beseeching his friends not to fall off and beseeching his driver not to lose her coach.

The ride seemed interminable. Sophie pulled her head back in, but was tempted to put it back out and scream her frustration when traffic slowed their progress significantly. The Strand was even more busy than usual, it appeared, and the closer they got to their destination, the slower the going became. Farmer's wagons, dray carts and private carriages— the street was seething with frustrated traffic. Sophie quickly grew too exasperated to wait, and climbed out to walk. As she drew closer to their destination, the source of the problem became apparent.

A massive, shifting crowd surrounded the tavern they sought. The rough but happy men were singing and spilling into the street, blocking the flow of traffic both ways. She fought her way towards the door of the Lady's Slipper, but stopped when she saw what awaited her there. Sir Harold Luskison stood there, stationed behind the infamous shoe, passing out rum punch as fast as he could ladle it.

'Thank Heaven that you are here!' he cried. 'The tavern owner is irate and has threatened to have me arrested. Here, now,' he called to the men surrounding him, 'clear the way, men. The lady deserves a cup.'

Sophie made her way to him and he poured her a cup. She tasted it; it was deliciously hot and wickedly rich. Sir Harold thankfully handed her his lilac and note. He tossed her a devilish grin as well, stepped away from the steaming cauldron, and bellowed, 'It's all yours, gentlemen!' The crowd roared with appreciation. Sophie didn't hear it; she was perusing her newest hint.

After you have quenched your thirst, feed your mind. Here's your clue: I was born a poet, but was the only one to know it.

* * *

She paused. This one had her stumped. Frantically she searched her memory, but she could not recall anything in Charles's past pertaining to poetry. She shared the note with Sir Harold, but he only shook his head. Then Nell asked to see it. She looked it over and then looked up, her eyes bright with pleasure.

'Happen I know this one! I heard two footmen talking of it in Lady Dayle's kitchens. Lord Dayle dressed up like Byron and showed up at the Mayfair Ladies Byron Appreciation Society. He even read a poem before he was unmasked.'

Sophie slapped a hand to her head. 'I cannot believe I missed that one.'

'I don't think the Ladies liked the idea of it getting around. Several of them actually swooned before they found him out.'

'But where, Nell?' Sophie clutched her maid by the arms. 'Where did they meet?'

'At that fancy bookstore. Hatchards.'

Sophie pulled her into a tight embrace. 'I don't know what I would do without you, Nell! Quickly! Let's go!'

They backtracked to the cab and talked the driver into turning it about. The rum punch must have given out, because traffic began to move again. Sir Harold rode with them as well, this time. They lost some of the dandies to the lure of free liquor, but Theo and even some of the men from the crowd were still following behind.

Traffic in Piccadilly was busy as well, and Sophie thought they would never get through. She was near to bouncing on her seat in her excitement, but at last the cab pulled to a stop in front of the bookstore.

A smiling Miss Ashford stood next to the entrance, waving her sealed sheet of vellum. She wore the brightest smile Sophie had ever seen on her and had a tight hold of Mr Huxley's arm.

'Oh, Sophie—such news!' she called. 'Mr Huxley and I are betrothed!'

Sophie gasped. 'But how wonderful!'

'Here,' Miss Ashford said, handing her the paper. 'I wish you will be as happy as we are.' She leaned forward confidingly. 'We are going to tour the Lake District for our bridal trip.'

'I have always thought there needed to be a good map made of all those trails in Cumbria,' said Mr Huxley as he held out his lilac sprig. 'Tell your uncle that I am sorry things did not work out as he wished.' He bestowed a satisfied glance upon the beaming Miss Ashford. 'I think it all came out for the best, just the same.'

Her uncle was not the man foremost in Sophie's mind. This time the clue was just one sentence.

* * *

The King is blue once more.

Sophie looked up into a group of expectant faces. 'Westminster!' she shouted.

They had found him at last. Charles stood at the King's Entrance of Westminster, addressing another crowd. He had a huge bunch of lilacs in his hand and he was standing next to poor King Alfred. The statue had been moved from its position in the Hall and was indeed blue again, from head to foot.

The cab's door opened and Sophie descended slowly, staring in amazement. They were all here. Everyone. Lady Dayle and Emily and her family stood near to Charles. Mr Fowler, her publisher, actually dabbed at his eye with his handkerchief. All the girls who had performed at the masquerade were grouped to one side. Mateo stood with his arm around an openly weeping man—it was her Italian *stuccatore!* She recognised some of the men from her workshop in Blackford Chase, and Mr Darvey stood in the middle of them.

Only Charles was apparently oblivious to her arrival. He had continued with his speech. Sophie blinked back further tears at the sight of him. He was smiling at the crowd and he looked so tall and handsome. The sun glinted off the chestnut in his hair.

'…and so I do withdraw from the political arena. I have resigned from my committees and given up my appointments.'

Sophie gasped. Her heart melted, but then she stilled. Could he truly be giving up his political career altogether? She hadn't… She looked wildly about, wondering if anyone else knew what a sacrifice he was making.

'Oh, no, Charles.' It was Lady Dayle's voice protesting.

He laughed. 'Do not worry, it is a fitting end to a haphazard career, in any case. I am sure the government will sail smoothly on without this sometime rake and fribble.'

'But Dayle, you cannot have considered us?' someone called from the side of the crowd. Sophie looked over and saw a gaggle of reporters, pads out, taking notes. 'Our readers love you. They will be bereft.'

'Our editors will be even more so,' another said in a loud, theatrical lament.

'You'll have to find someone else to be your whipping boy, my lads.' Charles grinned. 'Haunt someone else's footsteps from here on out, for mine will be traipsing down a different, and far more complacent, path.' He stepped away from King Alfred and grew more serious.

'For a long time I have walked in shadow. I have held the darkness and decay of the past too close to my heart.' He gestured towards Sophie and directed that open, satisfied smile her way. 'It took a very special lady to pound that truth into my head.' He held out his arms to her and the crowd parted to make way.

Still in a daze, she advanced, spellbound by the lightness of Charles's voice and the brightness of his clear gaze.

'I've been lost,' he said simply. 'Never knowing just who I was, or what I needed. Now I do not claim to be completely redeemed,' he said with a rakish glance at the crowd, 'for I am afraid that is a task which will take the right woman years to accomplish.' He grinned as the crowd laughed along with him. 'But the process has begun. I am found, because one woman cared enough to search. We did not make it easy on each other, I assure you, but at the last I stand before you, all of our friends and family, not as Viscount Dayle, not even as Mr Charles Alden. I stand here, just a man, desperately in love with a woman.'

The crowd roared their approval and Charles beckoned to Sophie once more.

'I give you all the incredible woman who showed

me how to find the sun again, how to hold on to the memories of the past, and let go of the pain, how to appreciate how blessed I am in the loved ones I still have. She has shown me that true generosity of spirit does exist in this world. She has demonstrated courage and fortitude and somehow, most miraculously, she has breached the barriers I had surrounded myself with and found something inside worthy of her love.'

He stepped into the crowd and walked toward her. They met in the middle. Sophie gazed at him in wonder. He handed her the bouquet, then, heedless of the many staring faces, he took her in his arms and kissed her long and hard.

The crowd cheered. He drew back and said to her alone, 'Some of those shadows will always be with me, I'm afraid. But I can see past them now, and it is clear that you are my future.' He touched her hair, ran a finger along the curve of her cheek. 'You will marry me, will you not?'

Sophie couldn't speak, couldn't believe it was true. She felt a sharp elbow in her back as Nell nudged her from behind, so she just nodded and kept nodding, for once in her life struck silent by happiness.

Charles did not appear to mind. He grabbed her up, whirled her around and claimed her mouth once more in a slow, most thorough kiss.

'She said yes!' someone nearby shouted, and a great roar rose up from the crowd. Laughing, the pair broke apart. Something soft landed on Sophie's nose and she looked up to see that everyone in the crowd had held a lilac and now they were tossing them in the air in celebration, surrounding them all in a soft, fragrant rain.

'A moment! Hold a moment!' The shouts, weak as they were, began to penetrate the noise of the crowd and to interfere with Charles's exultation. He tore his gaze from Sophie's shining face and glanced back towards the arching entrance way.

Cranbourne stood there, weak but upright, supported by a shorter man. Mr Wren, Charles presumed.

'I said, hold a moment,' Cranbourne said testily. Slowly the happy tumult abated and all eyes turned toward the man.

'I am the girl's guardian. She should seek my consent before she seeks to wed,' he said in a voice too frail to carry far. It carried far enough to rouse everyone's wrath, however. Hisses and boos met his statement and Charles saw his mother step towards the old man, her face as angry as he'd ever seen it.

'Why, you lowly little muckworm—' she began.

'A chance,' he wheezed. 'Just give me a chance to speak.' He waited until silence reigned once more. 'I do give my consent for Sophie to wed, but—' Everyone held their breaths. Charles struggled to hold on to his temper.

'I cannot condone Lord Dayle's retirement from service to the government. He is a good man. He has done nothing for which he need be ashamed.' Another cheer greeted this pronouncement. Charles just snorted. Sophie, however, was watching her uncle, and Charles knew what was about to happen when she tightened her grip on him.

'Lord Dayle has been under attack in the past months. He has been much maligned. Maliciously. He has been accused of many faults. Falsely. I know this to be true, because I am the one who perpetrated it.'

Charles looked to the left. The whole group of reporters was grinning and scribbling away as fast as their fingers would fly.

'It is I who am retiring from public life,' Cranbourne said. ' I hereby resign my positions, and although my word means nothing, now, I urge you to join me in my attempt to change Lord Dayle's mind.'

'What do you say, Dayle?' It was Sir Harold's voice coming from the back of the mob. 'The Tories stand in need of good men. Will you stay?'

Charles looked into Sophie's questioning gaze. 'I don't know,' he said to her. 'I was looking forward to finding new ways to make a difference.' He looked up and around at the grand buildings sur-rounding them. 'This was Phillip's path. Perhaps it will turn out to be mine as well. I just do not know.' He squeezed her hands. 'If I don't know what I want to do with myself now, there is one thing I do know for certain: that I want you beside me. For ever.'

Her dark eyes sparkled. 'You arc free now. Free to follow whatever path you wish. There is only one absolute necessity in your future.'

He grinned. 'What is that, my love?'

'You must kiss me again. Now.'

So he did.

Epilogue

'I do not know just how your mother did it,' Lady Dayle said to the chortling baby in her arms, 'but look, there you are.'

She indicated the elegantly framed picture hanging just before them. It was the portrait that Sophie had drawn of her, when she had acted as Dunyazade, all those many months ago. The viscountess had adored the picture as soon as it had come from Sophie's easel, but it was only recently that she had noticed this remarkable likeness.

'I must admit, I thought you were losing touch with reality when you told me of this,' Emily Lowder declared. 'I was prepared to break the bad news to your sons that their mother was showing signs of senility. But you were right! It is the very image of the child.'

That long ago night, at Miss Ashford's, now Mrs

Huxley's, masquerade, Sophie had indeed drawn Lady Dayle's secret dream: the viscountess surrounded by an unruly pack of happy grandchildren. Lady Dayle had adored it, and had had it framed and hung here in her sitting room. She had been admiring it once more just yesterday when suddenly the uncanny resemblance of the imagined child she held in the picture, to the baby currently residing in Fordham's nursery, had jumped out at her.

'It is unreal.' Emily exclaimed. 'How did she do it? Sophie could not have known, could she have?' She straightened, as if hit by a sudden thought. 'You've had the portrait of you and the boys moved back here from Sevenoaks, have you not?'

Lady Dayle nodded, puzzled. 'Yes.'

'Good, I want to get a look at it again.'

They went to the long gallery where all the family portraits were hung, taking the baby with them.

'Will he let me carry him, do you think?' Emily asked.

'He may, but will I?' Lady Dayle laughed. 'Oh, all right, but only because your own Edward is not here to protest.'

'Come here, you adorable bit of bunting,' Emily cooed. She dug her face in and covered his little neck with loud smacking kisses, making the next Viscount Dayle scream with delight.

'Here it is,' said Lady Dayle. They had reached the spot where the portrait had been restored to its former position. 'What did you wish to see?'

'I want to look at the image of Charles when he was younger,' said Emily. She stared at the painting, and glanced repeatedly at the boy in her arms. 'That's it,' she announced with satisfaction. 'She must have used the image of Charles as a boy for a model.'

'She could not have,' argued Lady Dayle. 'Sophie had never been here in the house that I know of. She never saw that portrait until I had it delivered to Sevenoaks.'

'Then how did she do it?' wondered Emily.

'I don't know, but perhaps it is better that we do not know.' She smiled. 'Hand him back to me now.' She took the baby away from her friend and held him up so he could see the painting on the wall. 'Do you see that boy there, the one with the wicked grin? That is your father, my boy.' She moved her hand. 'And that is your Uncle Phillip, right there. I'm sorry you will not have the chance to know him. He was a wonderful man and would have made a superb uncle.'

'Yes,' agreed Emily. 'He was just the type who would have lectured your parents endlessly about limiting the amount of sweets you were allowed, then he would have kept a pocket full of them just for you.'

'And this, you see, is your Uncle Jack. He is away right now, but will be home for the holidays.'

'Do you recall the day that we unveiled my drawing room? Who would have imagined, back then, that it would have worked out this way?'

'Oh, I don't know,' said Lady Dayle with a smile. 'I am sure that someone with a little imagination might have foreseen how happily it has turned out.' She kissed her grandson and looked back at the portrait. 'I do hope your parents do not wait too long to make the rest of that portrait into reality.'

The baby chuckled his agreement.

THE REGENCY COLLECTION

Your favourite historical authors
invite you to be whisked away into a
Regent world of lavish and lust…

The Regency Large Print Collection